The Art of Arrow Cutting

The Art of Arrow Cutting

Stephen Dedman

A Tom Doherty Associates Book / New York

THE ART OF ARROW CUTTING

Edited by James Frenkel

A Tor Book
Published by Tom Doherty Associates, Inc.
175 Fifth Avenue
New York, NY 10010

Tor Books on the World Wide Web:
http://www.tor.com

Tor® is a registered trademark of Tom Doherty
Associates, Inc.

Library of Congress Cataloging-in-Publication Data

Dedman, Stephen.
    The art of arrow cutting / Stephen Dedman. — 1st ed.
        p.   cm.
    "A Tom Doherty Associates book."
    Novel.
    ISBN 0-312-86320-9
    I. Title.
    PR9619.3.D387A89   1997
    823—dc21   96-53282
                                                           CIP

First Edition: July 1997

Printed in the United States of America

0 9 8 7 6 5 4 3 2 1

To Tanya,
for showing me some of the magic in the world,
and Elaine,
for giving me a home to come back to.

Contents

Acknowledgments

Thanks to Richard Curtis, Jim Frenkel, Tara, Ralph, Keira, Chris, Helen, Terry, Jack, Cappy, Scott, Harlan, Susan, Terry, Bill, Leanne, Robin, Richard, the IYHF, STA Travel, the strangers who paid my departure tax at LAX when I was broke, and to everyone who's ever given me a meal and a place to sleep.

The Art of
Arrow
Cutting

Tamenaga

Tamenaga Tatsuo had not worn a kimono since his daughter's wedding, three years before, and few of his employees had seen him in anything other than a thousand-dollar business suit. None, as far as Nakatani knew, had ever been invited to discuss business with him in the bath, and anything unprecedented made Nakatani nervous; he liked an ordered, predictable, comfortable world, and intended eventually to retire to one . . . if Tamenaga permitted it.

He was ushered into a change room by one of Tamenaga's attendants, an attractive woman whose age was unguessable and whose expression didn't alter by a millimeter as Nakatani undressed. She wore a white robe that might easily have concealed a small armory, and she made him feel very naked. It required all his willpower to walk ahead of her without turning around, particularly as she made no perceptible sound.

Tamenaga's bath was a Jacuzzi the size of a backyard pool, bubbling like a witches' cauldron. Behind Tamenaga stood another white-robed attendant, a muscular Japanese in his thirties.

Tamenaga himself sat at the far end of the pool with only his head, neck, shoulders, and arms showing above the foaming water; both arms and shoulders were elaborately tattooed. Nakatani bowed, trying not to stare at a detailed rendition of a spectacled cobra coiled around Tamenaga's left arm, the hood spread across the biceps.

"Good morning, Nakatani-san," Tamenaga said in Japanese with a trace of a California accent. "Won't you join me?"

Nakatani nodded, then slipped into the foaming water quickly, trying hard not to remember the stories he'd heard about ninja who could swim underwater for minutes at a time.

"What have you discovered?"

"Sir, I . . ." He kept his head bowed and stared at the markings on the cobra's hood—according to legend, the fingerprints of Buddha, for whom the snake had once provided shade. "I have checked everywhere. There is no question but that the girl stole it from Higuchi-san."

"And where is the girl?"

"I . . . haven't been able to find her. Yet."

Tamenaga nodded. "And where is my son-in-law?"

"Higuchi-san should be in his office, sir . . . he was there when I left him." Nakatani's eyes bugged slightly as the cobra's hood swelled and seemed to become scaly. "Inagaki and Tsuchiya are watching him. You didn't say you wanted him brought to you—"

"I don't," Tamenaga grunted, and was silent for a moment. "Does the girl know what she has taken from us, Nakatani-san?"

Nakatani's gaze followed the tattoo as it wound its way to just below Tamenaga's wrist. "It seems barely possible, sir . . ."

"There are some people for whom anything is possible, Nakatani-san," said Tamenaga smoothly. The cobra lifted its head and stared straight at Nakatani.

"Was anything else stolen?" asked Tamenaga.

Nakatani stared back at the cobra. It flicked its tongue at him and its hood widened.

"Was anything else stolen?" repeated Tamenaga sharply.

Nakatani pulled himself together as best he could. "No, sir."

"You're certain?"

"Nothing else is missing," said Nakatani, not taking his eyes from the snake's. "Maybe some cash of Higuchi's, but he says no—"

"Then she knew what she was looking for, neh?" Tamenaga brooded. His son-in-law was probably telling the truth this time: Tamenaga doubted that he had the imagination to lie competently. Certainly he'd never been able to hide his infidelities from Haruko (who was Westernized enough to be irritated by them), let alone from Tamenaga.

"She may not be able to use it," Nakatani ventured.

"She is extremely intelligent, even gifted, and would not have stolen it if she didn't think she could learn," countered Tamenaga, though he relaxed slightly. "But if we find her quickly enough, Nakatani-san . . ." The cobra turned away from Nakatani and flicked its tongue in the direction of Tamenaga's ear, as though whispering a secret.

When Nakatani had been ushered out, Tamenaga climbed out of the pool. The cobra coiled itself around his arm again and became a tattoo. "Call Hegarty, tell him to be in my office in four minutes. I want a good picture of the girl, and a hundred copies. Send some men to the airport, the bus and railway stations . . . and send them to LAX as well. She's had *hours,* she could be anywhere by now. It doesn't matter who you send, as long as they have eyes and aren't too obvious. Sakura, go and stay with my daughter. Buy her a black dress, something respectable, and put it on my account."

Amanda

When she first saw him, he was sitting along a low brick wall outside the Greyhound station watching the shape-shifting clouds and early morning moon, his long legs stretched out before him in obvious enjoyment of their newfound liberty, his long black hair fluttering in the cold October breeze, his scuffed and faded pack serving as a backrest, the strap of his camera case wrapped tightly around his wrist. He opened his eyes slightly as she approached, then opened them wide to let his pupils dilate in appreciation. His camera case was in his lap and open in a moment.

His name was Michelangelo Magistrale, and he was nominally a professional photographer. His father, on the rare occasions that he acknowledged his son's existence, called him a bum, which was at least as accurate. He had drifted cheerfully through twenty-three years, with little ambition and less greed; he had never been rich or considered himself poor, and not even his lovers had been able to hurt him seriously, though dozens had left him without his understanding why. He considered himself a pacifist; he carried no weapons and never consciously started a fight, but he had never lost one, either. He was essentially honest, but he had been questioned by police often enough to avoid them when he could. He had a cool head, a long reach, excellent reflexes, and the knack of anticipating his opponents by watching their eyes.

Strangers who noticed only his smoothly handsome face and beautiful hair tended to underestimate him, and Magistrale tended to agree with them. He was rootless by nature, a drifter, remembering faces and favors and little else, never planning or predicting the future, living from meal to meal and bed to bed. He rode the buses and trains rarely, preferring to hitchhike along the busier roads—but lifts to small towns like Totem Rock are difficult to find. When he saw the girl, the Greyhound ticket suddenly looked like a good investment.

Magistrale had recently worked in Nevada as a figure photographer for *Bandit,* a soft-core skin magazine; none of the women he'd encountered there (including the one he'd come to Totem Rock to see) had been remotely as attractive as the blonde who was walking toward him. She was wearing jeans and a sheepskin coat, a costume that almost completely hid her figure (the CIA should keep secrets so well), but her legs were long and she walked like a goddess—or at least like a girl who knows she's attractive. Magistrale could have recognized *that* even if she'd been wearing a space suit.

She didn't flinch or hide as he framed the shot, but she didn't smile; as he zoomed in on her face, he noticed that she was anxious, maybe even scared. Reluctantly, he lowered the camera. "Hi."

The girl nodded. "Do you have the correct time, please?"

He smiled. "If I haven't missed a time zone somewhere along the line, it's a quarter of nine."

"Just off the bus?"

"Yeah."

"From?"

"Toronto, I guess."

"You guess?"

He grinned. "Well, it's the last place I slept worth a damn—I mean, not on a bus seat. I stayed there for a week and bummed around, watched the leaves turning, took a few photos. It's a nice place, very clean. Where're you headed?"

She shrugged, almost invisibly. "Calgary."

"And what's in Calgary?"

"I just need to go there."

"Boyfriend?"

"No." She looked away, bit her lip. Her face, normally beautiful, was pale and drawn, and Mage decided he *had* to see her smile. "Where're you going?" she asked.

"God knows," he replied cheerfully. "I may stay here for a while and then head back down south. Or maybe go west. Vancouver or somewhere. Or maybe Calgary, now that you mention it."

"You're not from here," she said, and it wasn't a question.

"I'm kind of from everywhere. I was born in Brooklyn and I went to college in Boston for a year, if that helps, and my family's from Italy, as if it didn't show. My name's Magistrale, but my friends call me Magus, or Mage. How about you?"

"Vancouver."

"What? Oh. I meant . . . never mind." She was staring at the cafeteria, which shared a roof with the bus station, obviously watching the people inside.

"I need some money," she said suddenly. He glanced at the cafeteria window. All the customers were middle-aged or older, farmers or working stiffs in plaid shirts, and none of them likely to give a teenage girl money to run away with. He'd walked past the place after leaving the bus, and though he would have liked some breakfast and it was obviously much warmer inside than on the wall, he'd doubted he'd be made welcome. He turned his attention back to the girl and guessed her age as nineteen, almost certainly a college student. She was nervous, even jumpy, but she didn't show any of the obvious signs of drug use—most of which Mage knew too damn well from months of living in the poorer, more dangerous areas of dozens of cities. He wished he could see her eyes, but they were hidden behind her sunglasses. She was carrying a large handbag, but no luggage.

"How much?"

"I'm twenty-seven dollars short."

He nodded. Native New Yorkers are notoriously suspicious of anyone asking for money, and Mage, who had four sisters, knew from experience that pretty girls were no more trustworthy than any other human species . . . but he had about forty Canadian dollars, plus two hundred U.S. that he could exchange when the banks opened, and Carol sure as hell wasn't going to charge him rent; he could afford to blow twenty-seven bucks if it was going to make this girl happy. After all, he had been able to travel cheaply across America because people had trusted him, giving him lifts and places to sleep, and occasionally much more. He was able to repay them with good conversation, a little driving, some good sex, and *his* trust. Trust was better than money, any day.

"Look, I have a room here," she said, mistaking his hesitation for refusal. "Rent's paid to Friday week, if you want to stay." She reached inside the collar of her coat and removed a key on a braided thong. "Here's a key."

"What is it?" he asked. "Family trouble? Accident? Someone in the hospital?"

". . . hospital."

"Who?"

"Me. I have to go back there. I thought I'd be okay, but . . . oh, Jesus . . . !"

She began to cry, tilted her sunglasses up until they sat atop her head and rummaged in her voluminous handbag for a tissue. Mage watched her closely. He prided himself on knowing when people were lying, and she wasn't. If she was telling the whole truth, then he was a virgin and an only child, but she wasn't actually *lying*.

"What's your name?"

"Amanda," she snuffled. "Sharmon."

He reached into his denim jacket for his wallet and removed two tens and two fives. "Here."

"Thank you." She wiped her eyes and looked directly at him for a few seconds before lowering her sunglasses. She still wasn't smiling exactly, but she looked slightly more relaxed. "Thanks. I'll go buy the ticket now, bring you your change."

"It's okay."

"No, it's not. Look, do you have an address I can send the money to, pay you back when I can?"

He looked at her again and reached out slowly to remove her sunglasses. She flinched slightly but didn't try to stop him. "How're you going to get back here without any money?" he asked.

"I know some people in Calgary, or I should be able to hitch a ride." She rummaged in her handbag again and removed a diary and a pencil. "Address?"

"I don't really have an address . . . better send it to my Uncle Dante; I work for him sometimes. P.O. Box Eighteen . . . Eighteen something, Boulder City, Nevada."

"Nevada?"

"You're from there?"

"No . . . I've been to Vegas before."

He found a business card in his wallet and let her copy it. "This is probably the best thing about being Italian, having relatives everywhere. And don't worry about the money . . . just write to me, let me know you're okay and where you are. Maybe I could come and see you."

She nodded, finished writing and dropped diary and pencil back into her handbag. "I'll be back in a minute," she promised, standing.

"Hey! Don't forget your key!"

"Keep it. Stay in the room if you like. Or leave the key there so the landlady can get it; I'll only have to post it if you don't. Please?"

"What's the address?"

"Fourty-four-A North Street."

He nodded and pocketed the key. "Hey! Smile!"

She had reached the door to the station but she turned to look at him, smiling as best she could, and he took a long shot of her. Suddenly she laughed, and he zoomed in for a mid shot, then a close-up, and for an instant it all seemed worthwhile.

She returned seven minutes later with his three dollars. He shook his head. "Buy yourself some lunch on the trip."

"They'll feed me at the hospital."

He shrugged and accepted the change. She'd washed her face, redone her makeup and pocketed her sunglasses; her blue-green eyes were still red-laced and slightly puffy, and her eyelashes very short, but she looked much prettier. "Thanks again, Magus."

He kissed her forehead, and her golden hair, noticing that it smelled, or maybe tasted, slightly strange. Not bad, just unusual. "Don't mention it. It's my good deed for the year. Or maybe last year's . . . I'm a little behind. When's the bus?"

"Comes in five minutes: twenty-minute rest stop. Do you remember the address?"

"Forty-four-A North."

"Right."

"What hospital?"

"What?"

"What hospital? If I come to Calgary, I might drop in, see how you're doing."

"Calgary General. Eight forty-one Center Avenue East," she replied without any hesitation. They sat in silence for nearly a minute.

"You said you work for your uncle. What sort of work?" she asked.

"Yeah. Yeah, sometimes. I'm a photographer."

"What sort of photographer?"

"Whatever sort they're hiring. I do some wedding photos and portraits, but mostly it's nudes for the girlie magazines."

"Sounds like interesting work," she said, poker-faced.

"Not really, not for long," he said and shrugged. "The pictures never really look as good as I think they should, and if they did, the magazine probably wouldn't want them anyway. And most of the women you see down there are trying to raise some money after their husbands have blown it all at Vegas, or divorcées who think they're being independent, or losers who have never learned to do anything else with their bodies, let alone their minds. Would-be starlets on their way to Hollywood, small-time strippers, waitresses who got tired of waiting—"

"Are you *sure* you're Italian? You don't sound like one."

"You mean my accent? I've got what they call a quick ear."

"No, you're just . . . not full of macho bullshit, I guess."

He grinned. "I *was* about to finish up with 'but never anyone who looks as good as you,' but I guess you hear that a lot."

"No, not really," she replied. "Not recently."

"What is it with this place? Everyone under sixty split?" He'd seen too many small country towns and bankrupted cities where that had happened—and others where it hadn't, which were often worse. In his experience, little towns were even less friendly than the big cities, especially to impoverished strangers and beautiful young women.

"No . . . I just don't get out much, I guess."

"Well, let me know when you check out of the hospital and we'll change that. Or are you too busy?" No reply. "Studying? What're you studying?"

"Mathematics. Probability theory." There was the crunch of gravel behind them and the bus pulled into the parking bay, the door opening with a depressing wheeze. "Thanks for everything, Mage," she said and stood.

"My pleasure." He walked with her to the bus door, kissed her hand—it felt unusually cool—as she gave the driver her ticket, then stood back and craned his neck to watch her choose her seat. "The Lord giveth and Greyhound taketh away," he muttered, still wishing he could have made her smile more. He glanced at his watch: not quite 9:30, and over an hour and a half before Carol was due, but at least the bank should be open.

The senior cashier was mid-twentyish, with a city girl's bearing, a Northeastern accent, a pleasant smile, and no wedding ring; Mage guessed that some officious bastard had banished her to this ghost town and called it a promotion. He cashed a twenty-dollar traveler's check and asked for directions to North Street. Number Forty-four was seven blocks away, farther than he cared to walk carrying the pack. "Thank you kindly."

"You staying here long?"

"I don't know. How about you?"

"Until Christmas. Then I'm being transferred back to Toronto."

"Home?"

"Uh-huh. How about you?"

He shrugged. "I drift. I was in Toronto a week ago. Nice place."

"No home?"

"Not really." He grinned. "Most people say, 'That must be exciting,' or something like that. You look like you're sorry for me."

"I am. I mean, I just can't imagine that, not calling anywhere home."

"At least you're honest. Most people don't know what they want, and they don't dare wonder."

"And you?"

"I don't know either," he replied. "But I'm going to keep looking 'til I find it. Ciao."

He returned to the wall at eleven, armed with a cherry Danish and a new Vangelis cassette. He listened to the tape on his Walkman, watched the sky, and waited. A few minutes before noon, he removed the headphones and heard Carol's car, an ancient VW Beetle, long before it turned the corner and chugged to a stop. The door flew open without restraint and Carol emerged—she was short enough to get out of a Beetle quickly, if not gracefully—smiling broadly.

"Hi. Just put that in the hood and we can get home. I've been up since five and I'm just about dead; it's my week for mornings. How're you?"

"I'm fine." She was moving too quickly for Mage to grab her, so he picked up his pack and swung it into the luggage compartment. "Where d'you work?"

"The Stop-and-Rob down near the highway." She slammed the hood down and opened the door for him. "Four of us rotate, which isn't too bad, and we're all *very* dangerous during the graveyard shift. And I need the money—I mean, I kept the house and it's on the market, but you can't sell a house in this town and get enough to move anywhere there's any work. Okay, let's go. I'm going to make some breakfast and hit the sack immediately—and sleep. You must be bushed yourself after the bus trip. Oh, yeah—Jeannie, who has the shift after mine, wants to know if you can do a photo of her. She saw that thing you did of me, not the one for the magazine—you know, the one you took in that red dress—and she really liked it."

"I never wore a red dress in my life," muttered Mage, but Carol didn't hear him over the noise of the engine.

"So, what d'you want for breakfast?"

*   *   *

Now I really *am* going to go to sleep," she said nearly three hours later. "I oughta make you drink that coffee, too." She stretched lazily. "So, how come you're even better during the day? I thought magic needed a full moon or something."

"I don't know," he said, smiling. "Maybe I'm solar powered. And you're pretty magical yourself; it felt like you really *do* rotate."

"What? Oh!" She laughed and kissed his biceps—sliding up (or down) the bed to kiss him anywhere else would have been too exhausting. They lay there for several minutes silently, and then she asked, "What're you thinking?"

"Who says I'm thinking? I don't have the energy left to think—not that I'm complaining."

"Balls."

He stared at the ceiling. "You've got good shadows."

"Oh, yeah? What can you see up there that you can't see down here?"

"There's a leopard—see the spots?—and the Venus de Milo . . . well, she's a little lopsided. Maybe it's the Venus de Willendorf instead." She looked up, obviously puzzled. "The Willendorf Venus is a Cro-Magnon figurine, a fertility—never mind."

He rolled over and kissed her. She was twenty-nine, he knew, six years his senior, and she'd never been beautiful. She was proud of her body, particularly of her large, big-nippled breasts; he loved her smile, which was honest and almost pretty. When he'd photographed her for *Bandit,* he'd made sure that she smiled, joking and flirting and flattering her. Not that most of the readers gave a damn about prettiness—they wanted glands and genitalia—but Mage was a photographer, not a dissector. To him, a shot that didn't include the woman's face had all the erotic appeal of a guillotine. Despite his first name, no one had ever called him an artist, and he would have denied it if they had—but he had some of the vision that makes an artist, though not the technique, nor much desire to learn it.

"You know how to live," he said. "Nothing I know is of any use."

She laughed. "I'm lying here hardly able to move at half past three in the afternoon, and you say that nothing you know is of any use? If Roy had known how to do *that*, I would never've let him leave."

"Thanks." He kissed her again, then flopped back onto his side of the bed and yawned. "Guess I'd better get some sleep, too."

"What do you want for dinner?"

"Oh, God . . ."

"I don't feel like cooking, either. Pizza suit you?"

"Are you kidding? I used to live on the stuff, I love it. With extra anchovies, right? And tomorrow I'll go shopping and *I'll* cook dinner: Spaghetti Bolognese a la Magistrale."

Four nights, he thought. Four wouldn't hurt either of them. And then where?

Packer

George Packer had learned to fire a shotgun on his father's farm at the age of seven. Thirty-one years later he was an almost fanatical collector and target shooter, an itinerant farm-machinery salesman who also sold black-market firearms. He was of average intelligence, with a modest talent for mathematics, and no doubt he had a good Freudian reason for wanting to blow wet, messy holes in living beings.

At ten to midnight he sat in his car thinking of how much he'd enjoy blowing a hole in Gacy, the employer he didn't mention on his tax return. Gacy had told him to look for this blonde—which was okay by Packer—and given him a list of little towns on the Greyhound route. He'd also given him half the payment in advance—which was more than he'd get in a good month of selling combine harvesters—but he hadn't told him about the boredom. The girl had been missing for nearly two weeks now, and Gacy doubted that they'd ever find her at all—which, Packer guessed, was why *he* wasn't freezing his buns in Totem Rock, Saskatchewan, population 330, a few minutes before midnight.

And to cap it off, the Greyhound station and café were closed. Packer looked at the timetable and eventually deduced that since the bus was arriving at twenty to one, the station would probably open at 12:30 or so. He yawned, set the alarm on his watch for 12:25, pushed his seat back as far as it would go, loosened his belt and closed his eyes. His left arm dangled down, brushing against the stock of his favorite gun, a Mossberg 12-gauge with a winter trigger. He also had an HK-4 in his pocket "for luck." The rifles and SMGs in the trunk were unloaded and nominally for sale; the ammunition, much of it hand-loaded and illegal even in the U.S., was in his *other* suitcase.

He woke when the bus arrived, scratched himself and walked to the dingy office. Not surprisingly, no one was boarding or disembarking, but the clerk was busy with a few parcels. Packer bought himself a Dr. Pepper from the machine and waited.

"Help you?"

"Yeah, maybe," Packer replied and brought out the picture. The clerk was only a kid, nineteen at the most, which was good; he wouldn't have forgotten a girl that beautiful. "You seen this girl come through here? It's not that great a shot, I know, but she's about so tall"—he held his hand level with his mustache—"long blond hair, unless she's done something to it. . . ."

"You her father?"

"Uncle," Packer replied glibly. He was muscular and thick-featured, with colorless eyes and receding chestnut hair, and resembled the pretty blonde not at all. "She was running away from her father—you can probably guess why. But he's just died, and her mother—my sister—wants her home. You understand." The story was a good one, maybe too good for Gacy, and Packer wondered who'd thought of it. "You've seen her, haven't you?"

"I don't know. Like you say, it's a lousy photo. But there was a girl like that, a blonde, stopped off here . . ."

"When?"

The boy looked at him, his face darkening slightly with suspicion. "When did she run away?"

"Last year. She was working in Salt Lake City for a while. Least that was the postmark on her letters until a couple of weeks back, when she said her job had finished and she was looking for work somewhere else. I hoped she might come and see me, but like I said, it's been two weeks now. . . ."

The boy stared at him, then nodded. "About a week ago. What is it now, Wednesday?"

"By about half an hour, yeah."

"It must've been early last week. Monday, I guess. I haven't seen her since."

"You're sure?"

"Sure. No offense, but I'd remember her."

"No offense taken, you've been a great help. You wouldn't know where she would've gone?"

The boy shrugged. "Maybe to the motel, unless she's staying with a friend. Or there are rooms out at the other end of town you can rent by the week."

"Thanks," said Packer and returned to his car.

He'd neglected to ask one question. The boy only worked nights and so hadn't seen the girl catch the morning bus the day before.

Carol slipped out of bed as gently as she could and dressed in the dark. Mage, who had grown up in a small apartment with paper-thin walls, slept on without stirring.

He looked years younger with his eyes closed, she thought. Not boyish—he was too tall to appear boyish—but innocent, or cute, or peaceful. She wasn't sure there was a word for it.

Words weren't her native language. He slept soundly, snoring very softly. She felt that she could sit there for hours and watch him sleep—wait for a shadow of beard to appear on his chin, maybe. He was a sloppy dresser, but he was as fussy as a cat about the rest of his appearance; his first action on leaving the bed had been to shower and wash his shoulder-long black hair. She finished dressing, blew him a kiss from the doorway and quietly closed the door behind her.

He would, she thought, make a terrible husband—not that she was looking for a husband, of course.

A few hours later, Mage emerged from a dream of Amanda— an unsatisfying, vaguely disturbing dream of the scent of her hair and the sadness in her eyes—and remembered where he was. He lay there for a few minutes, then guessed that the day was about as warm as it was likely to get and hauled himself out from underneath the blankets and into his robe and size eleven moccasins. A moment later he was prowling around the apartment with a large mug of coffee. It was a small apartment, and thus the prowl was rather badly cramped.

She wasn't at the motel and she hadn't been there—unless the old man who ran the place was lying, of course. But that, Packer thought, was unlikely. He didn't know very much about people, but he was used to dealing with liars. That left only the apartments and then, he hoped, he could get the hell out of Totem Rock. He donned his army-surplus greatcoat, which— apart from being warm and weatherproof—was the only garment he owned that could hide a silenced MAC-11. Then he packed his bag and took it out to the car.

The car, he suddenly realized, might be recognized—it had Edmonton license plates and was newer than anything else he'd seen in town. Walking the necessary seven blocks would make him less conspicuous. It wasn't as though he was going to *need* the 12-gauge or the AR-15. Gacy had specified that the girl was to be brought in alive and uninjured; stressed it too, though he hadn't told Packer why. Packer suspected, quite rightly, that Gacy didn't know, and wondered who *he* was working for.

He pulled the cover back over the trunk and locked it down. It was weatherproof, like the greatcoat, but its real purpose was to hide the shotgun in the back seat. Then he shrugged, feeling the reassuring weight of the MAC-11 on its sling, and set off.

It was midday before Packer had his answer, and he didn't like it. The girl *had* been living there, briefly, but the caretaker hadn't seen her in three days. The rent was paid until the end of the week though, and she might be back. Who is she, your daughter?

Packer reassured the caretaker with the same story he'd told the Greyhound clerk and the motel manager (town this small, he thought, they probably compare notes on everything that happens, probably be talking about this for months), then decided to ring Gacy. He spotted a booth less than a block away and fumbled in his pocket for change.

"I think I found her," he said as soon as he recognized Gacy's voice.

"What d'you mean, 'I think'?" came the weary reply.

"Well, I found her."

"O-kaay! Where is she?"

"Uh . . ."

"She got away, didn't she?" Gacy didn't *say* "You dumb asshole," but he thought it very loudly.

"No . . . I don't know where she *is*, but she *was* here. I found her apartment, and I know the name she was using. It may even be her real one."

"What is it?"

"Well, it looks to me like that should be worth a bonus."

"Yeah. Maybe. *If* it helps us catch her, now you've let her go. What was it?"

"Sharmon. Amanda Sharmon. And I didn't let her go; I don't even know she's gone."

"What you don't know isn't worth shit."

"She's paid the rent here 'til the end of the week."

"She can probably afford to do *that* in every pissant town in Saskatchewan, you jerk. Could probably have bought the place. Why d'you think these guys want her?"

"I don't know. But she must be here. She didn't catch the Greyhound and there's no other way out of town."

Gacy sighed. "Maybe she bought a car. Maybe she hitched a ride—she's a looker, in case you hadn't noticed."

"A place this size, away from the highway? No cars for sale that I've seen, and nobody ever goes through here, not slow enough to notice."

"Hmm . . . so maybe she's shacked up with someone there. Have you seen inside the room?"

"No."

"Do it. Break in if you have to. And keep looking around town; if you're right, she's still there. Call me again tomorrow. At least now we know where she was—that's *something.*"

Packer found himself wishing he was wrong. "Okay. Thanks. Talk to you tomorrow." *Bastard,* he thought.

Carol glanced at the bedside clock, did a double take and then sat up, clutching the quilt to her chin. "You better get moving. Jeannie's coming over at seven."

"Jeannie?"

"The girl at work? Wants you to photograph her? She's coming over for dinner. You remember."

"Tonight?" he asked lazily.

"She's coming to dinner tonight. The photo you can do any-time you're here, or do you do *that* better in the daytime too?"

He grinned and sat up, stretching luxuriously. "Actually, yes. You don't have the lights here for portrait work, so I'll have to rely on the sun and use a flash for fill. She has the afternoon shift, hasn't she?" Carol nodded. "So I guess I'd better do her one morning. While you're at work. Is that okay?"

"You'll have to ask her," replied Carol offhandedly. "It's okay with me."

Mage disentangled himself from the bedclothes for the second time that day and walked toward the shower. "Is dinner formal?"

"No, but it's going to be cold. You'd better wear *something.*"

He laughed. "That's what I meant. I only have one set of clean clothes left. I meant to go looking for a laundromat this morning, but you didn't leave me a key."

"Oh, damn; I'm sorry. There's one—a laundromat, I mean—on North Street."

"It's okay. Tomorrow morning'll be fine. And I'll get that stuff for the spaghetti." He stepped into the bathroom and turned around. "And while we're on the subject, hadn't *you* better get dressed too?" He shut the door on her reply. Quickly.

Kirisutegomen

Morning came, and hid behind the clouds. Mage awoke after nine, rose slowly, dressed hastily, and began sorting through his clothes. The key that Amanda had given him fell from the pocket of his jeans; he picked it up and looked at it for a moment. It was shiny and seemed fairly new, with the Volkswagen-shaped head of a Lockwood but without a brand name. Obviously a copy. A letter "A" was stamped crookedly on one face; the other face was blank.

The thong looked less like leather than like plaited hair—dark hair, not the girl's blond—and it certainly didn't smell like leather, though it didn't exactly smell like hair either. He stood there for a moment remembering the cool, strangely flat scent of Amanda's hair . . . then shrugged and stuffed the key in the pocket of his jacket with his coins.

The laundromat was at 37 North Street, and Mage walked past the small apartment building at 44 North without particularly noticing it. It was only after he had bundled his clothes into the washer and reached into his pocket for coins that he found Amanda's key and realized where he was. He glanced around the room and frowned. The machine had a fifteen-minute cycle, the laundromat was chilly, and the plastic-seated chairs, with their uneven metal legs, looked far less comfortable than a Greyhound seat. The antique fluorescent tubes flickered arrhythmically like something out of *Alien,* making reading impossible, and there was no one else around to talk to (Mage had never actually picked up anyone in a laundromat, nor did he know anyone who had, but he lived in hope). Besides, Amanda might have left the fixings for a cup of coffee. He dropped the coins in the slot and ambled across the windy street without looking back.

As soon as he fit the key in the lock, he sensed that someone else—not Amanda—had been there recently, though he couldn't have said how he knew. The apartment was even colder than the laundromat had been, and switching the light on only made everything a more dismal shade of gray. The place was tidy, mainly because it was so empty; the only thing that seemed remotely worth stealing—an old portable black-and-white TV—still stared cycloptically at a slightly threadbare sofa and matching chairs, a standard floor lamp now visibly substandard, a recently re-re-re-painted dining-room suite, and a small, empty bookshelf. No pictures on the wall, no hints of personality. How could anyone, even a student, bear to live like this?

Cautiously he closed the door behind him, removed his gloves and placed his camera case on the bookshelf. A glass, a cup and saucer stood in the kitchen sink. He opened the small fridge and peered in at a half-empty container of blueberry yogurt (a cautious sniff suggested that it was only a few days old), a tub of margarine, a small wedge of Camembert cheese, two eggs, and three slightly limp carrots. The freezer compartment was empty except for a tray of ice cubes and a thick layer of frost. The motor muttered when he closed the door. The pantry contained a box of tea bags, three-quarters full.

There were two other doors leading out of the room; the first he opened led to the bathroom. There was a cake of Ivory soap in the shower, only slightly worn, and the rings from shampoo and conditioner bottles, no longer there. The cabinet was bare and the laundry hamper empty.

The bedroom contained a slightly sagging double bed, an empty bureau, and a closet that hid only a dozen wire coat hangers. There was a large box of tissues on the bureau, but nothing that was identifiably *hers,* no books or photographs, nothing beautiful or meaningful, nothing to return to. As though she'd come here with nothing but that handbag and left with the same, without time to impress her personality on the room at all. As though it were a cheap motel, or a set in a bad TV series. As though she didn't have anything of her own.

He shuddered and walked into the bathroom again, looking in the sink and the shower drain. Not a single hair.

He sat on the toilet and pondered. Even if someone had raided the place last night—and he realized suddenly where that impression had come from: small objects that had been put back slightly out of true with their dust shadows—nothing had been taken. If there had been anything to take, Amanda had taken it herself. Wondering what "it" might be, he returned to the living room, donned his gloves, shouldered his camera case and walked out. He was still musing as he crossed the road without looking, and he didn't notice Packer staring at him from inside the phone booth outside 41 North Street.

Mage dumped his damp clothes into the spin-dryer and was fumbling in his pocket for some change when he heard the door open and close behind him. He turned around to see a thick-featured, middle-aged man reaching into his war-surplus great-coat.

"Hi."

Packer smiled slightly and drew his MAC-11. Mage stared at it and swallowed, then stared down at his own left hand as though it belonged to someone else. He swallowed again and this time found some of his voice. "Uh . . . it's okay," he croaked quietly. "I don't have a . . . what do you want? If it's money, I'm sorry, but you've got the wrong person. I've just got enough for the—"

"Where is she?"

"—dryer and— Who?" He'd seen photos of Carol's ex; this definitely wasn't him.

"The blonde. The one whose apartment you just left."

"The . . ." He inhaled raggedly, nervously, and began again. "Who're you? Her father?" There was no discernible family resemblance, but he looked to be the right age, and Mage had known several pretty girls with uglier parents.

"Never mind that. Where is she?"

The washing machine clunked suddenly, changing its cycle, and Mage jumped, nearly losing control of his bladder. *"I don't know."*

"What were you doing in the apartment?"

"Nothing. She gave me the key. I wanted to see if she'd come back."

"So she's coming back, is she?"

"I don't know."

Packer grunted. "You her boyfriend?"

"Me? *No!* I just lent her some money . . ."

"When?"

"Yes . . . no, day before yesterday. What was that?"

"Tuesday."

He nodded. "Whatever you say."

Packer scratched his chin with his left hand; the gun, in his right, barely wavered. "So if she's coming back, she must've gone somewhere first, right? So where?"

"She caught a Greyhound, said she was going to Calgary."

"You're lying," said Packer flatly. "I already checked that."

"Well, that's what *she* told *me*. I saw her get on the bus and it was headed for Calgary, but I don't know where she went from there. For real, I don't know."

Mage stared at the gun, at the long magazine and the thick suppressor, vaguely recognizing it as an Ingram. What was that riddle? "How do you hit something with an Ingram at more than ten feet? You throw the damn thing overarm." Unfortunately, the muzzle was barely a yard away, no one could miss at that range. He realized that he'd answered all the questions and that now the guy would shoot him. What if it jammed? he fantasized. Machine-pistols were notorious for jamming, weren't they? His left hand, in his jacket pocket, clenched until he felt his nails bite into his palm, felt the jagged edge of the apartment key between his middle and ring fingers. If it jammed, he might—

Packer pulled the trigger. There was a *cl-* as the gun jammed on the first round.

They stared at each other for nearly half a second. Then Mage grabbed the strap of his camera case with his right hand and swung it like a flail. It hit the machine-pistol squarely, sending it flying from Packer's hand and over his shoulder until the sling arrested its flight and brought it back, hitting the gunman in the ass. Mage swung the camera case in as tight a circle as possible, twisting the strap around his wrist, and struck Packer in the temple with an audible crack. Packer fell heavily against the washing machines and slid to the floor.

Mage stared at the body until he noticed—with relief, heavily tainted by sheer panic—that the gunman still seemed to be breathing. Acting without conscious choice, his left hand unclenched and reached behind him to open the dryer door and remove the damp clothes. He snapped back to reality when his hand encountered warm, soggy denim, but he didn't take his eyes from Packer.

His choices were few, and it didn't take long to review them.

He collected his clothes hastily, took out his camera and flash for a few photographs of Packer (if his murdered body was ever found anywhere, he reasoned, at least the cops would know who to look for), leaped over the unconscious gunman and ran down North Street.

When he arrived at Carol's, it was five past ten. He barely had time to stuff the bags of damp clothes into his pack, gather whatever else he had and shut the door on his way out. He had decided that his only hope was to catch the 10:20 Greyhound to Calgary to try to find Amanda. If he found her, he could warn her, or ask her what was happening; if she'd lied but the gunman had spoken the truth, then Calgary would probably be the last place the mysterious "they" would look for him.

That a mysterious "they" was involved, and that the gunman was a mere employee, Mage had no doubt. Someone with a personal stake wouldn't have called Amanda "the blonde."

He arrived at the Greyhound station three minutes before the bus was due to leave and waved his ticket at the driver. There was no sign of the gunman.

5

The Hunter

The Greyhound was less than half full, and Mage curled himself into a double seat, hiding his face behind a copy of *Zoom*. He stared surreptitiously over the magazine at his fellow passengers, none of whom seemed to be carrying a concealed gun. Then, as soon as Totem Rock had dwindled to nothingness behind him, he closed his eyes, fighting to shut out the morning. At the first rest stop, he bought new batteries for his Walkman and phoned Carol.

"Hi. It's Mage. I . . ."

"Where are you?" She sounded resigned, ready to disbelieve whatever she heard.

"Ah . . . Swift Current, I think, wherever *that* is."

"I got back and saw your pack was gone. I thought we'd been robbed—"

Mage noticed the "we" and shoved it to the back of his mind. "You may be yet. There's some maniac in town with an Ingram, a machine gun—"

"I know what an Ingram is," she said dryly. "Who?"

"No one I've ever met. Short brown hair, little reddish mustache, big face, small mouth. Sunglasses, gray trenchcoat, combat boots. Late thirties, I guess—I'm no good at men's ages—height about five ten, and one-eighty pounds."

"Doesn't sound familiar. What happened?"

"He cornered me in the laundromat and grilled me. Would've shot me too, but his gun jammed. I . . . I knocked him out, believe it or not, and ran. Look, I know this sounds incredible—"

"Uh-huh," she agreed. "Did you call the sheriff or anyone . . . or are you in some sort of trouble?"

"I didn't think I was, but I sure as hell am now. No, I didn't call the sheriff, I didn't have time, and for all I knew, this guy *was* the sheriff."

"With a submachine gun? Where did you think you were, L.A.?"

"Look, I was too scared to be logical." The idea of voluntarily talking to a cop hadn't occurred to him until the bus was well out of town and he'd had time to recover some semblance of calm, and after a moment's rational thought, he'd rejected it. Even if the cops could protect Amanda, he'd decided, she might have her own reasons for not wanting them to find her.

Carol sighed. "Sounds like a guilty conscience to me. Whose daughter did you knock up?"

"Ha, ha. I . . ." He paused and thought. "I helped a fugitive, maybe. What d'they call that? 'Aiding and abetting'?"

"What?"

"Look, it's just a guess; that's all I can do at present. I don't know what's happening, but maybe if I can find her, she can tell me—"

"She? Oh, never mind. *I'll* call the sheriff, but I don't know where you are, right?"

"You *don't* know where I am! Jesus, *I* don't know where I am! Look, everyone's getting back on the bus; I'd better go. I'll come back when I can. Promise. Ciao."

He walked back to the bus, folded himself into his seat and listened to his Walkman, trying hard to relax. He traded cassettes with the twins in the seats behind him, then talked with one while the other dozed. They lived with their mother in Regina and were going to Calgary to visit their father. They were freshly sixteen and still innocence and baby fat, flirting like kittens playing with a ball. No makeup, no bras, no visible scars. The sleeper was Susan; the talker, Georgia. Mage would never see them again, and he forgot their names within a week—but he remembered their faces, and thousands of others, for the rest of his life.

I'm sorry, but Miss Sharmon checked out yesterday morning."

Mage refrained from swearing, with difficulty. He'd had to catch a bus and a train from the Greyhound station to the youth hostel, then walk nine blocks from the hostel to the hospital. He was tired and hungry, his legs and shoulders ached, and the adrenaline surge that comes with being shot at had dissipated hours before.

"Yesterday," he guessed, meant an overnight stay, presumably tests of some sort, but he knew that nurses didn't give medical information away, and this one didn't seem readily susceptible to charm. She was a fortyish, muscular, square-featured redhead who looked as though she should've had an Irish brogue but spoke instead with a hint of Quebecois accent and arrogance. He tried his best smile nonetheless and asked, "Did she say where she was going?"

"Are you a relative?"

So much for his best smile. He looked at the nurse's face carefully and saw the answer she had ready, saw the trap. "No. She doesn't have any relatives."

The nurse's face fell, very slightly: bull's-eye. "I'm sorry . . ." she lied. "We only give that sort of information to next of kin. If you were married—"

"How about engaged?"

"Are you?" she asked flatly.

"No, not really. I just thought she might have mentioned me."

"Well . . ." She glanced at the computer screen and shook her head. "There's no next of kin listed. If she'd put your name down . . . what *is* your name, please?"

"Magistrale. Michelangelo Magistrale. Middle initial G. Has anyone else come looking for her?"

"Not while I've been here, and there's nothing in her file."

"Can you tell me when she's coming back, then? Please?"

"No." But she glanced at the VDU, inadvertently telling Mage that Amanda *was* scheduled to come back sometime. But that wasn't enough to work with. "Sometime" could be up to a year away, and Mage rarely knew where he was sleeping more than a month in advance.

"Thanks." He was thinking furiously as he left the hospital and so didn't notice the tobacco-brown Toyota parked outside the entrance, or see the Japanese-looking man in the back seat with a Fujica camera.

"Was that him?" asked the driver, watching his passenger carefully in the rearview mirror. Yukitaka Hideo nodded. "Do we follow him, then?"

"No need, I think." The city catered well enough to pedestrians, but its malls and one-way streets made it a nightmare for drivers. "Go to Seventh Avenue and we'll see if he turns up at the youth hostel."

The driver was about to ask, "And what if he doesn't?" but decided against it. Yukitaka was rumored to be more than Tamenaga's bodyguard: there were many who called him Tamenaga's left hand. Tamenaga was the only human who knew just how true that was.

*   *   *

Mage was sitting in the hostel's laundry, listening to his Walkman and watching his slightly musty clothes tumble around in the drier, when the door opened. He jumped, reaching for his camera case, then relaxed. "Hi."

The girl—he recognized her as the warden's assistant, probably her daughter—was giggling too much to speak, so he continued. "Sorry, I was miles away. Is the place always this quiet?"

"Well, our busy season's in July, around stampede."

"July isn't much of a season."

"It's that or wait for another Winter Olympics. I mean, I like it here but you're right, it is sort of quiet. Where're you from?"

"New York," he replied, "once upon a time."

She shook her head disbelievingly. "So what're you doing here?"

"Looking for a friend."

"Anybody in particular?"

He grinned. "Yeah. Maybe she's been here. She didn't have much money last time I saw her. Her name's Amanda Sharmon. Blond, good-looking, about five-seven . . ."

"Doesn't ring any bells, an' it's a strange name. I think I'd remember't."

"Could you look it up? Please?"

She looked at him warily, then nodded. "Okay. You booked for dinner, didn't you?"

"Yes . . . oh, damn, is—"

"It's ready. That's why I came looking for you; don't flatter yourself. Come on."

Why's it so important you find this girl?"

"What?" Mage glanced up from the register and blinked.

"Why're you looking for her?"

He thought quickly. "She's sick."

"Oh, yeah? What've you got, AIDS or something?"

"Me? Hell, no."

The girl nodded suspiciously. "This is all so much bullshit, isn't it?"

"Well . . ." He held his hand up to the bottom of his sternum. "Maybe *so* much."

She snorted. "I knew it. If she's sick, why aren't you looking at the hospital?"

"I did," he replied, returning his attention to the register. Nothing. "They wouldn't tell me a damn thing. You wouldn't have a friend who's a nurse, would you?"

"No."

He shrugged. For all its skyscrapers, Calgary wasn't New York, but it wasn't Totem Rock either; the chance of a Grey-hound cashier remembering one girl, however beautiful, was negligible, and even the chance of finding the right cashier was damn slender. What the hell to do next?

"What time is curfew?"

"Two. Desk closes at twelve."

He glanced at his watch: ten past eight. "I'll be back."

The girl gave him a "Who cares?" shrug and he walked out, wondering vaguely if he were losing his touch.

To find a needle in a haystack, he knew, you use a magnet. Finding a blonde in a wheatfield might be infinitely more rewarding, but not as easy. There was a quarter-column of Shar-mons in the White Pages, seven with the initial "A."

He thought furiously. Was Sharmon her real name? Almost certainly. People rarely gave false names to hospitals. And even if it wasn't, he had nothing else to go by.

Was Calgary her hometown? Probably, but again, people usually went to the nearest hospital where treatment (what treatment? and for what?) was available. There were, he presumed, hospitals in Saskatoon and Regina, both of which were much closer to Totem Rock than Calgary. So she wasn't from Totem Rock. . . .

He remembered suddenly that there hadn't even been a telephone in her apartment in Totem Rock, just an empty jack. Of course there were unlisted numbers, and communal houses popular with students—was there a university in Calgary? He riffled through the phone book again until he found it. Maybe if he phoned the admin office tomorrow . . . what *was* tomorrow? He had to look at his watch to remember that it was Friday.

There had to be *some* way of finding her. Didn't there?

The tobacco-brown Toyota was parked across the road from the hostel when Mage returned. Yukitaka watched him enter the building, looked at his watch and nodded.

"Back to the hotel," he told the driver.

"But—"

"He won't be going anywhere else tonight. He'll be quite safe in there."

The driver shrugged resignedly and started the car. He didn't see the smile on Yukitaka's face, and would have been none the wiser if he had.

Amanda hesitated when the car pulled over to the curb ahead of her. It had local plates, but it was too new to belong to any of her student friends and Alex refused to drive anything Japanese because of the lack of legroom. She stood there, prepared to run, as the front passenger door opened.

"Amanda?"

The voice was familiar, and she nervously took a step forward. "Jenny?"

"Come on, get in. You must be freezing out there! When did you get back?"

She walked to the side of the car, glanced in and recognized Jenny's broad, rather plain features and huge round glasses. "Where did you get the car?"

"It's my boyfriend's," came the reply, with a slight undertone of giggle.

"Your—"

"Come *on*. I have to pick him up at work. I'll tell you all about it while we drive."

6

Ninjo

The dorm had six beds, all but one unoccupied. The exception, the lower bunk nearest the window, sagged slightly under the weight of a small rucksack that might have been black a thousand miles ago. Its owner hadn't appeared at ten when Mage dropped the key, his Saint Christopher, his passport pouch, his wallet and his watch into his camera case, switched the light off, scrambled into his sleeping bag, turned his back to the window and resolved to sleep.

A few minutes after two, he heard a faint scratching sound behind him and rolled over. The window was being edged open from the outside. He froze, then relaxed slightly when he remembered that he was on the second floor and that there were vertical bars outside the window, only slightly wider than his head.

The window continued to edge up, and a pair of black-gloved hands appeared between the sash and the sill. Mage unzipped his sleeping bag slowly, quietly; it would mean running through the hostel half-naked, but he was sure that stranger things had happened.

The window opened as far as it could, and Mage could see a face beyond the bars. The details were vague, but he noticed off-the-collar black hair and slightly flat, Oriental features. The head squeezed between the bars, then twisted until the figure's shoulders were parallel with the sides of the window. Mage watched, fascinated, as the intruder slithered into the room like toothpaste from a tube, then stood, closed the window quietly, crept over to the nearest bunk, placed the rucksack on the floor and unzipped his leather jacket.

Mage heard footfalls in the hallway outside—and so, apparently, did the intruder; he was out of his boots and into his sleeping bag so quickly that he almost blurred. The door opened a moment later and the warden looked in suspiciously. The intruder was lying in the sleeping bag with his back to the door, apparently dead to the world. Mage looked up blearily at the light. The warden glanced in his direction dismissively, then backed out of the room and shut the door. The intruder waited, then rolled over with a quiet sigh of relief.

"Sorry if I woke you, man, but I never was very good with curfews." He twisted around inside his sleeping bag, then dropped his black jeans on the floor beside the bed.

"Do you do this often?" asked Mage dryly, and just as quietly.

The intruder grinned. "Sometimes, yeah."

"Why didn't you use the fire escape?"

"Leads into the girls' dorm. Besides, it's a family tradition."

"Climbing walls?"

"No, that's my mother's side," the intruder said, dropping his socks on the floor. "I meant the window. Like when the fuzz busted the Family, they couldn't find my father. So they searched again and one of the cops saw long hair hanging out of this little cupboard above the hand basin. It looked much too small for a human being, but not for the old man." He shrugged. "It can be a useful skill. It's the only way he'll ever get into Heaven."

Mage closed his eyes. The story sounded familiar . . . and then he opened his eyes very wide. "Manson?" he whispered. "Charles Manson? He's your father?"

"Charles Willis Takumo, at your service, and good night." His roommate rolled over to face the wall and was silent.

Mage slept badly, and his little sleep was slashed and riddled with bad dreams. Excessively ordinary-looking assassins, armed with silenced machine pistols with muzzles like cannons, crept in through barred windows and locked doors and spin-dryers, while beautiful blondes disappeared as he reached for them, leaving only a few long strands of hair (and black hair at that). He was awakened by the scraping sound of the window being opened yet again.

"What's up, Charlie? Midnight snack?" he murmured, still half asleep, and rolled over. Takumo was in his sleeping bag, facing the wall—or at least something Takumo-sized was in the sleeping bag, and something black-haired and head-shaped was sticking out of the appropriate end. Mage glanced at the window and saw another pair of black-gloved hands easing it up from the outside. Oh, Jesus, he thought, what is this? A convention?

The sash rose by a few inches and the hands crept underneath it. Mage was horrified to see that they were just that—hands, ending at the wrists in bloodless stumps, but working as a pair. He looked beyond the window and saw a face, obscured by blacking. The hands opened the window and the head squeezed in between the bars. It was a broader head than Takumo's, with less hair, and though the skillfully applied camouflage blurred his features, Mage could tell that the man (head? head-man? manhead?) was older than Charlie—probably in his late thirties—and Asian. Probably Japanese.

The head floated into the room and the hands closed the window behind it. Then head and hands crept toward Mage's bunk, staying close together, almost as though they were connected by an invisible body, but hovering just above the floor. Mage tried hard to convince himself that he was still dreaming, and failed.

Takumo rolled over and opened one eye as the hands glided past his bed. He opened his mouth to speak, then closed it again. His left arm flopped over the edge of the bed, the hand describing a slow spiral until it reached his leather jacket.

The hands slid slowly and silently over to Mage's bed and reached for the strap of the camera case. Suddenly, without taking time to think, Mage grabbed one of the hands by the wrist. It squirmed in his grasp, but it couldn't match his strength. The right hand hovered out of Mage's reach, and the head appeared slowly above the bunk like a horrible moonrise. Mage lifted his head to grin nervously back at it and swung his pillow overarm. It enveloped the blackened face, batting it closer to the floor and temporarily blinding it.

Mage jackknifed his body out of the sleeping bag and dropped to the floor, armed only with the pillow. The head flew toward him, teeth bared in a snarl, and Mage instinctively shielded his groin with the pillow. The head avoided the shield and went for his forearm, sinking carnivore-sharp teeth into the muscle. Mage flinched, swung around and bashed the head into one of the wooden bedposts. The right hand wrapped itself around his throat while he struggled with the left. Mage swung the head into the bedpost again, dropped the pillow and pried at the choking hand. He looked around the room hurriedly for something that might be used as a weapon: an electric heater, a hand basin, a fire extinguisher, anything.

Nothing.

Takumo slipped quietly out of bed and crept toward him. Mage heard a faint *click* and saw a short black blade suddenly appear in Takumo's hand. Takumo looked at the struggling left hand and then at the bedpost. Mage blinked and nodded slightly. He waited until Takumo was in range, then swung his arm so that the left hand slapped the bedpost. Takumo lunged with the butterfly knife, pinning the hand to the post. The head opened its mouth to scream, and Mage brought his knee up into the base of its skull.

The head flew up with the force of the blow, then dropped, bouncing off the bed and onto the floor. The right hand relaxed its grip on Mage's throat, very slightly but enough for the photographer to pry it loose with both hands. The head rolled under the bed before Takumo could grab it.

"Nice friends you have," muttered Takumo.

"I thought he was with you!"

Takumo glanced at the right hand and noticed the gashes in Mage's arm, which were far too deep and bloody to have been made by human teeth. He suddenly felt very naked, and looked down. His cock was as rigid as an iron bar, if rather less useful, and his skin was goose-bumped and ivory-pale and slick with sweat.

The monstrous head flew out from under the bed and up to the ceiling, where it glared down at them. Mage tightened his grip on the hand, ensuring that it couldn't slip out of the glove.

The head swooped down at Mage's groin again, and the photographer slapped its face with the gloved hand. The head bit down slightly and the hand jerked violently, twisting out of Mage's sweaty grasp. The leather took the worst of the damage, but Mage could see what looked like drops of blood in some of the rents. The head retreated slightly, and Takumo high-kicked it with all his strength, sending it spinning toward the ceiling.

The right hand groped around the bedpost, apparently looking for the hilt of Takumo's knife. The head righted itself and drifted back to the corner of the ceiling, its features contorted by pain and fury and a good measure of confusion, as though it could not believe what was happening to it.

"You watch the hand, man; I'll watch the head," murmured Takumo.

The right hand stopped as though the head had heard him; then it, too, leaped toward the ceiling.

"I think they've had enough," whispered Mage hopefully.

The hand crept down toward the door handle and turned it. The door opened a crack, and head and hand vanished through it. Takumo kicked the door shut hurriedly.

"Do we follow them?"

"*What?*" hissed Takumo as he grabbed the only chair in the room and jammed it under the door handle.

"They may attack someone else."

Takumo stopped, then shook his head, feeling warm blood returning to his face. "No way. It was after you, wasn't it?"

"What gives you that idea?"

"It didn't attack *me*. Not even when I was fighting back. What's in that bag of yours, anyway?"

"Just my camera."

Takumo raised an eyebrow, diverting a stream of cold perspiration down the bridge of his nose. "Oh, yeah? What in hell've you been photographing?"

"If you'd asked me yesterday, I'd have said girls."

"I'm asking you now."

"I don't know."

Takumo nodded. Mage walked carefully toward the window—he was still shivering uncontrollably and his legs felt like overcooked spaghetti—and muttered, "I wish I'd gotten a shot of it. No one is going to believe this."

"Who were you thinking of telling?"

Mage slid the window shut, then shrugged. "I don't know. I wouldn't even know what to call it."

"It looked like some kind of Japanese vampire. Or ghoul. I used to know the name. But does it matter?"

Mage, who hadn't expected an answer, brightened. A name, he considered, could occasionally be as useful as a photograph. "It might."

"We can go to a library after they throw us out of here—and

they will, y'know. D'you have anything that can fix that window? Knife?"

"No."

Takumo reached for his jeans and removed a Swiss Army knife from a pouch on his belt. "Better get dressed first. There're innocent little girls out there; you could scare the hell out of 'em with that." He shrugged. "Whereas, who's going to tell anyone they saw a head and a hand floating through the place?"

"Can they get out? The head and hand, I mean."

"No problem. There's a transom above the main door."

"Sounds like you cased this place pretty well yourself."

"I've stayed here before," muttered Takumo. "Going to be lucky to leave with our membership cards this time, though."

"Is that all that's worrying you?"

"If I worry, I don't have time to panic."

"I fight better when I'm panicking."

Takumo smiled. "Besides, it wasn't trying to kill *me*. Someone *is* after you, neh?"

"Yeah."

Takumo sat on the bed and reached for his jacket. "I'm still on an adrenaline high—too buzzed to try to sleep. Tell me about it."

When Mage had finished, Takumo shook his head as though making sure it was still attached to his neck. "Far freakin' out."

"I'm finding it hard to believe, myself," replied Mage.

"Yeah, but having the beast with five fingers pinned to your bed makes it sort of hard to be skeptical. But you say this joker's gun jammed on the first round?" Mage nodded. "Weird. Maybe it wasn't loaded, or loaded with the wrong caliber ammo, or he still had the safety on—easy enough to do—or maybe he just wanted to scare you."

"He succeeded," Mage admitted flatly, wrapping his jacket tighter around himself. It didn't stop his shivering. He had never before encountered a threat that had followed him after he'd left town, and he would have liked to dismiss the whole affair as a serial nightmare, a shared hallucination, but his eyes had always served him well in the past and he found it difficult to distrust them now.

"And the horseless headman went for your camera case, not for you, like he wasn't heavily into killing you either. Did this lady give you anything?"

"Only the key to her apartment."

Takumo raised his eyebrows at that. "Did you try it?"

"Yes."

"Anything in there?"

"No . . . and it was only a cheap lock. Anyone with a credit card could've broken in. I think someone did before I got there and gave the place the once-over, but didn't take anything."

"How d'you know?"

"They didn't disturb the dust."

"*Man,* have you got some pair of eyes. So they were looking for something and it wasn't there, so they think *you* got it, right?"

"Looks that way."

"Or like they think you know where it is, so they don't want to kill you yet?"

Mage shrugged, an eloquent Italian shrug that exercised most of the muscles in his upper body.

"So wha'do we do now?"

Mage stopped in mid shrug and mid shiver. "We?"

"For sure. Like safety in numbers, dig? Like they're going to want my ass too."

Mage considered this. Takumo's appearance did little to inspire trust, even when he was dressed, and he was hardly inconspicuous—but he could fight, and maybe he knew something about the mysterious "they."

"Is Manson really your father?"

"I don' know, man. I was kind of young at the time. But it's what my mother told me, and I think she believed it. Like, I was probably conceived at the Family's monthly orgy at the ranch, Spahn Movie Ranch, before the Tate-LaBianca murders went down. My real father could've been any one of a half-dozen bikies—Straight Satans—or one of the Family males. I was born a couple of months after the arrest but before the trial. My mother thought they were all innocent and so she named me after Charlie . . . well, after one of his aliases." He grinned humorlessly. "She was sure she'd been careful, and said that made me a karma baby, or a miracle child, or something. Guess I'm lucky she didn't call me 'God' or 'Jesus.' God Jesus Christ Takumo. Got a ring to it, neh?"

Mage nodded. "And Takumo—isn't that a monster or something?"

"You speak Japanese?"

"No, I just know something about monsters—my Uncle Dante writes horror stories." He glanced at the helplessly wriggling hand. "Pity he's not here."

Takumo smiled. "Well, *kumo* just means spider. *Hirata-kumo* is a huntsman spider—you know, the kind that lassoes its prey—except that it's about a yard across. *Totate-kumo* is a trap-door spider, about the same size. Some of them can shapeshift into human. What do people call you?"

"Mage. Michelangelo Gaetano Magistrale, if that makes you feel any better."

"Mage? As in Wise Man from the East?"

"I'm from New York," Mage admitted. "The wisdom must've been an optional extra."

"Hey, you left New York. That makes you wiser than most." He stared at the window; the sky was as dark as despair.

"Four o'clock," said Mage.

"Three fifty-seven." Takumo grinned, holding up a digital watch with more functions than his Swiss Army knife. "Wonders of Japanese technology. What d'you want to do with the hand?'"

"What?"

" 'Here comes the sun,' " he sang softly. "I think the thing has to be home by sunrise or it'll start to bleed like a bitch. You want t'explain that to the warden?"

Mage stared at the hand, which was hanging limply, wrist down. There was a dark-red film on the blade, but the wound and the end of the wrist looked dry; the few drops of blood on the floor were his. Just looking at the thing made his savaged triceps hurt like hell.

"What d'you think it'll do if we open the window and let it go?" he asked.

"Let it go? You mean throw it out and shut the window behind it pronto? It probably can't find its way out without the head to see for it. What time is sunrise, anyway?"

"I don't know. I never was a Boy Scout."

Yukitaka sat in the Toyota drumming his fingers on the dash and waiting. Every few minutes he glanced at the tourniquet on his left forearm as though it were a watch. The sky was still black but the sun would rise in less than an hour. Yukitaka had a momentary vision of circling the world, constantly flying ahead of the sunrise, and he smiled briefly at the idea. Tamenaga could afford it, and might have done so had their positions been reversed. Or would he cut off his arm to save face?

There was a slight twinge as the knife was pulled out of his hand, but the pain troubled Yukitaka Hideo far less than the humiliation. He brooded on his failure as the hand flopped to the ground and began to creep across the frost toward the Toyota, its senses and its strength severely diminished by its distance from Yukitaka's head.

Yukitaka glanced at the dashboard clock again and cursed. He disliked English, with its complicated grammar and downright bizarre spelling, but he was frequently grateful for the swearwords. He opened the door and stepped out into the bitter cold.

He caught his left hand on his wrist like a falconer and hastily removed the leather glove. Hand and forearm bonded in a moment, without even a mark. He bandaged the hand as best he could, loosened the tourniquet and drove back to the hotel.

The sun rose just as Yukitaka was parking the Toyota, and he screamed with pain as blood squirted suddenly back into his palm.

Mage and Takumo watched the first dawn rays hit the clouds, nodded at each other in weary jubilation and crept back to their beds.

Gilded Honor

Mage's second dream of the morning was disturbed by the call to breakfast, for which he was silently but sincerely grateful. He sat up, saw the chair jammed under the door handle and jumped out of bed as hastily as possible to remove it. Takumo looked at him blearily and closed his eyes again. Mage glanced at the gash in the bedpost, shook his head and reached for his clothes. The urge to disbelieve everything that had happened the night before, to dismiss it as a dream, was strong, but he found it difficult to disbelieve or forget what he'd seen.

In the dining room, he rescued his breakfast pancakes from the mandatory drowning in maple syrup, poured himself a mug of coffee and sat at an empty table despite a vacancy opposite a pretty redhead. Takumo—his dark hair damp from the shower, his eyes bloodshot but wide open—appeared as he was finishing his second cup of coffee.

"Morning."

Takumo nodded. "I've volunteered us for garbage detail.

Hope you don't mind." Mage grunted. "That way, we get finished early and split."

"Where to?"

"The university, check out the library."

"Okay. After that?"

"Where would your girlfriend have gone?"

"She wasn't my girlfriend," said Mage automatically.

"Figure of speech. What else should I call her?"

Mage conceded the point wearily. "I don't know, and I don't know where she would have gone. Vancouver? Edmonton? The States? Back to Totem Rock?"

"Won't they be looking for her there?"

"Yeah, and everywhere else."

"Or waiting for you to lead them to her."

Mage's coffee suddenly tried to climb back up his throat. "Oh, Jesus." Several of his fellow diners turned around and glared. He wiped his mouth with his napkin and tried to smile.

"So sorry."

"You're probably right, but what else can I do?"

"Forget her?"

Mage smiled bitterly. "She's not someone you'd forget."

"Or fake it, anyway."

"Then they'll think I have whatever-it-is . . ."

"The three magic beans."

"The what?"

"Sorry. Your story smacks a little of 'Jack and the Beanstalk.' "

Mage carefully swallowed a mouthful of coffee. "I'm going to keep looking."

"Why? You only met her once."

Mage took another sip of coffee to give himself time to think. He was sure there was a good reason why he needed to find Amanda Sharmon, but he couldn't put it into words that made sense. He wondered if he'd fallen in love with her and decided that that probably wasn't it. Maybe it was just that he didn't know which way to run . . . no, that wasn't it either.

"It's starting to bug me," he replied finally. "I hate mysteries."

Takumo grinned. "Okay, I can relate to that. So. Where was she from?"

"Here."

"How d'you know?"

"She goes to the hospital here."

"What's wrong with her?"

"I don't know . . . but it's serious, and not contagious, so it's not AIDS. Cancer, I guess."

"Did she look sick?"

"No. Worried, but not sick."

"Hm. Accent?"

"Canadian."

"East? West?"

"I don't know. Anywhere except Quebec. I'm not very good with accents. She's a student, or she was, and she said she was from Vancouver originally. . . . Where were *you* going?"

"Back home."

"L.A.?"

Takumo nodded, drained the last of his tea and stood. "Let's go."

The dumpster was behind the building, where the sun didn't touch the frost until eleven. Mage walked carefully around the northwest corner, then stopped so suddenly that Takumo walked squarely into the Baggie of garbage in his left hand and almost tripped.

"Hey—"

Mage dropped his other Baggie and pointed. Long blond hair was hanging over the edge of the dumpster. Takumo stared. "Oh, man . . ."

They stood there silently for several seconds. "Did you ever see this Japanese horror movie," asked Mage nervously, "where this samurai comes home to his former wife and all that's left is her ghost, and her hair, and she—"

Takumo nodded. "Seven times. It's called *Kwaidan.*"

"Seven?"

"I was working as a projectionist at a film festival."

Mage nodded. Takumo dropped his Baggies and they both took a few hesitant steps closer to the bin.

"Actually . . ."

"Yeah?"

"I was thinking about the time the cops raided Barker Ranch and saw this hair hanging out of the medicine cabinet—"

"And it was your father. You told me."

"Sorry."

Another step carried them within arm's reach. Takumo learned forward cautiously and touched the hair. Nothing happened. He grabbed it, winding it around his fingers.

"I got it. Open the lid."

Mage shuddered slightly, reached for the handle and threw the lid up as forcefully as he could. It seemed to hang in midair for a second, then crashed backward resoundingly, leaving the dumpster open. Nothing happened.

Takumo tugged experimentally, and the hair slid over the edge and dropped to the ground. Both men stared at it; then Takumo knelt and took it in both hands.

"Don't say it," Mage said.

"Don't say what?"

" 'Alas, poor Yorick, I knew him well . . .' "

" 'I knew him, *Horatio,*' " corrected Takumo. Mage blinked. "I do Shakespeare as well as stunts. 'Whether 'tis nobler in the mind to suffer the slings and arrows of outrageous fortune, or to take arms against a sea of troubles, and by opposing end them?' " He studied the wig, turning it over in his hands. "Are you sure this lady was really blond?"

"Yes."

"How're you sure?"

Mage stared into his memory and saw Amanda's face as clearly as if it were a photograph. "Her eyebrows were pale. *Very* pale."

Takumo nodded. "Could this be her?"

"Presuming you mean 'hers' . . . yeah, I guess so. The length and the color are right."

"It's real hair," said Takumo. "Human hair. Very expensive. People don't just throw it away."

"How d'you know?"

"Ninja always used ropes of real hair, paid a fortune for it."

"You can tell by the feel?"

Takumo laughed. "No, but there's a label in here. See?" He stood and threw the wig to Mage. "Besides, I was a very low-budget ninja. Used ordinary nylon rope."

Mage looked at the wig. "No bloodstains."

"You really *are* paranoid, aren't you?"

"Maybe, but that doesn't mean they're not out to get me," replied Mage automatically. "And the same people were out to get her, too."

"It wasn't the *people* that had me going," retorted Takumo. "Hey, what if you're wrong? What if your blonde's just set you up to take the rap?"

Mage stared at him. *"Now* who's paranoid?"

"Hey, man, when you're five-foot-five, illegitimate, and named after the most notorious criminal in the local mythology, you have an excuse for paranoia that six-foot-three can barely understand."

"I'm six-one," replied Mage.

"Neat. So *you* can look inside and see if there's a body."

Mage gulped, then peered down into the bin. "Nothing but Baggies." He opened the other lid and stared into that half. "No."

"What if she's—"

"Don't even *think* it," replied Mage, shuddering. "Why

would they put her in a Baggie and leave her wig hanging out like a billboard?"

Takumo shrugged his eyebrows. "Shall we dump the trash and split?"

"Suits me," Mage said, unzipping a pocket in his jacket and stuffing the wig inside.

"What're you keeping that for?"

"Damned if I know," he replied and walked back to where they'd dropped the bags of garbage.

The woman behind the admissions desk at the university was thirtyish and tired-looking, but as helpful as she was permitted to be. Yes, they'd had a student named Amanda Sharmon. No, she wasn't still enrolled. No, she couldn't tell him why. Yes, there was a copy of her last-known address and phone number on file, and no, she couldn't give it out, but yes, they could attempt to relay a letter. Could they phone her, ask if she wanted to speak to a Mage—a Michelangelo Magistrale—and hand the receiver over if she said yes; it *was* an emergency. The woman looked at him, then nodded.

There was no answer, but the phone hadn't been disconnected. Mage thanked her and turned to leave, then stopped.

"Has anyone else been here recently to ask about her?"

"No," she said positively. "Why?"

"Just paranoia," he replied and grinned disarmingly. "Do you know who her tutors were?"

"No, but the math department would."

"Great. Where is it?"

She told him, and he thanked her with a smile and a slight bow before dashing outside to where Takumo was waiting.

"Why so happy?"

"They haven't been here yet. We're one step ahead of them!"

"Pun unintended, I presume," said Takumo dryly. "So where to now, kemosabe?"

"Math department. They'll be able to tell us who her tutors were, the tutors can tell us who her friends were, her friends—"

"You hope," said Takumo. "Do you need me, or shall I check out the library?"

"I think I'll be okay on my own." He glanced at his watch. "Meet you back here at one o'clock."

The timetable on the door suggested that Dr. Corwin should be inside; Mage had left college after only one year, but he'd learned how little *that* meant. He knocked tentatively and was rewarded with a loud grunt that might have been "Come in."

Corwin was a lanky, sandy-haired man in his forties. He looked up from the papers on his desk and over his thick glasses.

"Yes?"

"Dr. Corwin?"

"That's correct."

"I'm trying to contact a student of yours . . . well, an ex-student. Amanda Sharmon."

"I can't help you." He looked down at his papers again, dismissively.

"You remember her?"

"Certainly. Best student I've had in years. Damn shame. But I don't know where she is now. Sorry."

"Do you remember who any of her friends were?"

Corwin peered over his glasses warily. "Who're you?"

"My name is Magistrale. Last time I met Amanda, she told me she was coming back here to go into the hospital. I said I'd visit her there, but I missed her and . . ."

Corwin chewed his lip. "I don't know anybody who's seen her this semester."

"Please . . . it's very important I find her."

"Why?"

"I think I can help her."

Corwin snorted. "You a magician?"

"No."

"Faith-healer? Miracle-worker? Shaman? Witch?"

Mage bit back his anger, trying not to reveal his ignorance. "I said help her, not cure her."

Corwin shook his head.

"She didn't finish her degree," persisted Mage. "Some of her classmates should still be here. Some of her friends. One name. *Please.*"

"When did you last see her?" asked Corwin finally.

"Last week. Tuesday."

"How was she?"

"Worried."

"That's all?"

"Scared. Anxious. Broke. I gave her money for the bus. But she looked . . . she *didn't* look sick."

Corwin stared at him, his expression neither hostile nor friendly, the red pen in his hand swaying like a metronome, left, right, left, right. He hated making decisions based on inadequate data and was convinced that he usually made the wrong choice.

Mage, not moving from the doorway, looked around the room. Two walls were lined with bookshelves, one was mostly window, and the fourth was adorned with diplomas, certificates, and an Escher print: *Regular Division of the Plane III*. Men on horseback, tessellated together, reds going left, whites right. Mage decided that he didn't much like it, but he could see why it would appeal to a statistician. Or to a political scientist. He looked at Corwin, waiting for him to make a decision (preferably the correct decision); he shoved his hands into his pockets, indicating that he had no intention of closing the door, and discovered Amanda's key. His fingers twisted the cord around his fingers as Corwin wavered, left, right, left. . . .

"Jenny Holdridge," said Corwin finally.

"Thank you. Where can I find her?"

"The office should be able to find her, or if you're really in a hurry, she works part-time in the library."

"I am. Thank you. You won't regret this."

Corwin grunted a dismissal and dropped his gaze and his grimace back to the papers on his desk.

Did you phone your uncle?"

"Yeah. He hadn't heard from her. What've you found?"

Takumo munched at his salad like a ruminant, then answered, "*Found* is a little strong. I kind of focused on the idea that we weren't going to be going up against Godzilla or Ghidrah, that I should concentrate on something you wouldn't notice if you passed it on the street—assuming the street was in California, of course. It didn't narrow the field as much as I'd hoped . . . so I started with *Kwaidan* and some other Lafcadio Hearn stuff and went from there.

"The thing last night was a *rukoro-kubi,* a spinning-head goblin. It's a carnivore"—he took another mouthful of salad, with a condescending glance at Mage's hot dog—"and it usually eats carrion, insects, that kind of shit. When it attacks humans, it likes to go for the extremities—fingers, toes . . ." He crossed his legs suddenly. "You know. They're supposed to be rare, if that helps."

"How d'you kill them?"

"My, aren't we macho all of a sudden? You exorcise them—don't ask me how, I just *eat* Buddhist—or you stop the head from returning to the body by sunrise.

"Rukoro-kubi are *bakemono,* which are kind of like ghosts—except that they were never really human and they're not really dead—and kind of like goblins. Most bakemono don't look very human, but the more human they look when they want to, the more human they aren't, if you can dig that.

"*Shuten-doji* are bakemono too. They're your basic vampires, except that they can appear by day or night. Apart from that, they can do anything Count Dracula can do . . . including count. The best defense against them is to drop some rice in their path, 'cause they have to stop and count the grains. They're kind of your undead number-crunchers. Hell's accountants. *Mujina* are more like gorgons. They're false-faces, and the females like to look like pretty girls"—Takumo smiled sourly—"but their real faces are voids that can send you mad or just scare you to death. Don't ask me how to kill *them;* the book doesn't say.

"Then you have *neko, kitsune,* and *tenuki*—cats, foxes, and badgers. That, as you may have heard, is also the scale the Japanese use for women. They're all shape-changers—the monsters, I mean, not the women. Well, not all of them. They're also pretty neat illusionists. Cats are lords and ladies, upper-crust and powerful; foxes are minor nobles, like samurai; badgers are peasants, with a pretty crude sense of humor. They're all whimsical at best, malicious and chaotic at worst. You want to hear any more?"

Mage shrugged—a subdued shrug, involving only his shoulders and his face. "Do you believe this stuff?"

"I didn't yesterday. How much of it I believe now, I don't know. But believing in one bakemono's like eating one peanut. Like, say you believe in vampires. Or demons. Vampires can be turned by a cross, burned by holy water or the host. Demons can be exorcised. So either you throw out that part of the mythos—and a lot of horror writers do that, make vampirism a disease or a mutation—or you have to believe in God, or it doesn't work. Like, you can't have that kind of evil without some supernatural good to match it. Like yin and yang."

"What if it's only the vampires or the demons who believe in God and that's why they can be exorcised? Like faith-healing in reverse or—what's the word? A psychosomatic disease? That doesn't mean the god is real."

"Then how does the rukoro-kubi fly? Where does the magic come from?"

"Damned if I know," replied Mage wryly. "I take it you don't believe in that kind of god either?"

Takumo shook his head. "My grandparents—who mostly brought me up—were Buddhists, and my mother thought God was doing life for murder. I'm only a kind of half-assed Buddhist, like I don't eat meat or anything or kill or lie any more than I have to, and I pray to the Goddess every time I do a stunt, but I was never a Christian. What about you? You look like you were a good Catholic boy."

"Yeah, I guess I was, back before my voice broke. Then I got interested in girls, and they got interested in me." He grinned briefly. "And I didn't like the way the church treated women; I mean, Jesus obviously liked women, but all the Old Testament and Saint Paul bullshit about the husband being to the wife what God was to the church . . . my father shouldn't be left in charge of a toll booth, much less a family, and he used religion as an excuse for nearly everything he did, and the last thing I wanted was to be like him. Anyway, Mom started bitching when I didn't want to go to church any longer, and she wouldn't tell any of us about sex; sex was nasty and you didn't take precautions because that meant you'd thought about it beforehand—if it happened, it had to happen by accident. That's what innocence meant to Mom—hell of an attitude for a woman with four daughters, huh? But you can't *not* find out about sex in school, even if most of what you find out is wrong . . . and then after Gina got knocked up, we found out by accident that Mom was on the pill. Okay, so she had good reasons—five children, six if you include my father—but the bullshit, you know, the hypocrisy? And you find flaws like that in a religion, it disillusions you completely, you chuck the whole thing."

Takumo shrugged. "New Yorkers might, but not Californians. Like, we invented chop suey, remember? We'll marry anything to anything else. Gay churches, beach chess, billion-dollar counterculture"—he took another gigantic bite from his lentilburger and swallowed—"and the Ronald Reagan Library.

I guess that makes it easier for me to dig this. Anyway, you want to come to the library, see the books yourself?"

Mage nodded, cramming the last of his hot dog into his mouth. Takumo stood and asked, "You want to know why I think you gave up on God?" Mage raised an eyebrow. "I don't think you believe in anything you can't see."

Mage, unable to speak, merely shook his head. "Think about it," said Takumo, and walked out.

Takumo placed another three books on the end of the table and murmured, "Back in a minute." Mage nodded without looking up from the volume open before him, which described the Seven Fortunate Gods. He was—as Takumo had expected—particularly intrigued by Benten, Goddess of Love and the Arts and Patron of Women, who rewarded those she favored with physical beauty.

Takumo ambled casually toward the men's restroom, glanced quickly over his shoulder at Mage, then dashed between the bookshelves and hurried toward the exit. No bags were allowed into the stacks, and Mage had been forced to leave his camera case in the foyer downstairs. Takumo was fairly sure that the case wasn't locked—Mage often needed to be quick on the draw when a fleeting image presented itself—and though he swore to himself that he *trusted* the photographer, he didn't believe that Mage had told him everything. Maybe, he told himself, Mage didn't *know* everything. Maybe the blonde had slipped something into the camera case that Mage hadn't found, and then told the rukoro-kubi—maybe under torture, maybe not.

The case opened easily, revealing a Nikon camera with an 80-300 zoom lens attached, a flashgun the size of a mallet, two unopened boxes of 200 ASA film, and seven filters—all in their respective slots in the foam-rubber padding. Takumo pressed the lining of the case, looking for anything hard, but he knew that was too obvious. He was opening the battery compartment of the flashgun when a hand fell heavily on his shoulder. He froze. The hand, he noted with some relief, was apparently attached to an arm—or at least to a familiar-looking sleeve.

Takumo knew seven working defenses from that position, three of them particularly effective against a larger opponent, but he decided against using them.

"I think there are photocopiers upstairs," said Mage sweetly. "How was the book?"

"I didn't finish it. Who's the Japanese God of Thieves?"

"Hotei, I guess," said Takumo slowly. "He's the God of Gamblers and Patron of the *Yakuza*—professional criminals. Or there's Ebisu, who's the God of Merchants, which is equal time, neh?"

Mage released his shoulder and opened the flashgun, dropping three large rechargeable batteries into his hand, then letting Takumo peer down the empty tube. "Curiosity satisfied?"

"No."

"What else do you want to see?"

"If I knew that, man—"

"You wouldn't have to look. Right. You think there's something here that the rukoro-kubi wanted. I thought the same thing, so I searched this case before we left the hostel this morning, while you were in the shower. Okay?"

"Find anything?"

"Just what you see here, and my passport, unless he was after my Saint Christopher medal or . . . "

"Or what?"

Mage blinked, slipped the batteries back into the flashgun and closed the compartment, then reached into his pocket and withdrew the key, waving it before Takumo like a hypnotist's focus, studying it. It still looked perfectly ordinary.

"Or this. Amanda's key."

Takumo, taking care to move slowly, placed his hand, palm up, beneath the midpoint of the key's swing. "Can I see it?"

Mage hesitated.

"Hey, man, I risked my ass for you last night! A good New Yorker would've let the freakin' thing kill you! Okay, so maybe I'm one of your mysterious *they,* maybe you've been set up, sure, sure. What's the worst that can happen? I take the key, give you the vibrating palm and split? If I could do that, man, I could do it flipside just as easy, dig? I turn into a rukoro-kubi and my hand flies out the door? Which, in case you hadn't noticed, weighs half a ton? If I do that, man, you can keep my body for transplants; don't forget to cauterize the neck. I mean, hey, I heard your laser pistol here charging up then, you can burn my shadow onto the wall if I—"

"Okay." He dropped the key into Takumo's hand. "Sorry."

"It's cool." Takumo bowed his head to stare at the key. "Looks ordinary enough. You say it opened her door?"

"Yes."

"Damn. I was hoping it might fit some luggage locker in Grand Central Station," he said in a better-than-average imitation of Peter Lorre's Joel Cairo. He turned the key over with his thumb and stroked the thong. "This feels like hair."

"Human hair?" asked Mage.

"I think so, yeah. It isn't yours?"

"No."

Takumo nodded. "Thanks for the trust."

"No. Keep it. Or post it back to Totem Rock if you like. It hasn't exactly brought me any luck. I'll meet you later . . . what time's the bus?"

"Twenty past nine, but—"

"Damn. When's the next one?"

"Tomorrow morning, ten thirty-five. Why?"

"Amanda's friend, Jenny. She's working until half past nine. Can you afford a hotel for the night, or shall I meet you in L.A.?"

"I can find a place to sleep," replied Takumo, closing his hand around the key. "Meet you at the bus tomorrow at ten. Okay?"

"Okay."

Takumo looked down at his clenched fist. "You're sure about this?"

"I'm sure," replied Mage, glancing at his watch. A quarter to seven. "You want to eat?"

8

Days Are Numbers

Jenny Holdridge was somewhere between cute and cuddly—that is, between ten and twenty pounds overweight. Her body language was casual but slightly clumsy, her clothes baggy and badge-encrusted, her shoulder-length brown hair reminiscent of a freshly unmade bed. Her eyes were obscured by large school-marmish spectacles, and her mouth was too small for her face, but her dimples were easy to read. Mage liked her at first sight and realized that the feeling was mutual; he doubted that Jenny had an enemy in the world.

And here I come to change that, he thought bitterly. He'd introduced himself as a friend of Amanda's, and she'd believed him. He'd offered to take her to dinner but she'd suggested they grab some take-out and eat it at her place instead—most of the good places had closed by nine anyway.

"You should try Washington," he'd told her. "Everything outside of Chinatown is strictly breakfast and lunch. I do remember one Mexican place with a sign in the window saying that it was open for dinner, but they'd been closed down and someone had thrown a brick through the sign."

She'd laughed. Her teeth were white and perfect. "What were you doing in Washington?"

"Seeing the Smithsonian."

"Spaceships or dinosaurs?"

"Spaceships mainly. I'm not a technology freak—I understand how a camera works and that's about my limit—but I always wanted to get into space, go to the moon . . ."

"Why?"

He shrugged. "I don't know. I guess I'm a born tourist, always have to be somewhere else, see somewhere new."

"Where'd you bump into Amanda?"

"Totem Rock."

"Where?"

"It's a little town, about half a day east of here."

"What was she doing *there*?"

"I don't know. I met her outside the Greyhound station when she was on her way back here. Coming back to the hospital. She was renting a grotty little apartment—"

"You mean smaller than this?"

"And grottier. It looked like she lived there alone—" he began, then reconsidered. "Actually, it looked like no one lived there at all. Certainly not for very long. Does she know anyone there?"

"I never heard of the place . . . but she didn't mention any friends outside the university. I guess I just assumed she didn't have any."

They sat on the living-room floor to eat; the kitchen table was covered with computer printouts and books. Mage looked around the room, deciding that the unicorns—glass unicorns, ceramic unicorns, soft toys, posters, a calendar, a mobile—were Jenny's, while the Salvador Dalis, fractal images and chess prizes were Amanda's. He was trying to guess the owner of the framed print on the wall—a very attractive witch working at a cauldron, all darks and brooding reds—when Jenny remarked, "You said Amanda came back here?"

"What?"

"To the hospital."

"Yes. Didn't she call you or anything?"

"No," replied Jenny. She sounded disappointed and puzzled.

"Has anyone else come here looking for her?"

"No."

Mage waited, eyebrows raised slightly.

"Oh, it's funny, and it's probably nothing, but I felt, I don't know, as though someone were watching the place. And there've been phone calls, you know the sort, only a silence on the other end. And . . ."

"Yes?"

"The other day—Tuesday—I think someone took my photo. Someone in a brown car. It wasn't you . . . ?"

"No. I only arrived yesterday."

"Did Amanda say when she was coming back?"

"She was at the hospital Tuesday and checked out Wednesday."

Jenny took another slice of pizza and stared at it as though it were a Rorschach. "That's not like her. She must really be down."

"Was she down a lot?"

"Not as much as you'd think, not as much as I'd be if I had what she had." Mage silently but sincerely damned her fear of words. "And it was weird, but she seemed to cheer up just before she left, as though she'd found a cure or something. She was reading a lot of medical texts, interspersed with math— population dynamics mostly, and Von Neumann's *Theory of Games*. And playing chess, blindfolded, with anyone who'd sit still long enough. I didn't."

Mage nodded; Jenny didn't look like the sitting-down type. "I noticed all the prizes."

"Oh, they're old. She lost interest in competing—said it took too much time—though she was a minor celebrity when she was fifteen, sixteen. That trophy, the queen"—she pointed with the wedge of pizza—"was from the '93 U.S. Open in Vegas. I guess that's when she became interested in blackjack instead."

"Blackjack?"

"Uh-huh." She shrugged slightly; her glasses slid down her nose and she pushed them back up with the pizza crust. "She started spending her time at the blackjack tables between chess matches. She said she was interested in the math of it, the probabilities, more than the money. She didn't win an outrageous fortune or anything, but she won consistently enough that the pit bosses started to wonder about her. She said that the last time she was there, the manager of one of the casinos actually took her to dinner and asked about her method. I don't know what she told him, but I think she kept seeing him, though she didn't talk about it much."

"Did she have a method?"

"For blackjack? I don't know, but I think she was looking for one. She liked to know how everything worked—and what the probability was that it *wouldn't* work. Alex once complained that she played chess like a computer, but I think that was because she kept beating him."

"Who was Alex? Her boyfriend?"

"No. She didn't have any boyfriends, apart from maybe Tony, the guy in Vegas. All the boys we knew treated her like she was contagious." She shrugged again. "But I can sort of understand. Who wants a relationship with someone who's going to die in . . ." Words and Jenny failed each other again. Mage waited silently. "Alex was our math tutor, Alex Corwin. I think he loved Amanda, in his way; she was the student every professor dreams of. A prodigy. She had a *feel* for numbers, and patterns, that I can't really understand; to her, they were some sort of magic. You could give her a number—a phone number, say— and she'd tell you whether it was prime or not, or if it was a cube . . . that sort of thing. A computer can do that, of course, but it does it by trial and error. You can't ask a computer what's interesting or unique about a number."

"Were you a prodigy?"

She laughed. "Me? No, I've always had to do everything the hard way, but that's more useful; you can't program a *feel* into a computer, or teach it in schools. It was a toss-up between this and history, but you can't get a job with an arts degree. Pretty corrupt, right?"

"If corrupt means compromising," said Mage slowly, "doing something you don't like doing just for money, then I guess most of us are corrupt sometimes."

"How about you?"

"Yeah, me too. I like traveling, taking photos, but sometimes I make more money by staying in one place, or taking photos that I don't like . . . though I don't need a lot of money and I move on when I have enough."

"You never wanted to settle down?"

"Not yet. Someday maybe; I don't know."

"When you find the right girl?"

Mage studied her and realized that she was referring to Amanda, not to herself. "Maybe . . . but I don't think so. The right girl would like traveling."

"What if you weren't going in the same direction?"

"I don't know; if it were the right girl, I guess I'd turn around, go where she went—but I've never found the *one* right girl, anymore than I've ever found the *one* right place. It's not that I never love—I don't sleep with *anyone* I don't love. But I love easy. So sue me." He smiled. "Or better still, tell me more about Amanda."

Jenny hesitated: Mage could see the question that hovered on her lips, and he was trying to think of the answer when she asked, "Like what?" instead.

"What *exactly* was wrong with her? She wouldn't tell me."

"Leukemia," she replied—quietly, as though the cancer came when it was called.

Mage nodded gently. "And where did she go?"

"Down south."

"The States?"

Jenny nodded.

"Another hospital?"

"I don't know. She didn't give me a forwarding address or anything."

"Does she know anyone down there?"

"I don't think so, apart from Tony . . . not very well, anyway. I don't remember her getting letters or long-distance phone calls, and she didn't use E-mail much."

"When did she leave?"

"End of semester."

So she went south, maybe to Vegas, then to Totem Rock, then back to Calgary. Mage shook his head. Perhaps there was a pattern there that Amanda could've seen, but it seemed perfectly random to him. . . .

She knew she was being chased. Okay. She didn't want anyone to find her, not even him. Again okay. But had she set him up? Did she expect him to divert her pursuers, maybe die in her place? *That,* he refused to accept. She hadn't looked the kind, and Mage trusted his eyes—trusted them more than any facts.

"What's wrong?"

"Wrong?"

"You looked sort of stunned for a minute there."

He shook his head. "No, I'm okay. Maybe a little tired."

"You want to stay here the night?" she asked. "Amanda's bed's made up."

He smiled. "Thanks."

It was only a single bed, made exclusively for sleeping in, but sleep eluded him. Every footfall upstairs, every gurgle of water in the pipes, rang in his semiconsciousness like a burglar alarm. The temptation to creep into Jenny's room was almost overpowering, and he spent his wakeful moments wondering why he didn't simply yield to it. He doubted that she'd scream rape, but she might throw him out—and quite apart from the possible dangers, it was bitterly cold outside; he could even see snow falling past the window. Furthermore, he suspected that Jenny also had a single bed, and the occasional creak and murmur from her room suggested that she was a restless sleeper.

The sun was rising over Calgary and Mage was finally falling asleep when Yukitaka Hideo was ushered into Tamenaga's quarters by the blank-faced Sakura.

Tamenaga was naked except for a *fundoshi,* an ornate loincloth, and his tattoos shone slightly with sweat: the cobra on his right arm, the meter-long centipede, or *mukade,* on his left, the weighted chains around each wrist, the python coiled around his hairless chest, and the vest of ninja ring-mail. Yukitaka bowed and waited.

"So," said Tamenaga softly, his face almost as unreadable as Sakura's. "You failed."

Yukitaka nodded and apologized profusely in hurried Japanese. To his immense relief, Tamenaga did not interrupt him. A less indispensable employee would have been silenced in mid sentence. Yukitaka knew of no rukoro-kubi outside of his own family and doubted that any others survived. Rukoro-kubi could live for years without a taste of human flesh, but they soon lost their ability to heal, eventually bleeding to death (their deaths, if not disguised, were usually taken for particularly gruesome suicides; their bodies were always cremated).

Rukoro-kubi females could interbreed with human males, but their offspring were mostly mere humans, or sometimes deformed monsters; no human female had ever carried a rukoro-kubi baby to term, and few survived the pregnancy. Yukitaka Hideo's parents were long dead; his sister, Sumie, worked as an industrial spy in Tokyo. None of her employers knew her secret;

none had dared to ask. Occasionally she would visit Hong Kong and feast on children and junkies in the slums, her attacks mistaken for rat bites.

Sakura, behind Tamenaga's back, opened a mouth to yawn silently. There is little love lost between monsters, but Yukitaka disliked Sakura less than any human female, and she returned his indifference and small respect in full measure.

"I accept your apology," Tamenaga said politely, "but I am curious. Who was the knife-fighter?"

Yukitaka bowed deeply, more to hide his relieved expression than as a gesture of respect. "His name is Charles Willis Takumo. He's a small-time stuntman from California, mostly impersonating women and children, or playing at being ninja."

"Japanese?"

"Half Japanese. His father is unknown; probably an American hippie. His mother left him with her parents, who raised him. She died in a commune in '75, and her father died in '88. His grandmother is in a hospital, nearly senile. Takumo has no other family, no wife, no regular job—he is currently suspended from the stunt performers' union for taking drugs—and no allegiances. So, in short, another drifter."

"Where did he meet Magistrale?"

"I don't know. They spoke like strangers. It seems that they met for the first time in the hostel, by coincidence."

"Coincidence?" Tamenaga raised an eyebrow slightly at that. "Coincidence, like a gun jamming so opportunely?"

Yukitaka was silent.

"It seems," said Tamenaga quietly, "that the girl diverted us and that we have underestimated Magistrale-san."

"The girl," said Sakura politely but flatly, "is no longer a problem."

"And the knife-fighter?" asked Yukitaka.

"A *chambara* actor," replied Tamenaga dismissively, "using an amateur's weapon. Hardly worth your time, Yukitaka-san— but you're welcome to him when this is all over, if you wish."

9

Journey of the Sorcerer

Takumo greeted him cheerfully, "Goood morning, sunshine," and grinned. " 'Some were born to wild delight, / Some were born to endless night.' "

Mage grunted, amazed and secretly pleased that the stuntman had turned up instead of taking the key (which he obviously thought valuable for reasons that entirely escaped Mage) and running. "As a matter of fact, I . . . oh, never mind. Where did you sleep last night?"

"On a waterbed. A *heated* waterbed. A—"

"Oh, shut up." Mage shook his head and walked over to the vending machines, returning with a caffeine- and sugar-rich Classic Coke. "I thought you were broke. How the hell did you afford a place with a waterbed?"

"Didn't cost me a cent." He reached into his pocket for Amanda's key and threw it to Mage. "Take a look at that."

Mage glanced at the key, then looked Takumo up and down. "You went to a wife-swapping party? I thought those went out with the seventies."

"*Look,* man. You got the eyes. *Use* them."

Mage shrugged and looked more closely at the key. It was shiny and new-looking, like Amanda's, with the same Volks-wagen-shaped Lockwood head with a crooked "A" stamped on one side, and the rough edge, whatever you called that, that looked a little like the Manhattan skyline. So why had he thought it was different?

He blinked and stared hard at the key, trying to remember. Was his imagination running away with him, or had the edge previously resembled the east coast of South America? Hadn't this large shark's tooth previously been M-shaped? Hadn't . . .

"It's a different key, isn't it?"

"Is it?"

He glanced at the braid of black hair. *That* hadn't noticeably changed. "It looks different . . . at least I think it does. I didn't look at it that closely before, I could just be imagining it. I've been under a lot of stress lately," he said dryly. "Did you get an-other key cut?"

"No."

"Then it's the same key—"

"Yes and no. It *changed.* It changed to fit the lock. Like it evolved or something."

Mage shook his head. "No, that's impossible. It must be a coincidence, a key that fits two different locks."

"Four."

"Four?"

"There were two locks on the door—one of them a dead-bolt—and they were different brands, not meant to take the same key. The windows had security mesh screens, and okay, maybe they were all designed for the one key, but that still makes *three* locks, and the garage door makes four. Okay, all the locks were stiff and kind of reluctant, but the one key shouldn't have *fit* them, let alone opened them. I haven't tried it on any car doors, but I don't see why it wouldn't work on those too."

Mage stared at the key, fascinated. "How did you think of this?"

Takumo shrugged. "Naturally devious, I guess. I was wondering what could be so hot about a key to start all this hassle. Like, it's a key, its purpose in life is to open something, unless you need it to launch a nuke or something, and I didn't want to think of that. So I wondered what that something it could open might be, and I started to think of doors I'd *like* it to open, and after about three or four, I thought 'All of the above,' and . . . so then I thought, like, 'Why not?' And then I saw this pad with the 'To Rent—Fully Furnished' sign . . . and I kind of extrapolated from there." He grinned. "Neat, huh? The ultimate skeleton key, worth a small fortune."

"No."

"Okay, a large fortune, an *outrageous* fortune if you're heavily into possessions. I don't like to steal from—"

"No," repeated Mage.

"Will you believe it if you see it?"

"Maybe, but that's not why. It isn't ours, and even if you're right and it *is* some sort of magic, we're not going to use it."

"Why not?"

"Amanda had it," the photographer reminded him, "and she had to borrow thirty bucks to get out of town, so it didn't make her rich. I don't know how long she had the key, but no one remembers her having money, and no one planned on sending her any Christmas cards, so it didn't make her healthy, either. Jenny told me she had leukemia, but Amanda wasn't telling Jenny everything, any more than she told me everything, but she was crying when I saw her, so it certainly didn't make her happy. Now, Amanda was a mathematician and I'm not, and maybe I'm screwing up cause and effect here, but I don't want to use that key *at all* until I see her again."

"Yeah, okay. Like the Hope diamond."

"What?"

"You know how it's supposed to be cursed? Like ever since

it was stolen, everyone who owned it found a nasty way of dying young. So, after the French Revolution—Marie Antoinette had inherited it—the diamond disappeared for about forty years, then someone gave it to a diamond cutter in Amsterdam to cut down. Which he did, but his son stole it and took off for London. So the cutter committed suicide, and the son's money ran out, but he couldn't work up the nerve to sell the diamond. He ended up taking a job as a street sweeper—with a diamond worth about half a million in his pocket."

Mage shivered.

"Maybe magic has a way of doing that," Takumo mused. "Like, maybe there's a price tag, a catch, a first and second law of thermodymagics, or something. Conservation of power. Action and reaction. Yin and yang." A shadow fell over him and he looked up to notice the bus driver staring at him. "Then again, what do I know?"

"About magic? More than I do," said Mage quietly after the driver had turned away. "Doesn't this scare you shitless?"

"No," said Takumo cheerfully. "I always wanted there to be magic in the world. You?"

Mage shrugged. "I was doing okay without it."

"Are you sure about that?"

Mage slept until they reached the border, while Takumo kept watch—an unnecessary precaution as it happened, but it made for a more interesting journey.

The Rocky Mountains at close quarters are as frightening as any monster. Man's first goddesses, Takumo knew, had been earth mothers, bountiful and supportive, but his first gods were mountains, arrogant and unproductive—except, perhaps, of smoke and lava and falling rocks. The goddesses were to be thanked and loved; the gods, appeased and feared.

Later races of men, more confident, reduced their gods to human scale and placed them atop the mountains, new gods on the shoulders of old—Zeus on Olympus, Yahweh on Sinai. Still later, of course, men even less prone to awe would regard mountains as mere obstacles, to be flown over or tunneled through—but not Takumo, who had never regarded his economy-sized physique as the measure of all things, had never felt the modern urge to leave nothing standing on earth that was taller or older than himself. He despised flatness and sameness, preferring mountains, and dinosaurs, and the towering redwoods that had miraculously survived the Reagan era. Takumo's deities were not economists, but giants: gods, goddesses, and Godzillas. He felt no urge to swim the deepest oceans or to cross the burning deserts, any more than he would have willingly killed the last whale. It was enough for Takumo to know that they were there.

Charlie? You okay?"

"Yeah, fine," replied Takumo quietly without taking his eyes from the view. "Why?"

"You weren't breathing."

"Prana-yoga. Breath control. It's good exercise. Helps you concentrate, and comes in real useful when there's a smog alert. Remind me to teach it to you sometime." He watched the sun setting and smiled. "You know, the nearest thing I ever had to a religious experience came when I was flying over those mountains."

Mage, who had wakened in time for lunch, merely nodded.

"It was early morning," Takumo continued, "about four o'clock, the time when the nightmares come for me whether I'm asleep or not, and I had the window seat, and all I could see was this magnificent triangular shadow. And I thought, 'Oh man, we're flying *much* too close to that mountain.' Like, I'm not scared of flying, but this was awesome, so I just had to shut my eyes—and it was four A.M., like I just said, and I always planned to die in my sleep.

"So I sat there, and a few minutes later I opened my eyes again and there was the mountain, still—same size, or maybe bigger. Okay, so a mountain range isn't one mountain wide or anything, and so I shut my eyes again, and I think that this time I fell asleep. When I looked again, it was a little lighter, but the shadow was still there, big as life. Bigger. Big as life and death and sex in one. Man.

"So, like, I just sat there and meditated quietly, and the shadow just sat there like all the bad karma in the world, and finally the sun came up, sweet as a kiss—and I looked out, and the ground below us was flat, not a mountain in sight. I must've sat there for hours, and had seven years' growth scared out of me, staring at the shadow of the wing of the plane." He laughed. "One day I'm going to have to really go into the mountains. The Japanese used to think there was a god—well, a *kami,* demigod—in every mountain. A yama-no-kami. Did you ever read this Hermann Hesse story called 'Faldum'?"

"No."

"It's about a man, a kind of wandering-magician type, who comes out of nowhere really and rolls up at a fair in this village called Faldum. He sees these girls looking in a mirror and making wishes, so he makes the wishes come true—one wish for everyone in town. So there's one guy who wants to stay there forever, so he wishes that he gets turned into a mountain. And he does. The rest of the story is about the thousands of years it takes for the environment to recover. I really dug that story." Takumo shook his head nostalgically. "Hey, if you had one wish, what'd you wish for?"

"I don't know." Mage shrugged. "I guess I never really thought about it. To see the world? No, they'd probably dump me in orbit without a space suit. Isn't that the thing about wishes? Be careful what you ask for, 'cause you might get it?" Mage knew the truth of *that* well enough. "A solar-powered Lamborghini? No, not a Lamborghini, a Winnebago, something I could sleep in . . . no, something two people could sleep in."

"Only two?"

"Yeah, only two of us—at a time, anyway. I'm not greedy. Or Californian."

Takumo smiled. "Then why don't you just wish for the perfect woman?"

"They're all perfect," Mage replied without cracking a smile.

In every city and town where the bus stopped between Calgary and L.A., Mage asked after Amanda—to no avail. Even in towns where the population doubled every time a bus went through, no one remembered seeing a tall, beautiful blonde.

The weather became warmer as they traveled south, but the air also became dirtier, and Greyhound stations, like airports, are usually located in the poorest and ugliest part of any city. Mage, who had never been prone to depression, was looking extremely dispirited when they finally disembarked in Santa Monica. Takumo's small apartment, however, was an eye-opener; tatami on the floor, posters on the walls and ceiling, paper lightshades, a large-screen (Japanese) TV and VCR, a laser-disc player, a futon and a Wing Chun wooden dummy in the bedroom, bookshelves randomly stuffed with paperbacks and laser discs and incense burners. The kitchen contained enough knives for three productions of *Julius Caesar.* Cushions of various sizes were piled in the corners, but there were no chairs, and only one low table.

"When do I remove my shoes?" Mage asked.

"Now, if you would," replied Takumo, glancing at his time-dishonored Reeboks.

Mage shrugged and complied. "You must be better off than you look."

"If you mean moneywise, yes, I am. Or I was, anyway. I haven't worked much recently."

The photographer walked into the sitting room and stared at a row of movie posters. *Age of the Sword* ("When the ammunition had gone, but the fallout hadn't."). *Moon Camp. Robocop 3. Red Ninja. Red Ninja II. Jonin* ("Master of Ninjitsu—and a Hundred Ninja!"). "You used to show these movies?"

"I was in them."

"As a ninja?"

"Yeah, sometimes. I'm pretty good at the spectacular stuff, chambara fighting, particularly *yadomejutsu,* arrow cutting."

"Arrow cutting?"

"Parrying arrows, *shuriken,* throwing knives, stuff like that—or catching them, if you want to be really flashy. My grandfather taught it to me; he said it was good practice for baseball. Unfortunately, it doesn't work with bullets." He removed his sneakers and socks, shut the door behind him, and then stood on his head and wiggled his toes. "And I double a lot for kids because I'm small, and sometimes for women."

"What were you doing in Calgary?"

"Passing through. I'd been doing a lousy movie in Edmonton. You know the aquarium in the mall, the one with the sharks? I was doubling for the star because I made the sharks look bigger. They were making it in Canada because it was cheaper—no union problems—and I needed the work. I was suspended from the union back in June and I was getting low on cash."

"Why were you suspended?"

"Drugs."

Takumo didn't seem the sort to need cocaine, or any other stimulant. "Grass?"

"Codeine. I don't use grass when I'm working. Like, I hurt my back doing some spacewalking stunts in *Moon Camp,* and the X rays didn't show any damage, so no union benefits, but the pain got to me occasionally. They threw me off *Ronin,* which was a real bummer, but I was nearly finished. I played one of the *komuso* in the first scene, so you don't get to see my face, but it's the biggest break I've had since . . . do you know the book?"

"No."

"There's a copy on the shelf there. Don't drool on the autograph."

Mage glanced at the library, which seemed to be the only chaos in the room. The copy of *Ronin*, in a Ziploc bag, shared a shelf with Musashi's *The Book of Five Rings, The Complete Works of William Shakespeare, The Encyclopedia of American Crime, The Dinosaur Heresies,* several *Swamp Thing* and *Sandman* trade paperbacks, ten volumes of *The Year's Best Fantasy and Horror,* dozens of half-inch-thick Japanese comics, and a French-English dictionary.

"French?" Mage asked.

"For sure. I speak Spanish too—comes in useful around here—and Japanese, of course. Plus some Korean and a smattering of half a dozen other languages, enough to get by in. That was the downfall of the ninja, y'know. They were perfect spies in a one-language culture, but when the Europeans came, the ninja didn't know what they were stealing. You want some tea?"

So. What're you going to do now?"

"Huh? I mean, I don't know. I've never been good at planning ahead."

Takumo was sitting comfortably in a lotus position, his eyes closed, his face impassive. "Even if she's here, man, you'll never find her. The city's too big, and I don't just mean crowded, I mean *big,* dig? Like imagine if you'd dropped Manhattan from low earth orbit and let it splatter over the landscape; *that* kind of big, but messier. So where're you going next?"

"I don't know. Back to Nevada, I guess, assuming I live so long."

"You can stay here for a couple of days if you like. We should be safe. There's a good alarm on the door, and security screens on the windows—I went on a heavy paranoia trip a year back, all on behalf of my lady, who split a few weeks later." He nodded in the direction of a photo on the bookshelf.

"She's lovely. What's her name?"

"Mike—Californian for Mika. *Nisei* Japanese. She came to me for *taijutsu* lessons and moved in. And out." Takumo's face remained neutral, though there was an edge in his voice. "But the place is secure," he continued, with a very slight stress on the noun. "And I've hidden a few gimmicks here and there. I know I should have some trapdoors and secret passages too, but the landlady wouldn't take it too well. Will you be okay on the floor? It never gets that cold here."

Mage nodded. "Thanks."

"It's cool," replied Takumo, still staring into some inner universe. "So, have you finished that roll of film? I'd like to see this mysterious Amanda."

10

Slings and Arrows

Takumo rose late, spent half an hour sparring with the wooden dummy and the rest of the morning meditating, then showered and dressed. "I've got to go and collect my bike. I don't like leaving it in the carport when I'm out of town, and I have a friend with an empty garage. You can come with me if you like, but you probably won't get back before the weekend. All the buses spend their time driving past the county court so the drivers can see themselves on the news."

"*All* the buses?"

"Okay, *both* the buses."

Mage laughed. "What sort of bike?"

"Kawasaki Ninja," Takumo replied, grinning. "I'll be back before sunset." He donned a leather jacket, boots and gloves, and a helmet with a tinted visor. Black-clad from head to toe, he resembled a very tough shadow. "If you need to go anywhere, lock the door on your way out; you shouldn't have any trouble getting back in."

* * *

Tamenaga looked up from the printout, his face carefully neutral. "You're certain of these figures?"

Lamm nodded. He rarely spoke to people, not even to his boss; he was a hacker, not a talker. Tamenaga returned his attention to the printout. "Good work."

"Easy."

"I may need you again tonight."

"Sure," Lamm replied, walking out. Tamenaga stared at the figures for another moment, then reached for the scrambler phone.

"Get me my daughter."

"Yes, boss."

He put the receiver down and allowed himself the luxury of a smile. A few seconds later the phone rang.

"Haruko?"

"Hai?"

"Pyramus is going to get the contract; the Senate should pass it next week. I'll start forcing their stock down immediately; begin buying all you can when it hits two twenty-three. If you don't have a thirty-one-percent share when they close Monday, call me and I'll do something to delay the bill."

"Okay. Anything else?"

"No, not at the moment. How's Nakatani doing?"

"No problems yet, but I don't think his heart's in it."

Haruko carefully kept any hint of reproach out of her voice. Nakatani may have lacked the instincts that made a good casino manager, but she was aware of his usefulness to the Tamenaga family. She suspected he would have been opposed to having Tony Higuchi killed; the murder may have been justified as a face-saving measure, but it was a bad business decision, and to Shota Nakatani, business was sacrosanct. In that regard, at least, he and Haruko were well suited to each other.

"Higuchi will be difficult to replace," her father conceded.

"Yes," Haruko agreed softly. The gambler had been a capable lover when he could be persuaded to stay at home—skilled, uninhibited, reasonably considerate, and almost as good as he thought he was—and she hadn't gotten laid since the night of the funeral. She wondered how good a lover Nakatani might be. His American wife had divorced him three or four years ago now, and she knew he hadn't been patronizing any of the Sunrise's professionals or her father's enslaved *karayuki*.

"Have you any suggestions?" asked Tamenaga.

"What? No . . . no, I don't know of anybody."

"None of the pit bosses?"

"Possibly . . ." said Haruko dubiously.

Tamenaga grunted. "I'll see if I can find somebody. I'll call again tomorrow." He hung up and reached for the remote. The television was, as always, set to the stock-market channel; Tamenaga stared at the screen for a few seconds, then reached inside his kimono to touch the loop of braided black hair he wore around his neck.

The slight regret he felt for having had his son-in-law killed was nothing compared to his genuine dismay when the Sharmon woman had stolen Higuchi's focus and escaped. The gambler's street smarts and instincts had been useful to his business, but Amanda was a fellow mathematician, a fellow prodigy, perhaps potentially even his own equal, and easily worth a dozen Tony Higuchis . . . but Haruko would never understand that.

Takumo returned at five, and the evening passed without event except for a minor argument about the ethics of vegetarianism. They watched *The Crow* on HBO and a late-night showing of *The Man with the X-Ray Eyes*. Mage fell asleep three minutes after Elvira's introduction. Takumo draped his sleeping bag over him without waking him and turned the volume down, then watched the movie to the end, quietly performing one-handed push-ups during the commercials. Mage woke briefly when Takumo turned the television off. "Wha—?"

"Good night."

Mage shook his head and began undressing. He was about to remove the key from around his neck, then reconsidered. His last thought before falling asleep was that he hadn't called Carol since before arriving in Calgary and he'd better let her know where he was.

They were awakened by a peremptory knock on the door. Mage glanced at the clock on the wall, blinked, then realized that the numbers ran counterclockwise. He wondered whether that was meant to represent Japanese left-handedness or Hollywood perversity and decided that he didn't need to know that badly, not at a quarter to eight. The knock sounded again and he groped for his pants, but Takumo was already halfway to the door, walking quickly but silently across the tatami. He peered through the peephole, shrugged slightly and opened the door a crack. "Yes?"

"Charles Takumo?" The voice was muffled, but it was unmistakably a cop's. Mage scrambled into his pants.

"I have that honor, yes."

"May we come in?"

Takumo hesitated, then nodded. "If you will excuse me; as you may observe, I am not dressed. One moment, please." He shut the door quietly, then turned to Mage.

"Real cops?" whispered Mage.

"They *look* real enough," said Takumo, his expression grim.

He walked into the bedroom and returned to the door a moment later wearing a black kimono with a startled-looking dragon on the back. He stopped at the door and murmured to Mage, "Sorry there's no fire escape . . ." before sliding the chain across.

"Thank you," he said without moving from the doorway. "Excuse me, but do you have a warrant? If not, would you mind removing your shoes? They scuff the tatami."

The cops glanced at each other. "No, we don't have a warrant," said the elder. "We just want to ask you a few questions, and we'd rather do it inside than out. Is that okay?"

Takumo glanced at their feet and then, impassively, at their faces. After a few seconds, the elder cop swore and bent down to untie his shoes. The younger watched Takumo carefully, apparently expecting him to kick his partner in the face.

By the time they entered, shoes in hand, Mage was fully dressed and packed. "You'd better hurry," Takumo told him casually. "You'll miss the bus. Now . . ."

The ruse failed. The elder cop smiled slightly and asked, "Michelangelo Magistrale?" He pronounced it Maji*strail,* and Mage was about to correct him—and then realized that he'd taken the bait.

"Yes," he replied wearily. "I'm Magistrale. What do you want?"

"Just a few questions." The cop looked from one to the other.

Takumo stepped cautiously toward the kitchen. "I was just about to make some tea. Would you—"

The younger cop rolled his eyes; the elder smiled. "Going somewhere, Mr. Magistrale?" He pronounced it almost correctly.

Mage shrugged. "Nevada," he replied. "I have family there."

"Just passing through, then?"

"Yes."

"From Canada, wasn't it?"

"Yes."

"Calgary?"

"I spent a night—no, two nights—in Calgary, yes. What—"

"Do you know this girl?" The cop handed over a grainy, badly lit head-and-shoulders shot, probably a passport photo greatly enlarged; it showed what might have been a younger Amanda, with much shorter hair.

"It's hard to tell," said Mage noncommittally. "The photographer should be, uh . . . who is she?"

"Her name's Amanda Sharmon."

"I've met her," he replied neutrally.

"In Calgary?"

"No, as a matter of fact. Before I went to Calgary."

The cop turned to Takumo and tossed the photo to him. Takumo caught it neatly. "No."

"No?"

"No, I don't recognize her. Who is she?"

The cop ignored him and addressed Mage again. "You want to come down to the station, or you want me to arrest you? I will if I have to."

"On what charge?"

"Murder," replied the cop flatly. "Okay?" He turned to Takumo. "Thanks for the offer. The tea, I mean. Maybe some other time."

The smog was thick and gray, reducing visibility to one or two blocks; Mage stared at the pale, pearly disc of the sun without discomfort for several seconds before realizing that it wasn't the moon.

"So, are you planning to leave town today or something?" the taller cop asked. Mage remained silent. " 'Cause if you are, we may have to arrest you. Just in case."

"Am I entitled to a lawyer?"

The cop rubbed his jaw thoughtfully. "Y'know, that's a good question. I know you are if we actually arrest you, but . . . you know the answer to that one, Harry?" The younger cop, concentrating on the road, merely grunted. "Harry here's studying law. D'you have a lawyer?"

"No."

"Never needed one?"

"No."

The cop nodded. "Well, I don't think you're entitled to a P.D., they're pretty damn busy, but I'll ask the captain for you. I wouldn't sweat it, though. It's just questions."

"But if I get the answers wrong, I'm under arrest?" asked Mage.

"Something like that, yeah," the cop replied, not unkindly. "So, you're from New York?"

"Yeah. Brooklyn."

"Been here before?"

"Only passing through." He glanced out the window. There were more pedestrians than he'd expected; he'd been told no one ever walked in L.A. Maybe they were homeless.

"What were you doing in Canada?"

"Visiting a friend."

"In Calgary?"

"No."

"Relax." The cop glanced in the mirror and smiled. "Whaddaya got to worry about, anyway?"

When was the last time you saw Amanda Sharmon?"

Mage rolled his eyes and then closed them; there was nothing in the interrogation room worth looking at. "The first, last and *only* time was in Totem Rock, Canada, on Tuesday, October nineteenth."

"Where's Totem Rock?"

"A few hours south and east of Calgary. I don't know what province—Alberta or Saskatchewan, I guess—and it isn't on a lot of maps. Ask Greyhound; they got me there."

"What were you doing there?"

"Visiting a friend."

"Why? Was she sick?"

Mage shook his head. "No. Just lonely."

"Her name?"

"Carol Lancaster. Sixty-six Maple Street."

"Addr—" The lieutenant shut his mouth with a slight snap. Mage guessed his age at between twenty-six and thirty, his ambition grandiose, his patience limited. "Phone number?"

Mage reached into his pocket with exaggerated slowness and withdrew his address book. "May I see that?" asked the lieutenant. Mage opened his eyes and handed it over with a slight shrug. The lieutenant opened the book to "S," was disappointed and flipped a few pages back to "L."

"Try 'C.' I don't bother much with surnames."

Mage waited while the lieutenant copied down the number, opened the book to "A," grunted, and then handed it back. "We have statements that you asked about Amanda Sharmon at the hospital, the university, and the youth hostel."

"Yes."

"Why?"

Mage shrugged.

"Was she lonely too?" the lieutenant asked sarcastically.

"Anyone who has to ask a stranger for bus fare to the hospital isn't exactly overburdened with friends," Mage replied heavily. The lieutenant flushed slightly. "And she was also sick— or so everyone's told me. She didn't *look* sick."

"What was wrong with her?"

"A friend of hers told me she had leukemia; I don't know whether that was true or not. No one else would tell me anything."

"Uh-huh. Why did you go to Calgary, Mr. Magistrale?"

Mage decided not to mention the gunman. "To visit Amanda."

"Did Miss Lancaster know this?"

"*Ms.* Lancaster—she's divorced—and no."

The lieutenant nodded. "A nurse at the hospital says you implied that you were Amanda Sharmon's fiancé."

"I didn't intend to; she must have misunderstood me." Suddenly Mage's nerve failed—cops, red tape and the threat of jail scared him far more than guns or ghosts, and the LAPD was not renowned for gentleness—and he blurted out, "Look, I could help you a whole lot more if you'd just tell me what the *hell* is going on! The cop who picked me up said there'd been a murder. Is Amanda dead?"

The lieutenant ignored him. "Where were you on the night of the twenty-second? That's Friday last."

Mage took a deep, slow breath. "In Calgary."

"Where in Calgary?"

"In Amanda's old apartment; I don't remember the address. You can check with her housemate, Jenny Holdridge. If you haven't already."

"*I* haven't checked with anybody. All I have is the file that the Calgary police passed on to us. *They're* the ones who want you extradited, but I won't do it unless we can see just cause. I presume you don't want to go back to Canada just yet? You left rather quickly."

"I'd exhausted my options."

"What?"

"For finding Amanda. No one seemed to know where she was."

"You hadn't arranged to meet her?"

"I'd said I *might* come to the hospital."

"You still haven't told me *why.*"

Mage shrugged. "Whim, I guess."

"Whim?"

"I didn't have any plans, a job, anywhere else to go. She was attractive, and photogenic, and friendly; I'd never been to Calgary—" He stopped; the lieutenant looked as though he'd never indulged a whim in his upwardly mobile life. Changing tack, without any real hope that it would work, Mage added, "And she needed help. A friend."

The lieutenant looked at him skeptically, then shrugged. "Okay, Mr. Magistrale. I am formally placing you under arrest pending your extradition to Calgary. You have the right to remain silent . . ."

Takumo unzipped the pocket of Mage's jacket and pulled out the blond wig. He stared at it for several seconds, then walked into the bedroom and stuffed it into a drawer with his movie souvenirs. If all else failed, he could tell the cops that he'd worn it when doubling for an actress.

He wondered why he was protecting Mage after only three days' acquaintance. He was still wondering when the cops—the same pair—knocked on the door again. The elder showed him the warrant and let him read it, while Harry carried the backpack and camera case down to the car.

"The jacket there—that's his as well?"

"Yes."

The cop nodded. "Anything else?"

Takumo glanced around the room and shook his head. "He traveled light."

"Yeah, that figures. Thanks." The cop took the denim jacket, slipped back into his shoes and reached into his pocket. "Here. He said this was yours, asked me to give it back to you." He threw Takumo the key and shut the door behind him.

Takumo twisted the braided hair around his fingers, stared at the key, and thought very hard.

11

Kelly

To Mage's delight, the assistant P.D. was a woman in her late twenties; women, experience told him, were far more likely to believe him than men were. And she was attractive . . . or maybe "striking" would have been more apt. She towered above Mage; he guessed her height at six-foot-four, minus two or three inches for her afro and her heels, but still his height or taller. Though she was slender, her hands and wrists and her carriage suggested strength. She wore gray, which looked wrong against her mahogany skin; her suit seemed more a part of the detention-room walls than of her. No wedding or engagement ring or any other jewelry, not even earrings, and no makeup except the dark-red varnish on her short nails. She didn't offer to shake hands, and Mage decided not to stand; she didn't seem to be the sort to respond to chivalry.

"Michelangelo Magistrale?" Her voice was crisp, businesslike, rather deep. Not a California accent. Washington or Boston, probably.

"Yes." He tried to smile, and failed.

"I'm Kelly Barbet. Public Defender's Office." She placed the folder in her hand on the table, faceup, and looked at him with her first hint of uncertainty. "Well?"

Mage shrugged eloquently. "What do you want me to say? I didn't do it, I didn't see her in Calgary. Hell, I didn't even know she was *dead* until the cops told me! When did she die?"

Kelly opened the file to the first page. "The condition the body was in, it was hard to tell. Probably sometime between midnight and one A.M., but it was cold that night and it could have been two or three hours earlier or later. Do you have an alibi for the night?"

"On the twenty-third?"

"No, the twenty-second."

Mage blinked. "The *morning* of the twenty-second?"

"Yes. Where were you?"

"In a youth hostel."

She looked down at the file. "On Seventh Avenue?"

"Yeah, that's the one."

"That's where they found her body. On the twenty-fourth."

Mage thought, and suddenly turned pale. "Where . . ."

"Where what?"

"Where did they find the body?"

"In the garbage bin, outside."

He vomited.

Are you okay now?" she asked when he returned from the washroom.

"Do I *look* okay?" he asked sarcastically, then shook his head. "Sorry. Charlie volunteered us for garbage detail that morning. I must've been a couple of feet from her body and not known it. Jesus."

"Who's Charlie?"

"Charlie Takumo. I met him in the hostel; I was staying with him when the cops picked me up."

"Did he know Amanda Sharmon?"

"No. Well, not as far as I know. Look, is this necessary? I told you I didn't know she was dead. Hell, I spent the whole next day looking for her, you *know* that . . ."

"The prosecution could say you were trying to create an alibi."

"Yeah," he replied, disgusted. "Okay. Look, just as a matter of interest, how was she killed?"

Kelly sighed, flipped the file open and began turning pages. Suddenly she looked up, her face gray. Mage stared at her, then stood, drawing himself up to his full height.

"Look," he said, "whatever it is, *I didn't do it!* I'm not going to make any sort of confession, any sort of bargain; *I didn't do it,* and if you can't believe that, then get me a lawyer who can!"

They glared at each other for several seconds, then Kelly shut the file. "Okay, sit down. You've made your point."

Mage didn't budge. "Was she raped?"

"No. No evidence of penetration . . . not recently, anyway."

"Mutilated?"

"No, nothing like that. She was strangled, but that isn't . . ." Kelly grabbed the table with both hands and took a deep breath. Mage was startled to notice tears in her eyes. "Did you know she had leukemia?"

"I heard."

Kelly nodded, her face bleak. "She didn't have it."

"What?" Mage blinked. He had already been astonished more often in the past few hours than he had in as many years; he'd been forced to believe in monsters and magic, and his credulity was beginning to wear thin. One more shock, he thought, and he would have trouble believing that the sky was blue. He searched through the mental haze for the most likely explanation and asked, hopefully, "She didn't have leukemia?

Then what was—I mean, why did she have to go to the hospital?"

"Oh, she had leukemia *then,*" said Kelly sourly. "But . . . the body . . ."

"You mean it wasn't her?"

"No, it *was* her. Her roommate identified her, and they checked the dental records just to be certain. It *was* Amanda Sharmon—and she didn't have cancer."

Mage sat, bewildered. "I'm lost." Kelly didn't reply. "How is that possible?"

"I wish I knew," Kelly said, a little too sharply.

Mage looked at her closely, putting his own fears aside as best he could. Maybe she'd lost someone to cancer—or some part of herself, he thought, noticing the defensive way she crossed her arms tightly across her breasts.

"I'm sorry," he said softly after trying to think of something more intelligent or meaningful. "I'm sorry she's dead, and I'm sorry—oh, hell, how do I say this?" He bit his lip and tried to start again. "*I* didn't kill her, I don't *know* who killed her, I met her only once and I don't know very much about her at all, and . . ." He shook his head, drew a deep breath. "If she'd discovered a cure for cancer, I don't know what it was, but I don't think it makes her murder any more tragic." Kelly looked up, her expression unreadable. "And if that gives you a reason to hate her killer, fine, we have something in common. Are we going to stand here and spit at each other, or are we going to try to find him?"

Kelly was silent for a long, agonizing moment and then asked, "Him?"

"Figure of speech. I don't know anyone with any reason to kill her, I didn't know her well enough. It might have been a he or a she or . . ." *it,* he thought, remembering the rokuro-kubi. "I just lent her some money, tried to help. Maybe if I hadn't, she'd still be alive, but I didn't murder her."

* * *

There were few doors in the world that could open quickly enough to suit Kelly Barbet, and her bad days resembled a blooper reel from *Star Trek*. Lieutenant Holliday had long expected her to hurtle bodily through the glass door of his office, and was occasionally tempted to help her. This was one such occasion. Kelly, leaving, slammed the door so hard that the partition walls were still rattling when she collided breast-first with Johnny Knapp.

"Miss Barbet?" he said after each had taken a great step backward.

Kelly, who liked the tall Iowan, reduced her internal thermostat to "Simmer." "Yes?"

"Harry and I arrested your Mr. Magistrale, and I was wondering if I could talk with you about him." Kelly nodded. "If it helps, I don't believe he did it. I don't know what he *has* done, but he didn't kill that girl."

"How do you know?"

Knapp shuffled slightly. "This whole damn city is full of actors and fakes. You get used to it. Well, I never saw a performance like his, and if he was acting, he's the best in town. Miss Barbet, I swear to God he didn't know that girl was dead."

Kelly considered. Mage's shock reactions had seemed genuine, but she lacked the faith in her judgment, her ability to read people, that Knapp had in his. "Would you be prepared to tell a jury that?"

"Well, I would if I thought it'd help," replied the cop without any hesitation. "But like I said, don't ask me anything else, and I don't know as it's in your best interests to give him a polygraph test, because he's all keyed up about something—I mean, he's afraid of all *this*, even more than everyone else is, but there's something more. . . ."

Kelly nodded slightly. Polygraphs—popularly and inaccurately known as "lie detectors"—measured emotional responses. A polygraph test on an individual who was already emotionally overloaded would be inconclusive at best.

"What do you think he's done?" she asked.

"I don't know as it's anything he's *done*," said Knapp slowly. "I think it's more likely something he knows. Or something he *saw.*"

12

Turn, Turn, Turn

Elena Dobrovolski was born in L.A. in 1952 and had never left the city. Her parents had escaped from Stalin's purge of the Ukraine, never having previously traveled farther than fifty miles from their home. In 1983 they had retired and flown to Miami for a holiday. Their plane had crashed; that week Elena moved out of her apartment, finding another within a block of the bakery where she worked. She bought her food in the grocery store next door, and twice a year she walked downtown to buy new clothes. She had gone through school with Takumo's mother; she had been plump then, and now she was immense. She had never been to Chinatown, much less to China, but she knew the I Ching better than anyone Takumo had ever known. He visited her whenever he wanted advice, a shoulder to cry on, or wholesale quantities of blueberry doughnuts.

"So, Charlie," she asked while she made the coffee. "What is it this time, your heart or your stomach?"

Takumo thrust his tongue deep into his cheek and said, "Actually, I have this friend . . ."

Elena chuckled. "Now where've I heard *that* before?"

Takumo retrieved his tongue and said softly, "Okay. A friend of mine *is* in trouble—honest—and I think I can help him, but it's rather complicated. Can I ask the I Ching a question without actually putting it in words?"

"Sure. What kind of trouble?"

"He's been arrested. He's innocent, but the circumstantial evidence against him is . . . scary."

"How d'you know he's innocent? Is that what you want to ask?"

Takumo caught that one with his eyebrows and considered it. "No, I don't think so. I feel kind of honor-bound to trust him; doubting him would be too much like backing out. But I *know* things about him that I can't explain, and that I wouldn't ask you to believe. Is that okay?"

"Sure," she said diffidently. Takumo wanted to explain further but couldn't find the words. He twisted the thong around his hand, took the coins from Elena and closed his eyes.

Fire on the Mountain . . . the Wanderer. I guess that's you—and six in the second place, let's see . . .'The Wanderer comes to an inn, with his property, and wins the loyalty of a young servant.' "

Oh, wonderful, thought Takumo. If the Wanderer is Mage—and the description certainly fits—then I'm a servant. Great.

"Does this answer your question?"

"Not very much of it."

She shrugged. "You want to throw another hexagram?"

Takumo smiled slightly. " 'Ask the next question.' "

"Sorry?"

"Never mind."

*   *   *

Shih Ho. 'Biting through brings success. It is favorable to let justice be administered. Six in the fifth place means bite on lean dried meat, receive yellow gold. Be constantly aware of danger. No blame.' "

They sat there silently for several seconds. Then Takumo sighed. "I'm a vegetarian, I don't like money, and I don't know from justice."

"Yes you do."

Takumo scooped up the coins and jingled them in his hands. " 'Bite on lean dried meat'?"

"I don't know. Maybe you have to do something you don't want to, something you've given up . . . or fight something that's very old."

He closed his eyes, seeing a hand pinned to a bedpost with a butterfly knife, struggling like a fish in the sunlight. He had promised long ago never to use that knife, except to bluff. Bite on lean dried meat. . . .

"And yellow gold?"

"Does your friend need money?"

"For sure. Bail's set at twenty thousand. Where'm I supposed to find that, in a stick of beef jerky?"

He heard the coins jingle and clatter as they hit the floor, and suddenly he knew the answer.

He opened his eyes. Elena was staring at the hexagram. "It's the same, isn't it?"

"Yes. Shih Ho, six in the fifth place."

Be constantly aware of danger, he thought. Wonderful. "Thanks, Elena."

Boss? So sorry to disturb you, but there's a Mr. Leasor on the phone—chairman of Pyramus Industries. He says he needs to talk to you."

Tamenaga glanced at the figures on the TV screen. "Put him through."

"Yes, boss."

Leasor's accent was pure west Texas, a lazily arrogant drawl. Tamenaga had never spoken to the man before—he was accustomed to thinking of companies as ordered collections of numbers, not accumulations of people—but he knew enough about the chairman to know that the laziness was a ruse; Leasor worked hours that would have won the admiration of the most tyrannical Tokyo employer and had never backed away from a fight. The arrogance, Tamenaga suspected, was real.

"Mr. Tamenaga?"

"Speaking."

"I'll come straight to the point; I suspect your time's worth just as much as mine. Why are you trying to buy my company?"

"You are misinformed," replied Tamenaga coolly. "I have bought no shares in your company. Good day, sir."

"Wait just a goddamn minute," snapped Leasor. "I know, I know, you don't own any shares; your daughter does. I've heard that one before, and I didn't believe it then—"

"My daughter is twenty-six years old," replied Tamenaga. "At such an age, she is entitled to buy and own shares in her own right. She is also a native of this country; theoretically, at least, she could become *President,* were that position not clearly reserved for Caucasian males. She did not ask my advice, and I cannot say that I would have recommended the purchase if she had—but her husband was a degenerate gambler, and I suspect that she has acquired a taste for risky investments."

"You mean a *kabuto.*"

"The word is *bakuto,*" corrected Tamenaga. "A bakuto is a gambler; a kabuto is a helmet, similar in shape to the ones American soldiers now wear—an excellent design, I understand. And if you are implying that my son-in-law had connections with the yakuza or any other criminal organization, I would recommend you keep such opinions to yourself; my daughter is still in mourning and such a slur would be certain to upset her. Do you understand?"

"You want to talk slurs? We're looking at a major defense contract here. Do you think we're going to get it if the public thinks we're run by Japanese?"

You'll get it, thought Tamenaga. It's a good bid from a reliable company, and at least as important, it creates enough jobs in the right districts to get it through both houses. "You produce tractors," he replied, a hint of boredom creeping into his voice. "Rather good tractors, or so I've heard, but definitely on the plowshares side of the swords-to-plowshares equation. I can understand that you would be experiencing financial difficulty at a time when so many farmers are already so deeply in debt, but I fail to see how this may be considered—"

"We've put in a bid to build a new APC, as I'm sure you know damn well."

"Really? It is possible—indeed, likely—that I own shares in the corporations from which you will be buying the electronics, or any optical equipment; I have never heard anyone object to these being supplied by the Japanese. I may even be able to get you some ashtrays at considerably less than the twenty thousand dollars that I hear the Pentagon is accustomed to paying. But apart from these incidentals, I assure you again, I have no financial interest in your corporation or your bid. Good day."

Las Vegas.

Takumo had visited the concentration camp where his grandparents had been interned during World War II, stood on Salem's Gallows Hill, picketed munitions factories, camped at Spahn Movie Ranch, crossed Wall Street, biked hastily through Newark and Detroit, read the disused theater marquees in Times Square and the warning signs outside Alamogordo, and even traveled to the Mexican *teocalli*. None of them scared him as badly as Vegas.

Unreal city. . . .

He sat on the toilet, staring at the poker machine inside the door, and suddenly understood the fear. The concentration camp was derelict. Gallows Hill, Spahn Ranch, and Alamogordo had been touched by evil, but the evil was gone. New York was scary, sure, but people still *lived* there. The Toltecs had stood atop their pyramids and sacrificed their teenagers for victory in war, but that didn't make them inhuman—Americans had sat in their Pentagon and done much the same. It was stupid, and maybe evil, but it was *about* life.

Las Vegas was about money.

Las Vegas was Midas, starving as his food—and then his children—turned to gold.

Las Vegas was buying and selling husbands and wives; weddings as instant as a Polaroid photograph, divorce as easy as signing a check, sex . . . well, you got what you paid for. Las Vegas was cheap restaurants hidden inside casinos, and poker machines on lavatory doors. In Vegas you were expected to eat money, fuck money, and apparently shit money as well. Take away the money and there would be nothing but desert. The new "Family Entertainment" attractions only made it more frightening, as though the city were buying the souls of the children as well as their parents'. Takumo closed his eyes, wrapped the braided hair around his left hand, gripped the key tightly, dropped a nickel in the slot and pulled the lever.

A lemon, a cherry, and another lemon. Not even good fruit salad.

He stared at the key and again at the machine. How had he opened the locks at the house?

He tried again. Again, nothing.

He bit his lip. What had Mage told him about the idiot with the Ingram? He'd imagined the gun jamming—a simple enough thought. He hadn't had to understand the firing mechanism. Takumo had used the key in much the same way: a key opened doors. He hadn't had to see each tumbler in the lock, hadn't *seen* the key mutate. . . .

What did they say about the great Zen archers? That they closed their eyes and *saw* the arrow hit the target. Takumo closed his eyes and tried to imagine three cherries.

A cherry, a club, and a diamond.

He reached up and touched the corners of his eyes, twisting slightly until he saw three cherries. He focused on that image, pushed a coin in the slot and pulled the lever.

Nickels spat into the cup with a clatter and rolled out onto the floor around his ankles. He scooped them up, stuffed them into his pockets and sneaked into the next cubicle.

An hour later Takumo changed twelve hundred and seventy dollars' worth of quarters for large bills and left in search of another casino. He noticed a party of Japanese tourists on the far side of the street and decided to follow them. They were wearing new jeans, souvenir T-shirts and Oliver North haircuts, and there was no chance that he would be mistaken for one of them by any remotely observant croupier—but they were the only camouflage available. A few minutes later he was delighted by his choice.

The Sunrise was a new name on an old building; the previous owner, Takumo guessed, had died or been bought out, maybe both. The Japanese-ish decor was unsubtle and mass-produced but possibly genuine, and the "geisha" were more probably from Vietnam or Hong Kong, but Takumo particularly liked the statue watching over the tables. Americans might have thought it a curious place to put a Buddha, but Takumo knew better; the fat, grinning monk was Hotei, God of Gamblers and Good Luck.

Takumo grinned back. He bought fifty ten-dollar chips and walked over to the roulette table, beaming at the coolly pretty croupiers and the security cameras.

*   *   *

All of the phones on Tamenaga's desk were fitted with scramblers, of course, but his private line was a masterpiece of Japanese technology, as secure as any in the White House or the Pentagon. Anyone attempting to listen in would be exposed to subsonic frequencies that caused severe disorientation, acute headaches, temporary hearing loss, even epileptic seizures. Only Tamenaga's most trusted employees had access to the private line; it rang, on average, less than twice a year, yet this was the second time in as many weeks. Tamenaga, who had been studying the day's Nikkei Dow gains, let it continue ringing for a few seconds while he composed himself.

"Yes?"

"Boss?"

"Certainly," replied Tamenaga sourly. Nakatani sounded distinctly anxious, almost panicky. Maybe Haruko had been right; he wasn't suited to the day-to-day running of the casino. On the other hand, this was the first time he'd called. "What is it?"

"It's Takumo, boss—the actor whose records you wanted? He's here—and he's winning."

Tamenaga's silk shirt strained and two buttons popped as the python tattooed on his chest suddenly came to life. He felt the prick of the mukade's legs along his left arm, the slither of snakeskin on his right.

"Boss? What shall I do?"

Tamenaga closed his eyes and forced himself to think. The cobra slid out of his sleeve and flicked its tongue at his black-pearl cuff link. "How much has he won?"

"Between eight and ten thousand. He's being careful, only playing red and black and changing occasionally. He's raised his bet to five hundred, and he loses sometimes . . . but never very much. He *has* to be cheating somehow." There was an element in Nakatani's voice that was almost reproachful, a hint of "What haven't you told me?"

How much *have* I told him? Tamenaga wondered. He knows about the focus, but does he know what it can do? And the stuntman—how much did *he* know?

If he was winning at roulette in Tamenaga's casino, too damn much. It was the only trick Higuchi had ever learned—the gunrunner had been a competent organizer and a pretty good gambler, but no magician.

Tamenaga cursed. It was like fighting a hydra: you killed a head and two grew in its place. The Sharmon woman, a brilliant mathematician, had stolen the focus from Higuchi after he'd been stupid enough to tell her about it, so it had been logical to assume that she was the leader. But Sharmon had used it to cure her cancer and then passed it to Magistrale before they found her. Now Magistrale was in jail in L.A. . . . and Takumo was using it. We waited too long, he thought. We assumed the focus was safely in the LAPD's property store; we should have checked sooner. It would have been worth the risks. . . .

"How long has he been there?"

"Nearly an hour now."

"Whom do you have in the casino?"

Nakatani hesitated briefly. "Inagaki and Tsuchiya."

Tamenaga shook his head as the cobra coiled itself around the receiver. Inagaki Kenji was one of the bouncers, an obvious heavy; Takumo would spot him immediately. And Tsuchiya Shimako . . . Did the stuntman have a weakness for women? Or for anything else the Sunrise could provide? If so, it wasn't in his dossier.

"Any Americans?"

"Judd . . . and the gun nut."

"Packer?" Oh, yes, he'd sent the Canadian there to run up a debt to the syndicate. Tamenaga considered. The man was sloppy but wonderfully nondescript; Takumo hadn't seen him before, and he wouldn't be traced back to the casino. "Okay. Keep Takumo there as long as you can—let him win, offer him a room, dinner, women, whatever. He . . ." Tamenaga cursed mentally, and the cobra spread its hood and stared balefully at the handset. Takumo was a stuntman, accustomed to taking risks, but he wasn't avaricious; he would probably stop and leave as soon as he had enough for Magistrale's bail. Or would he become intoxicated by the wealth? Or by the joy of winning? Would he try to take as much from Tamenaga as possible? Tamenaga doubted it. "Just keep him as long as you can, whatever it costs. I'll have Oshima fly there immediately—"

"What if he leaves?"

Nakatani must have been panicky, to consider interrupting his employer—unless Takumo was leaving already. "Let him go," said Tamenaga. "Try not to kill him, but don't let him—or the money—reach L.A. When they bring him in, I want *you* or Sakura to search his body—not Judd, not even Shimako. And keep me up to date. Good-bye." He smashed down the "Call" button on the intercom with the heel of his hand and said without pausing for breath, "Call Sakura, tell her to go to the airport; call the airport and have the Learjet ready . . . and call Greyhound and Amtrak, ask when the buses and trains leave Vegas for L.A. If you can delay them without causing suspicion, do it."

Then he closed his eyes and concentrated on his mantra. His tattoos responded to anger or fear rather than to any act of will; controlling them required controlling his emotions. Tamenaga breathed slowly, deeply, trying to forget the monsters that crawled about his body, trying to deny them life.

It was only a whirring shuriken-shaped blur, then a pale, pearly meteor, then an ivory ball clicking and rattling its way around the indistinct numbers on the wheel. Takumo closed his eyes and concentrated.

"Twenty-one."

The crowd sighed. Takumo's eyes opened, smiled, and tried to count the chips as they were pushed into his square.

"Place your bets, please."

No *way* could he count all that between spins; he scooped the chips off the board and began a hasty stock-taking, feeling like a shuten-doji in a sushi bar. The crowd, which had been waiting to see how he would bet, nervously placed a few small chips on the table, obviously expecting the wheel to stop on a house number.

"Four."

There was some muttering, mostly in Japanese, and a few in the crowd drifted away, slightly disgruntled. The croupier, doing her best to conceal a smile, raked in the chips. Takumo, who had been careful to lose occasionally, dropped two ten-dollar chips onto black and returned his attention to his counting. To his vague surprise, the ball stopped on fifteen and paid off. He grinned quickly at the statue of Hotei and finished counting. Fifteen thousand dollars and change . . . well, nearly fifteen. He wondered whether it might be wise to leave for another casino— and rejected the idea. He didn't look like a man who could afford to gamble fourteen grand; he was better dressed than Howard Hughes had been when he owned much of Vegas, true, but he was far too young and looked far too hungry.

He only needed another five thousand (*only*, he thought with a mental sniff; he had owned five thousand *only* twice in his life) to pay Mage's bail. And then what? he wondered. What about court costs? Or a plane ticket (to where?) and a forged passport? Or . . .

"Place your bets, please."

He gripped the key tightly and dropped five hundred onto black. Hotei smiled.

13

Dante

Mage had been in jail before on three occasions—twice for hitchhiking and once for innocently accepting a ride in a stolen car—but he had always been released the next day. As far as he knew, this didn't constitute a criminal record, but he had told Kelly and the cops about it anyway.

His current cellmate was a sullen young Hispanic who spoke English rarely, and replaced "c"s with "b"s whenever he did. He reminded the photographer of a Monty Python sketch; fortunately, Mage was feeling far too drained to laugh. He lay on his lumpy bunk and stared at the space just before his eyes, focusing on nothing and trying not to wonder what slings and arrows fortune had in store for him next. He'd slept on softer floors, but at least the bunk was less confining than a Greyhound seat, and he supposed he could become accustomed to it in time . . . and it looked horribly as though he would *have* the time: years, possibly a lifetime, in which he might never get out of jail.

The cops had asked him some pointed questions about the

tooth marks on his arm; he'd replied that while he wasn't certain, Carol might have absentmindedly bitten him while making love, and he'd pointed out the scratch marks on his back and the faded bites on his shoulders. That had ended the questions on *that* subject, even though the cops hadn't seemed completely convinced.

Kelly had told him the forensic tests had suggested that Amanda had been strangled with a long blond wig and that there was no trace of skin or hair beneath her nails—from which the coroner had concluded that she'd been attacked by someone she knew.

"She *lived* in Calgary, for Christ's sake!" Mage had exploded. "I wasn't the only person there that she knew—I was probably the person she knew *least!* And how was she strangled?"

"What do you mean?"

"Was he standing behind her, or in front?"

Kelly leafed through the file. "It doesn't say."

"Ask. If he was behind her—"

"Well, that would help explain why she didn't scratch him."

"Look, they can't have it both ways. If she didn't scratch anyone, but I have scratches on my arm—"

"It looks more like a bite. Don't worry—bite marks aren't admissible as evidence."

"How do you bite the arm of someone behind you? And why would I be behind her? Uh . . . let me rephrase that. What was she wearing?" Kelly opened the file again. "Okay, forget I asked. Was she naked?"

"No. Fully dressed."

"Okay. Gloves?"

Flip, flip. . . . "I don't think so, or they wouldn't have expected to find anything under her nails. Ah, here it is . . . no. No gloves."

"Hmm. It was cold that night, too. May I look at that? Please?" He pored over the pages, then smiled grimly. "No gloves, no scarf, coat on but open. What does that suggest to you?" Kelly looked blank. "Forget that you're an Angeleno, try to think like a Canadian. To *me* it suggests that she'd just come into the warm from the cold, but either she hadn't been in for very long or she wasn't staying long, because she didn't completely remove her coat . . . or maybe she was in a car, a warm car but without much room. The front seat, and someone in back . . ." Suddenly Mage *knew* who, or what, had strangled Amanda Sharmon. Hands without a face to scratch, gloved hands that could have hidden on a window ledge. . . .

"Proving what?" asked Kelly.

"What?"

"Okay, so she was strangled in a car. What does that prove?"

"I don't *have* a car."

"Neither did she."

"That isn't the point. I said, she had friends in Calgary. Classmates, tutors . . . *someone* must have a car that she would've gotten into willingly. Jesus, even in darkest *Brooklyn,* most murders are done by friends or relatives, not by strangers."

"I know that," snapped Kelly.

"Good. So tell the cops and get me out of here!" When Kelly had hesitated, he'd sighed and asked, "What is the evidence against me? I confessed to having met her, I asked after her in Calgary—before and *after* she was killed."

"The photographs—"

"Oh, have they been developed? I'd like to see 'em. Okay, so I photograph women. It's my hobby; sometimes it's my job."

"There's no hard evidence," Kelly said heavily. "That's why they granted bail. Forensics is checking your clothes and your gear for her fingerprints, stuff like that, but they probably won't find anything conclusive, even if you're guilty; she didn't bleed, so no bloodstains, and if they find her prints or hair, well, that only proves that you met her. They didn't find anything on *her* that linked her to you either, except your name in her address book.

"But that's not why you're the perfect suspect. Who else is

there? Family? Her parents and sister died in a car crash when she was fifteen. Boyfriends? She didn't have any. For all anyone knows, she may have been a lesbian—but if she was, she was well closeted, because we can't find anyone who claims to've slept with her, not of any gender, not in Calgary or Totem Rock or anywhere else; no one in Totem Rock even *knew* her, except her landlady, who barely remembered her. Her roommate? No apparent motive, and again, she knew almost nothing about Amanda's private life except that she had a friend, possibly a lover, in Las Vegas, whom we've been unable to identify. Her professor? He has an airtight alibi; besides, he's nearly twice your age and has a spotless record, while you . . . you're a drifter, you're promiscuous, you come from one of the roughest parts of New York City, you're nearly broke—it looks like someone went through her handbag before they threw it out—and your last steady job was as a photographer for a porno magazine. And with everyone thinking that the Mafia controls pornography, even your name is a liability."

"It's a soft-core magazine—it's even legal in *Canada,* for Christ's sake—and I'm Italian. Gravesend Italian. The Mafia's Sicilian."

"What's the difference?"

"Have you ever known an Italian who could keep an oath of silence?"

Kelly had actually smiled, but swallowed it quickly. "Seriously, Mr. Magistrale, you're the sort of person that jurors expect a murderer to be. One reporter in Vancouver's already trying to cross-reference your travels with unsolved rapes, murders and missing-persons reports. Okay, it's not justice—it's the antithesis of justice, in fact. Trial by media, guilty until proven innocent, and yes, it stinks, but you can't afford to ignore it, especially not if you're broke."

"So what do we do?"

"We keep you out of court if at all possible. *You* take a polygraph test."

Mage thought quickly. "I thought they were inadmissible as evidence."

"They are, but a negative test may be enough to convince a judge to deny the deportation order. Fortunately, you won't be facing a jury *here*." Her expression showed all too clearly what she thought of California juries.

"What'll they ask?"

"What? Well, they'll talk to you for a few hours, working out some good yes-no questions—say, were you in the youth hostel on Seventh Avenue on the twenty-second, rather than where were you on the night of . . . Then they'll attach the polygraph, ask you a few test questions, four or five, to gauge your responses—is your name Michelangelo Magistrale, were you born in New York? Then they'll ask you if you killed her, when you last saw her alive, where you were and what you were doing at the time of Amanda Sharmon's murder." As she'd more than half expected, Mage grimaced. "That's the tough one, right?"

"Yeah."

"Whatever it is, it can't be worse than murder . . . or are you trying to protect someone?"

"No, it isn't that. It's just a lot harder to believe."

"What?"

"Never mind. Can I have some time to think about it?"

Well, he'd had time—nearly a day now. There'd been no news from Charlie, either.

"Magistrale?" He looked up to see a guard standing outside the cell. "Visitor," the man grunted.

"Who?"

"Says he's your uncle. Come on, I haven't got all bloody day."

Mage stood, glanced at his cellmate and muttered, "Don't go away, I'll be right back." He was pointedly ignored.

"What's *he* in for, anyway?" he asked the guard as they walked toward the visitors' room.

"Murder, same as you. Shot up another gang with a Kalashnikov, killed three." He said it flatly and without qualification —meaning, Mage realized, that his victims wouldn't be missed; three or four pushers fewer in L.A. was a difference that made no difference, and the shooter would be unlikely to make it into the papers, let alone the six-o'clock news.

The murder of a beautiful and brilliant girl with terminal cancer, on the other hand, was great for ratings. He shrugged and they walked the rest of the way in silence.

Dante Mandaglione was short and stocky, with thinning brown hair and an accent wavering somewhere between Sydney, Australia, and Boston, Massachusetts . . . but he spoke gutter Italian fluently, and he bawled out Mage with a speed that would have done credit to an auctioneer on amphetamines. This ritual over, he sat back and took a deep breath, and Mage asked, "How's the family?"

"Eh, they're okay."

"You mean you haven't told them yet?"

"Well, I'm breaking it to them gently," Mandaglione admitted. "Your father hasn't been well, Mikey. Which is no miracle —the man makes me look like number-nine vermicelli. Seems like you got your mother's genes. *She* knows something's up, all right, but she doesn't know the size of it; never did have much of an imagination, thank Christ. I hope you haven't made the New York papers?"

"I don't think so. Dad only reads the sports pages, anyway." He was more concerned about upsetting his sisters than his parents—and he knew Mandaglione knew that—but there was no point in saying so.

"Well, you're not likely to make the front page, not while Wall Street's having convulsions. When's the trial?"

"Three weeks at the earliest. If I can get bail, I'll try to delay it; if not, I'd like to get it over with."

"Well, I can't help you there," Mandaglione said glumly. "I

can't raise a tenth of that—and all you have is your camera, right?"

"Right."

"The family might be able to—"

"*No.*"

"That's what I thought you'd say."

"If they ask, tell them bail was denied. I won't take their money; this is *my* mess."

The two men sat there in embarrassed silence for half a minute. "Thanks for coming."

"Ah, don't mention it. I heard there was a sale on at Dangerous Visions."

"Good. I could do with something to read."

"What shall I get you?"

"Something escapist." Mandaglione laughed. "But not another copy of *Inferno,* and nothing of yours. If I want murder mysteries or horror stories, I just have to look around. If you can get it . . ."

"Yeah?"

"Something on Japanese mythology—something *good.*"

14

Dangerous Visions

Twenty-two thousand dollars, plus change: to Takumo, an outrageous fortune. He looked at the chips, glanced at the croupier—who was smiling nervously, her manicured nails hovering just above the felt (fingertips *on* the table, Takumo knew, signaled that a player was cheating)—and decided to call it quits. For one thing, he wasn't sure whose luck he was playing with here, his or Magistrale's; for another, money didn't really interest him. American currency was as ugly as a gun; the display outside Binion's Horseshoe Casino, a million in ten-thousand-dollar bills, looked to Takumo like so much computer printout. He could imagine someone wanting to collect Canadian banknotes, however worthless they might be as money, but U.S. bills looked as though you were meant to rid yourself of them with all possible haste. He cashed his chips and resolved to do exactly that.

A stunning silk-clad hostess tried to stop him, offering him a free dinner, a free room . . . gifts usually extended to big losers. Maybe they expected his luck to change. Despite her obvious charms, he declined politely and hurried out before she could offer anything further.

He arrived at the Greyhound station with forty minutes to spare and disappeared into the toilets to compose himself. In his agitation, he had not noticed a man following him from the Sunrise.

Sitting on the toilet, trying to ignore the smells of fresh poverty and despair, Takumo counted the money again as quietly as he could. Twenty-two thousand, three hundred and seventy dollars; he had been in movies that he would have sworn had cost less. He folded the large bills carefully, tucked them into the inside pocket of his leather jacket, closed his eyes and meditated.

Packer looked under the cubicle door, saw the sneakered feet and swore silently. He was carrying only two guns: a Metzger Arms Spectre 15 and a Smith & Wesson Model 38 Bodyguard. The Spectre was silenced, but it was only loaded with 9mm Parabellum hollow-points; a round fired through the door would be unlikely to kill his victim. Besides, knowing his luck, he'd probably put a bullet through the money. He backed away from the door, faced the mirror and waited.

It was a long wait. Four times men entered the room and left while he stood at the hand basin. Packer peered under the cubicle door twice to convince himself that Takumo hadn't teleported out, or become invisible, or whatever it was ninja were supposed to be able to do. Inagaki had warned him about this one, reminding him to stay well out of his reach—as though Packer was planning to risk a repetition of that embarrassing incident in Totem Rock.

Finally the door opened and Takumo emerged, his face calm. Packer turned off the taps and walked over to the hand drier, increasing the distance between them, then reached into his jacket for the Spectre.

It was the silencer, slowing down Packer's draw, that saved Takumo's life. He saw the gunman fumble and turned to face him . . . but they were standing nearly three yards apart.

Packer pulled the gun free and was bringing it to bear when Takumo reached for his wallet. "Okay, man, it's yours."

"What?"

"Easy come, easy go," said Takumo wistfully and threw the wallet toward Packer's knees—throwing it at his face or groin might have caused him to duck, or to fire reflexively. The gunman looked down and Takumo clenched his fist around the key, closed his eyes and *thought* himself into a textbook-perfect flying forward kick. An instant later he felt his foot connect with the gunman's face and prepared himself for a roll.

When he opened his eyes again, the world had disappeared.

Michelangelo Magistrale . . ."

Carol looked up. "What?"

"Isn't that the name of the guy who was staying with you? The photographer?"

Carol nodded. She hadn't heard from Mage since the day after he'd left; a cop had called the day before, asking her what she knew about his movements but without telling her why. She hadn't told him about the gunman and was wondering if that had been wise when Jeannie said, "It says here he's murdered someone."

"*What?*"

Jeannie put the newspaper down on the counter, open to the story. "Says he murdered a girl he met here in town. Did you know her?"

Carol looked at the photograph of Amanda and shrugged. "I might have seen her in here . . ." She smiled sourly. "Looks like a passport photo. Mage always said if you looked like the picture in your passport, you were much too sick to travel. I don't recognize the name."

"Me neither." Jeannie read the rest of the story and shook her head. "Guess you were lucky it wasn't you."

Packer, dazed, opened his eyes and tried to focus but found nothing to focus on. He looked around the featureless expanse of whiteness and finally saw the Spectre lying somewhere beyond his feet. He sat up slowly, shaking his ringing head, and touched his face. His nose was bleeding, his cheek swelling, and a few of his teeth felt loose. He tried to remember what had happened. That little Jap had come out of the crapper and—

Where the hell was he? Was he dead? If this was Heaven, he didn't like it at all; if it was Hell, he supposed he could tolerate it for a while. He turned his head painfully and saw Takumo standing—crouching, rather—on apparent nothingness. "What the fuck . . ." Packer began, slowly bringing his body around while reaching for the .38 in his ankle holster. Takumo spun on his left heel, and his right foot lashed out toward Packer's chin, knocking the gunman back to the floor. Packer barely had time to grunt before the whiteness dissolved into supernovae, which vanished into darkness an instant later.

Takumo dropped to one knee and ran his fingers lightly over the floor. The tiles and the grouting were still *there*, whatever that meant; they simply weren't visible. What the freakin' hell had happened?

He looked at himself and then at Packer. The gunman had apparently seen the same infinite blankness—or at least, Takumo told himself, he'd seen something changed, something unexpected. He vaguely regretted having to knock the man out again, but he seemed more of a liability than a help. With a slight sigh, he proceeded to search the gunman's body. First priority was the holdout pistol in the ankle holster; he removed it, glanced at it incuriously, swung the cylinder out and emptied it onto the floor, then threw the gun underarm toward its partner.

It bounced off an invisible something with a clang of metal on metal before dropping out of sight well short of the floor. Takumo stared at the nothingness, then at Packer, and then stepped carefully over the body and tiptoed cautiously toward the place where the revolver had disappeared, remembering stories of explorers lost in the Antarctic whiteout walking blindly into crevasses. To his relief, the floor (floor?) remained solid and level beneath his feet.

His flailing hands bumped something cold and angular before he saw it and he groped around until he recognized the shape and texture: the corner of a hand basin. He peered into the invisible sink and there saw the gun floating in mid blankness. He picked it up—it was slightly wet—and dropped it on the floor. He then circumnavigated the room slowly. As near as his hands could tell, nothing had changed except the appearance. He came to a cubicle door and hesitated before opening it. What the hell had he done?

Be careful what you wish for. . . .

What had he been thinking? His foot into Packer's face. . . .

What had he *seen?* He'd controlled the poker machines by seeing cherries, the roulette wheel by seeing the ball next to the number. For the kick, he'd concentrated on—

Oh, *shit!* he thought. A diagram. A page from a textbook. Two sketched figures on a blank background.

Takumo looked down at himself and his sense of humor took over briefly. Lucky my clothes aren't just painted on, he thought, and burst out giggling weakly, hysterically. Suddenly he stopped and listened, with a strong feeling that there was someone else in the room, someone watching him and laughing. Silence. He sat there for a few seconds, concentrating on his breathing—then, feeling much better, he unwrapped the braided hair from around his wrist, stuffed the focus into his pocket and opened the door.

The toilet was still there. Apparently, whatever he had done had stopped where his line of sight stopped. At least I didn't blow away the world, he thought, and sank to the floor, eyes shut. It's still out there somewhere, if I can just find the right door.

There was a groan from Packer. He dashed over to the body and pried open the gunman's left eye. Still unconscious, and—Takumo estimated—liable to remain so for a couple of minutes. "Unpleasant dreams," he murmured, and began searching the man.

A spare clip for the Spectre and a small folding knife concealed in the belt buckle were the only weapons—unless you counted a half-empty packet of Camels and two matchbooks with a Sunrise logo as lethal. His pockets contained no wallet and no I.D., only a few loose coins—some American, some Canadian—and a room key for the Sunrise Hotel. His watch was a battered digital with a cammo band, with stopwatch and multiple time-zone functions and an alarm set for twenty-five past midnight. He wore no dog tags or jewelry, and had no obvious tattoos. His sleeveless safari suit was fairly new but inexpensive, off-the-rack and years out of fashion, and probably chosen chiefly for its numerous pockets; his shoes were old, severely scuffed, and looked like government issue, probably army surplus. His chestnut hair was close-cropped and receding, his nails short and clean, his hands large; his palms were fairly soft, but his knuckles had lived in interesting times. He was muscular, with a slight paunch, and looked to be in his late thirties. The only useful information that Takumo could glean from his search was that the man had recently been to Canada, and possibly was Canadian; he had a distinct and unpleasant feeling that *that* should mean something to him, but it didn't. The blank surroundings made thinking difficult. . . .

He retrieved his wallet and pocketed it, picked up the pistols and the empty magazine and dumped them in a toilet bowl, then stood approximately where he had been standing when Packer had first pulled the gun. He closed his eyes and concentrated, drawing on his memory of the room, then reached into his pocket for the key.

A moment later he opened his eyes again. The room was no longer blank, but its lines and curves were extremely soft, and his reflection (thin and fuzzy except for the face) was frozen onto the mirror like a Hiroshima shadow. The "Vacant" signs on the doors were barely readable; the instructions on the hot-air hand drier were mere squiggles. He tried again and succeeded in sharpening some of the edges, but the overall effect still resembled the cabinet of Dr. Caligari.

Finally he retreated into a cubicle, pulled his jacket over his head and *imagined* the mirror shattering, *saw* the fluorescent tubes explode. When he opened his eyes again, it was reassuringly dark. He walked to the door with mock confidence and closed it behind him. He had seven minutes before his bus left for L.A. Let the gunman explain the mess when they woke him up.

He sat in the Greyhound station waiting, hiding his face behind a paperback copy of *The Story of the Stone*. It wasn't the face of a man who'd just won twenty-two thousand dollars; it was the face of a frightened boy who's just discovered that he can't do magic . . .

. . . but maybe, just maybe, he knew someone who could.

15

Negatives

By the time Oshima Sakura arrived in Las Vegas, Packer was being strapped onto a stretcher by paramedics while grim-faced cops placed his guns in Ziploc bags. Twenty minutes later she was on the phone to a furious Tamenaga.

Have you decided yet?"

"Decided?"

"About the polygraph."

Mage shook his head. "You don't have any better ideas?"

"No," replied Kelly. "And forensics has developed that film; the cops have the negatives—evidence—but I asked for a set of the prints. Who's this?" She handed over three eight-by-tens, and Mage winced.

"Oh, Jesus . . ."

"Strange name," said Kelly. "Spanish?"

"Very funny."

"He looks dead."

"No, just . . . unconscious. I knocked him out."

"Why?"

"He was pointing a gun at me."

"What sort of gun?"

"Machine pistol, with a silencer. An Ingram, I think."

"M-10 or M-11?"

"I don't know. It could even have been an Uzi, or almost anything; all I know about guns I got from watching movies and being mugged, and this one was a damn sight bigger than anything I've ever had pointed at me before."

Kelly nodded. "And you don't know who he was?"

"No."

"Had you seen him before?"

"I don't think so, and I have a pretty good memory for faces . . . though it's not a memorable face."

It *does* look like government issue, thought Kelly. "Accent?"

"Canadian. Probably western provinces; I heard similar accents in Calgary."

"And you knocked him out?"

"The gun jammed. I hit him with my camera case."

"And this is the story you were scared we wouldn't believe? The reason you won't take a polygraph test?"

"No," said Mage glumly. "If I told you the *incredible* part . . . oh, forget it."

Kelly shrugged. "Why was he pointing a gun at you?"

"He said he was looking for Amanda."

"Do you think *he* killed her?"

Mage didn't, but that wasn't any reason to say so. "That . . . hadn't occurred to me. I suppose he *might* have. I didn't see him in Calgary . . ."

Kelly looked at the photo and grimaced. "Maybe we should start at the beginning again. Now, when and where did you first meet Amanda Sharmon?"

*   *   *

Mage had told the story as far as his checking into the youth hostel in Calgary and was wondering whether or not to mention Takumo's unorthodox means of entry when there was a knock on the door. A sour-looking cop entered.

"Miss Barbet?"

"Yes?"

"There's some guy here with twenty thousand bucks, says he wants to pay Mr. Magistrale's bail."

"My uncle?"

"I dunno. Is your uncle Japanese?"

"No, Australian," replied Mage warily. A Japanese bailing him out? The rukoro-kubi, or one of its friends, setting him up?

"Skinny little guy, about your age."

Mage grinned in mingled relief and incredulity. "Name Charlie Takumo?"

"I didn't catch his name. You want out or not?"

"Sure I want out." He turned to Kelly. "I also want my stuff back; can you arrange that?"

"I can try."

For reasons that Kelly didn't pretend to understand, the LAPD's Scientific Investigation Division wanted to keep Mage's camera case (but not his camera), his jacket, his sneakers, his backpack, his belt, and *both* pairs of jeans. He stalked out barefoot, wearing black track-suit pants and a faded NASA T-shirt, camera in one hand and carry-bags in the other, ignoring Takumo's smiling assurances that his outfit would be utterly inconspicuous in L.A. The smog had cleared, the sun was out, the sidewalk was hot, and he jogged to Takumo's bike to avoid burning his feet. When a pretty girl wearing a muscle shirt and bicycle pants came jogging the other way with a friendly smile, Mage grudgingly decided that he could probably learn to tolerate the city, eventually.

Kelly and Takumo caught up with him half a block later. "Where are you going?" Kelly asked.

"To buy some shoes," Mage groaned, examining his scorched soles. "*And* some jeans. Doesn't this count as cruel and unusual punishment?"

Kelly ignored that. "Make certain they give you a receipt; I should be able to make forensics pay for them."

Mage grinned toothily. "Where's the most expensive jeanery you know?"

"Rodeo Drive," replied Takumo. "Like, I never shop there myself, but it must be. You prefer mink or sable?"

"Do you have the cash?" Kelly asked.

"Some. Do they take cash in Beverly Hills?"

"I wouldn't know." She caught Mage by the shoulder, turned him around. "Michael . . .Mage . . ." and then the right words abandoned her. "Will I see you again?" seemed sentimental; "Are you going to jump bail?" was unprofessionally gauche. She looked down at his camera. "Shouldn't you have a lens cap on that?"

"What?" Astonished, he stared at her; unable to see her face, he looked at her hand on his arm, and understood. "I keep losing the damn things. There's a UV filter on it. It'll be okay," he said gently.

She nodded sharply. "I'm in court tomorrow, a rape case, but can I meet you sometime, talk about the polygraph?"

"Where?"

"My office?" She reached into her handbag and withdrew a card. "This is my pager number. Call me when you decide. Okay?"

They watched her walk back to her car, and Takumo handed Mage a black motorcycle helmet. "What's in the envelope?" he asked.

"Prints. You wanted to see those shots of Amanda, didn't you?"

"For sure. How'd they turn out?"

"I'll have to crop them . . ." when this is over, he thought, but closed the helmet visor on the words. Takumo nodded and threw his leg over the seat. "Where to?"

Kelly looked over her shoulder and watched them ride away, trying to keep a cap on her anger—which was directed not at Mage, but at herself. All the evidence, circumstantial as it might be, pointed to Mage's guilt—no, to *Magistrale's* guilt, she thought. And all her feelings contradicted the evidence.

And now *another* drifter turns up, having known Mage—*Magistrale*—for little more than a week and drops twenty thousand in cash on the police blotter for *Magistrale's* bail, and where the hell did *that* money come from?

"Okay, she's gone," said Mage as they rounded the corner. "Where the *hell* did the money come from?"

Takumo grinned and swallowed it before opening his helmet. "Las Vegas."

"*What?*"

"I used the key," he said and laughed. He drew a deep breath, then burst out laughing again. Mage stared at him, and started laughing just as Takumo stopped. "I should've thought of this before," Takumo explained as he parked the bike. "Don't know why I didn't. Key. *Ki*—kay eye—is Japanese for . . . there really isn't any word for it in English. Literally, it means 'breath,' but it's usually translated as 'spirit,' or 'inner force.' It's from the Chinese 'chi,' as in tai chi. Used properly, it enables you to exceed your human limitations." He chuckled. "Whoever made this talisman had a seriously twisted sense of humor."

"Twisted? Braided. But you haven't explained—"

"Later, okay? It's a long story, and I'm not sure I believe all of it myself. But . . . here." He fished in the pocket of his jacket, retrieved the key and slapped it into Mage's hand. "I think you could use it better than I did."

Mage opened his mouth to ask another question, then closed it again. The hot pavement wasn't a good locale for an argument, so he followed Takumo at a jog. Despite his shorter legs, the stuntman was a fast walker; if he hadn't stopped to look in the window of a martial-arts supplier and burst out laughing again, Mage might have lost him.

"What's the joke *now?*"

Takumo pointed at the "Ninja" T-shirts and appliqués. "Those. It's like carrying a big neon sign saying 'CIA.' Far out." He shook his head, still chuckling, then proceeded into the shop next door. "Jeans, sneakers—you need anything else?"

"Some answers would be nice."

"What size?"

Mage glared at him, then grabbed three pairs of Lee's from the rack. "Look after these," he snapped, handing the envelope of prints to Takumo, and disappeared into the changing booth. Thin and long-limbed though he was, he still found it difficult to buy jeans that fit without surgery; he had concluded years before that most jeans were designed for soprano weregiraffes. He was zipping up the first pair when there was a knock on the door.

"Yes?"

"Mage?"

"Yeah?"

Silence. He sighed and opened the door. Takumo thrust the photograph of Packer at him and murmured, "This guy . . . Crewcut . . ."

"I told you about him."

"I saw him in Vegas. He tried to— Hey, can you hurry it up a little?"

Okay," said Takumo as soon as he'd kicked the door shut behind him. "Sorry, but I'm still a little shook-up—a *lot* shook-up—and I thought that doing something halfway normal might calm me down. I'd done my yoga, my exercises, some *kuji-kuri,* I'd meditated, but when I saw that photo, it—"

"You saw this clown in Vegas? You're sure?"

"Yeah. He looks a little different, mostly because now he has a bruise on his face suspiciously like a size seven sneaker sole, but he still had Canadian coins in his pockets. His behavior hasn't changed, either; he pulled a gun on *me* too." He chained the door behind him, kicked his sneakers off and walked toward the kitchen.

"Sit down and tell me about it," said Mage. "*I'll* make the tea."

Takumo smiled weakly. "That's cool. Okay . . ." He told the story hesitantly and Mage listened without interrupting. Two cups of tea later, he finished with, "For all I know, he's still there. But the key is yours, Mage. Like, I thought I'd wished both Foot-face and myself into the Phantom Zone; I don't have the control."

"*You* don't? Jesus, you're the one who meditates—"

"*You're* the one with the eyes. I think that's how this magic works—you have to *see* and *believe*. Of course, I could be wrong."

"Great."

"You have a better idea?"

Mage stared at the photograph of Packer and shook his head. "What d'you know about photography?"

"About as much as you know about *ninjutsu*. Okay, like I know which end of a camera you point, and I can usually tell which button to press, if there aren't too many of them."

"If I'd given you this roll of film to develop and print—"

"I'd have taken it to a drugstore."

"And if there weren't a drugstore? If you were in a fully equipped darkroom, with no one to help you?"

"I couldn't do a freakin' thing."

"You'd probably totally wreck the film by trying—and possibly the darkroom too."

"Yeah, I can dig that. I've seen beginners with *nunchaku*."

Mage pulled the talisman from his pocket and swung it

around his finger. "Okay, you've used this to pick locks and to rig a roulette wheel. What else can it do?"

"Jam a gun?"

"What? You've done that?"

"No, I didn't think of this at the time," said Takumo quietly. "More's the pity—but what happened before that Ingram jammed on you?"

Mage closed his eyes and concentrated. "I . . . stared at the guy—no, at the gun. I'd answered all his questions and I realized that that was it, he was going to kill me . . . and I was still staring at the gun, like it was more dangerous than he was, more real. I remember wondering what would happen if it jammed— I'd heard that they were easy to jam—"

"And then it jammed. Were you holding the key?"

"Yeah."

Takumo grinned. "Did you see it jam? Before it *did?* Did you visualize it?"

Mage nodded dumbly. Takumo's grin broadened. "Don't tell me *that's* not a useful trick. Like yadomejutsu, Second Dan: the art of *bullet* cutting."

Mage opened his eyes and stared at him balefully. "Wonderful. Magic that works only when someone is shooting at us and we can take time out to visualize. Just what we need."

"Hey, it's a beginning!"

"Wouldn't we be better off knowing *who* was going to be shooting at us?"

"For sure, but—"

"Okay. What was your impression of this Canadian?"

"Dumb," replied Takumo without hesitation. "And he probably gets off on Rambo movies."

"Dumb, yeah. A magician?"

Takumo grimaced. "Not even a sorcerer's apprentice. Like, he couldn't turn a car into a garage."

"So it isn't his. The key, I mean." Mage started, then slapped his forehead. "I'm an idiot! He didn't even *know* about the key!"

"What?"

"He goes to Totem Rock; he's looking for Amanda, and he finds me because I've just come out of Amanda's room. He calls Amanda 'the blonde,' so it's obvious he doesn't know her. I tell him I *have* her key and he doesn't even *ask* me for it!"

Takumo considered this theory for several seconds, then nodded. "Maybe. Or maybe he was going to kill you and take it anyway . . . but it still would've been easier if he'd asked you to hand it over. You're probably right."

"Okay. I thought, back then, that he had to be working for someone else. Now I'm convinced."

"For sure," said Takumo. "He's not a boss."

"How d'you know?"

"No authority. You work with directors, film crews, you know when someone's used to being in charge, who takes shit from whom. Like this clown *needed* that gun; take it away and he couldn't order a Big Mac with fries. But if he isn't the boss, who is? And what was he doing in *Vegas?* Can he teleport?"

Mage started again, kicking his empty cup over. "Oh Jesus . . ." They sat there silently, nervously looking around, for nearly half a minute before Takumo smiled. "Hey, it's cool. I just remembered. He had a key to the Sunrise."

"Sunrise?"

"The hotel, the casino. Where I won the money. Like, he must have seen me there . . ."

"How did he know you?"

"Maybe the rukoro-kubi told him," said Takumo after a moment's thought. "Or maybe the rukoro-kubi told his boss, who told Crewcut. Freakin' hell, if this key is worth what I think, there could just be a multimillion-dollar bounty on our heads. This guy's met you, tries to anticipate us . . . it doesn't work, does it?" Mage shook his head. "Okay, now it's your turn."

Mage stared at the poster for *Jonin*. "What about the rukoro-kubi? A boss?"

"No way."

"I agree: another employee."

"So where does that leave us?"

"At the Sunrise Hotel, maybe. Why would he—Crewcut—be staying there? The Sunrise caters to Japanese. Not the casino—they'll take money from *anyone*—but the hotel. It has a deal with a tour company in Tokyo."

"How d'you know this?"

"When I was working for Dante, most of the girls I met were from Vegas. They used to tell some pretty wild stories."

Takumo decided not to ask for details; he rightly suspected that the New Yorker was trying to be diplomatic. He was well aware of the reputation of many Japanese tourists, particularly in all-male packs, and was also aware that it was often justified. "So?"

"So maybe Crewcut works at, or for, the Sunrise."

Takumo considered it. "He digs guns. Maybe he sells them to Japanese tourists. A handgun will sell for ten or twenty times its original price in Tokyo; bullets can go for twelve bucks *each*. So what was he doing in Canada?"

"Looking for Amanda. Maybe she used the key to cheat the Sunrise; Jenny said she spent a lot of time in Vegas, gambling, winning a lot, maybe that was how she did it." Mage lay back on the tatami and stared at the ceiling. "But then why was she broke when I met her?"

Silence.

"It's the only lead we have," said Takumo. "What do we do with it?"

Mage sat up suddenly and grinned. "Can I use the phone?"

16

Names

"If I asked you why you wanted to know," Mandaglione wondered aloud, "would I be sorry?"

"Only if we answered."

Mandaglione shrugged eloquently—the first and only suggestion of a family resemblance that Takumo had noticed—and reached into his briefcase, removing a manila folder full of photocopies. "You're lucky. The local news back home has been full of the Sunrise for the past week and a half, ever since the manager blew his brains out."

Mage and Takumo glanced at each other, and Mage whistled softly. "Are they sure he did it himself?" asked Takumo.

"Fairly sure. He died in his bathroom, with the door locked on the inside. There was no sign of a struggle, and the wound *looked* like it was self-inflicted. The only window was eight inches wide and twelve floors up, and the screen could only be removed or replaced from the outside." He shrugged again. "On the other hand, there was no suicide note—at least no one's found one yet—and he was shot with a World War One Nambu with no identifiable prints, even though he had another gun, a Detonics nine-millimeter, in his shoulder holster." He turned to Takumo. "Does that make sense to you?"

Takumo smiled bleakly. "I'm not an expert on suicide. Was he Japanese?"

"San Francisco Japanese. His name was Tony Higuchi." Mage started at the name "Tony," but said nothing. "Good name for a casino manager," Mandaglione continued. "Sounds nice and Italian—the Mafia probably love him—but his grandparents came from Osaka."

"Then the Nambu may have belonged to his grandfather," said Takumo. "He may have been keeping it for this one use: an honorable weapon for a more honorable death. Suicides tend to be very fussy, even tidy, and that's not just a Japanese trait. Suicides everywhere tend to use clean knives or razors, to remove their glasses before jumping or their clothes before stabbing themselves." He noticed that Mage was looking slightly green. "Suicide is, above all, a form of communication."

"I think I'll stick to word processors," replied Mandaglione dryly.

"They're certainly easier to correct," agreed Takumo. "Did this Higuchi own the casino?"

"Officially, no."

"Unofficially?"

"Officially, Higuchi was the casino manager. He used to be a successful gambler; in fact, he used to be a lot of things, but gambling is the only one he stuck with. I never actually met him, but I have friends who did; said he could skin them alive at almost any game you could name. Apart from having one hell of a poker face himself, he was damn good at reading people . . . well, men anyway. I hear he had a serious weakness for pretty blondes, spent a fortune trying to impress them. But the Sunrise was rarely ripped off. Higuchi could spot a cheat or a thief as soon as one walked in, and he handpicked the staff, never forgot a name or a face. The other thing he knew well was guns;

he'd been accused of gunrunning a few times, starting back when he was a supply sergeant in the Marines, but never convicted of anything above a misdemeanor.

"The casino's owner, at least on paper, is a cleanskin named Shota Nakatani, no criminal record, what we'd call 'a fit and proper person' back home. He runs a package tour business for the Japanese—"

"Based in L.A.?" asked Takumo.

"Yeah."

"I know him. Or of him. Like, I never actually *met* him, but I worked for him. As a tour guide."

"Why'd you quit?"

"I got a better offer. A movie." And just in time, he admitted silently. If he'd received one more freakin' request for consumer advice on handguns, or directions to the nudie bars and strip shows, he would have told Nakatani-sama where he could stick his freakin' bus.

Softly, Mandaglione persisted. "Did you notice anything illegal?"

"A lot of the tourists were popping pills—amphetamines, I guess—but I don't know if Nakatani was supplying them. And his souvenir shops . . . well, the markups were unreal, but that's true for most tourist traps, neh?"

"Did they sell guns?"

"Not that I saw, but I only went in there once. Some of the staff looked more like *sumotori,* with manners to match, and you could've hidden a tank under the counter—I could barely see over the thing. I know a lot of the men bought handguns from *somewhere.* Why?"

"There's pretty good evidence that Higuchi started out shipping guns and ammunition to a Tokyo yakuza syndicate, probably the *Sumiyoshi-rengo.* He was actually caught twice, but the cases were thrown out of court—once on a technicality, no probable cause, the other time when a star witness failed to show. Rumor has it that he also runs—sorry, ran—small arms to some of the opium barons in Thailand and Burma."

Takumo showed his teeth. "How was he paid?"

"Handsomely, I presume. Traditionally, in gold."

"So why suicide?" asked Mage.

"Ah, there's the rub." He turned to Takumo. "Did you ever hear of Tatsuo Tamenaga?"

"No."

"When you were working for Nakatani?"

"No. Who is he?"

"Higuchi's father-in-law and—again allegedly—the major shareholder in the Sunrise Hotel after Nakatani himself. By all accounts, he's a financial wizard; he lives in this multimillion-dollar palace up in Glendale and calls himself an investor. No one ever sees him; I have photos here of Nakatani and Higuchi, even of Higuchi's wife, but none of Tamenaga."

Takumo nodded. "He didn't show at Higuchi's funeral?"

"No."

"What about the wife?"

"By all reports, she's holding up very well," replied Mandaglione dryly. "It was probably an arranged marriage, and like I said, Higuchi had a yen for blondes. Millions of yen, if necessary."

Mage blinked. "When exactly did he die?"

Mandaglione flicked through the pages. "Just a second . . . eh, here's Nakatani. Ah. Between midnight and two on the eleventh."

Mage calculated. That was eight days before he met Amanda, which didn't prove anything one way or the other, but he remembered Jenny saying something about Amanda dating a casino manager named Tony. Takumo handed him the photograph of Nakatani, who was far too slim and handsome to have been the rukoro-kubi.

"What else do you know about Tamenaga?" Takumo asked.

"Only what I got from the newspaper morgues. He was born in Tokyo in 1938 and orphaned in the war. Apparently he was some sort of mathematical genius even as a kid and they brought him over here to study, then sent him back home to help with the Reconstruction. After that the stories become a little vague. He returned to Japan in '59 and started work as a currency buyer for the Sumitomi Bank. Two or three years later he was working at another bank, then at a brokerage firm—Nikko, I think. Now this is unusual behavior for a Japanese—they tend to stay with the one employer for decades, even for life; they rarely quit and are as rarely fired. Tamenaga had at least four employers, possibly more, in ten years and no one seems to know why . . . but in those ten years, he mysteriously amassed a fortune. Then he went into business for himself—the real-estate business. He still owns some of the most valuable properties in Tokyo, many of which he bought at bargain prices."

Takumo whistled. "You mean he's yakuza?"

"Me mean? I'm not saying anything; I'm sure there are *some* honest people in the real-estate business. I think I met one of them once. But a friend of mine, who shall remain anonymous, described Tamenaga as a power broker, a man who can hire and fire yakuza—"

"A *kuromaku.*"

"Yeah, that was the word he used. According to . . . my friend . . . Tamenaga borrowed his employers' funds to bankroll yakuza loan sharks and split the profits. His employers, when they caught him, didn't have him arrested—the yakuza are too powerful; even the big companies pay protection. But they started watching him and he moved on. Then when he'd accumulated enough, his yakuza contacts helped him clinch the occasional real-estate deal by intimidating the original owner, or by providing him with information for blackmail. Of course, I can't *prove* any of this.

"Then, in '72, Tamenaga returned to America, in time for his daughter to be born here. He invested in an import firm and brought in electronics from Japan—calculators, security systems and surveillance equipment. Of course he cleaned up. By '77, he was a silent partner in a lot of businesses, and owned a few outright. He bought the mansion in Glendale, put in a security system that made Jerry Falwell's place look like Central Park, and effectively retired. Then his wife died in '81—auto accident, no suspicious circumstances—and Tamenaga disappeared into his fortress and hasn't come out since. Of course, he still keeps a Learjet at the Burbank Airport, and his employees fly it from time to time. And he keeps his passport up to date, just to prove he's alive.

"That's all I could uncover on a day's notice. I hope it helps—but I wish to hell you'd trust me." He turned to Takumo. "Where did that money come from? Yakuza loan sharks?"

"I won it at the Sunrise."

Mandaglione turned to his nephew imploringly. Mage nodded.

"Okay, Mikey. If that's the way you want it. I'll be going back home tomorrow morning. Call me if you change your mind."

17

Threads

"Did you get any joy out of that?" Takumo asked as he bolted the apartment door behind him.

Mage sighed. "Not much. Jenny Holdridge, Amanda's friend, told me that Amanda was seeing a casino manager from Vegas named Tony, but that was all she knew. Amanda had gone there to play chess originally and became interested in blackjack, and this Tony became interested in her. Maybe she was using the key to take money from the casino, maybe he had something to do with having her killed, sent the rukoro-kubi or Crewcut after her or something, or maybe that was Tamenaga's doing. It doesn't explain why she was broke and in Totem Rock, but it's the only link I can think of."

Takumo shook his head. "If that's a link, then this"—he held his hands a foot apart—"is a chain and I could beat someone to death with it."

"Yeah, maybe."

Mage collapsed onto the cushions and closed his eyes. He had never been a logician, or even a strong thinker, and he wished he could have told his uncle more of the truth; Dante Mandaglione liked mysteries, enjoyed piecing together elements to make a plot, rejecting stories that lacked internal logic. Unfortunately, Mandaglione was enormously skeptical of the supernatural, as befitted a fantasy writer. He would need the evidence of his own eyes. . . .

Eyes. He couldn't think like his uncle, couldn't think in words, but a diagram, something he could *see*— "Do you have any scrap paper?"

"Sure. By the phone."

Maybe a diagram would help. At the top of the page he wrote "AMANDA," underlined it and added "Mathematical prodigy," "Leukemia," "*Cured* leukemia—magic?" and "Murdered (by rukoro-kubi?)." Next to this he wrote "TAME-NAGA," "Mathematical prodigy," and drew a double-headed arrow between the two.

Takumo was right. It wasn't much of a connection.

He wrote "Canadian" under Amanda's list, then "CREW-CUT," "Canadian," "Sunrise Casino," and added "Sunrise Casino" to Tamenaga's column. It still didn't add up to much.

"RUKORO-KUBI." "Japanese." "Killed Amanda?"

He couldn't prove *that* either. He thought for a moment, then added "Killed Higuchi?" and drew arrows between that and "Sunrise Casino." It seemed easy enough for the rukoro-kubi to have entered a locked room via an eight-inch-wide twelfth-story window that opened from the outside, or to have locked the door from the inside to cover his tracks before exiting via the window. He added "Magic" to the list and returned his attention to "AMANDA." "Key—Magic."

"Key—whose?"

Ah, there's the rub, as Mandaglione would have said. He fingered the braided hair around his neck. Where would Amanda have gotten such an item? Inherited it from her parents? And how had she learned to use it? And if she'd had it earlier, why had she had to undergo chemotherapy, or radiotherapy, or whatever it was you did to relieve leukemia and make your hair fall out?

He reached for the photograph of Amanda and stared. How long had she had the key? How long did it take to almost but not quite grow your eyebrows back? A few days? You could grow a mustache in two weeks. Call it a week. Could she have taken the key from Higuchi? Maybe the key would explain Higuchi's success as a gambler. And his death; if he'd lost it, wouldn't that have been a reason for suicide? Or for whomever he owed money—probably Tamenaga—to kill him?

He fingered the key again, wondering where Higuchi might have come by it. Made it? Stolen it? Won it in a poker game? Been given it as a wedding present?

He stared at the diagram again. What else might Amanda and Tamenaga have in common? "Charlie . . ."

"Yeah?"

"Dante called Tamenaga a financial wizard. What if he were *really* a wizard?"

Takumo laughed. "Man, just because *we* don't know how to make money, doesn't mean it takes supernatural powers."

"I'm serious. The key must come from somewhere. Someone had to make it. You said yourself it was a Japanese-English pun—"

"A thong in a thkeleton key," quipped Takumo. Mage winced. "Okay, man, sure someone made it . . . but not Tamenaga-sama. Unlocking doors, winning at roulette, jamming guns, picture-perfect jump kicks, even curing leukemia. . . . Statistical freaks, outrageous fortune, absurd luck; the Seven Fortunate Gods used to grant that sort of favor like your God turns wine to blood—no offense. In extreme cases, they steered some mortal help in a worshiper's direction—a Samaritan samurai, a doctor, an ally. If all else failed, they might teleport someone to safety. This key does nearly all of that like some magical Swiss Army knife, and even the Magnificent Seven didn't give away talismans like that without some freakin' heavy dues; they liked their ego massage as much as any self-respecting gods, and that meant that people had to plead a little occasionally." Takumo glanced at his watch, pulled his T-shirt over his head and walked toward his bedroom. "With this, there's no pleading required; you're like Hamlet's lawyer, you can circumvent God or any number of gods—"

"Until the battery runs flat," said Mage grimly, "or the bill arrives."

Takumo stopped, raised an eyebrow and nodded. "Karma debt."

"Or something more concrete. Besides, maybe we're not circumventing your gods." Mage glanced at the diagram, sighed and squeezed the paper into a ball. "Maybe we're going exactly where they want us to go."

Mage woke trembling and sweating and glanced at the clock. Ten past eight—no, it was much too dark, even for smoggy L.A. Ten to four. Jesus.

He lay there, eyes open, and tried to remember his dream. Amanda—younger and happier—waltzing with Tony Higuchi over a black- and red-tiled floor. Sometimes they were naked, showing tattoos over Higuchi's arms and shoulders, Amanda's blond pubis. Sometimes there were numbers on the floor. Soon the dance became passionate, then frenzied, while the floor spun about them. Amanda scratched Higuchi's back deeply, her long nails staying in his flesh. Her legs wrapped around his thighs; his small cock stabbed into her (now utterly hairless) vulva. An ivory-colored bishop appeared behind them, blessing them as blood ran down Higuchi's legs and pooled at his feet. Higuchi stroked Amanda's hair, which came loose in his hand and wrapped itself around his wrist and both their throats. There was a sudden painful burst of silence, and half of Higuchi's head disappeared—

That was all he could remember—and more than he wanted to. He closed his eyes, breathed deeply and tried to relax.

Tamenaga, too, was having a sleepless night. He had called for his pillow girl at eleven and dismissed her forty minutes later. In that time she had not seen him, though he had seen her, had watched her in the shower, had watched Sakura search her. In fact, the girl (he had never asked her name) had not seen Tamenaga's face since the day after she arrived from Manila, and had never seen him naked; Tamenaga kept his bedroom as dark as possible, preferred sex with the woman facing away from him, and disliked mirrors. Occasionally he lost control sufficiently to bring his irezumi to life; a few of his women had been bitten by the cobra or attacked by the python before he'd managed to will them back into motionless ink. No price would have convinced them to return to his bed after this, and he had given them to Sakura and Yukitaka. One day he would have to ask them what they were doing with the bones.

This girl had been with the house for nearly a year now, and he was almost fond of her. She was petite, attractive, obedient, and a competent masseuse. Tamenaga preferred his women to be active participants. He had tried coupling with Sakura's mindless victims and found it absolutely unsatisfying. He also refused to have the girls blinded: it reduced their resale value. He did not insist on virginity; his only requirements were good health, good looks, and a complete ignorance of Japanese. Lack of English was also appreciated. He paid the karayuki traders well, and they asked no questions.

Tonight the girl had crept timorously to the door, knowing that she had been unable to satisfy the kuromaku. Tamenaga had not lost control; indeed, despite the girl's erotic skills, he had barely been able to maintain an erection. He had gruffly ordered her not to send for one of the other girls (he kept a stable of six) and had hit the showers as soon as she was gone. Then, clad only in a towel, he had stomped into his office and slumped into his swivel chair.

He closed his eyes and fingered the thong of braided hair he had worn around his neck from the age of six. The *oyabun* of the local yakuza gang had been running a gambling house; Tamenaga Tatsuo, already orphaned, had come begging for food and corrected the oyabun's calculations. The oyabun, Utsugi Dan, had kept him on and encouraged the gamblers to bet against his mathematical skills, giving him problems to solve mentally, and checking the answers on paper or with an abacus. Later Utsugi had employed him as a treasurer; Tamenaga had memorized the oyabun's financial records, eliminating the need for paperwork that could be used as evidence against him.

Utsugi's major source of income was the black market in food; people were trading antiques, family heirlooms, gold, pearls, *anything* for food. The talismans, and the accompanying scroll, had arrived in a small wooden box as part of a job lot with other stolen antiques. Utsugi had been more attracted by an old scroll of *Ukiyo-e*, erotic art, and a *tessen* decorated with a map of Japan, but he expected the empire to fall within a year and he was confident of his own ability to sell *anything* to the invading Americans. Tamenaga had opened the box a few weeks later and read the scroll. It described the talismans as payment from the god Hotei to an obsessive roadside gambler and hinted at their power to focus the wearer's ki. Tamenaga had kept them, replacing them with braided locks of hair bought from a young girl, and he practiced using them to influence dice.

The scroll was lost in the bombing of Tokyo, as was the overconfident Utsugi, but Tamenaga had thrived. He had taken the foci with him to America, explaining them away as a memento of his mother. There he had discovered higher mathematics— algebra, probability theory, calculus. Geometry and trigonometry failed to excite him; he preferred numbers and abstractions. He fell in love with computers, primitive as they were at the time; it was a love that would be reciprocated nearly forty years later, when he used the focus to discreetly manipulate the stock exchange computers and hasten the Wall Street crash of '87.

After returning to Japan, he renewed his links with the yakuza—now stronger than ever, thanks to the black market and U.S. military intelligence's need for somebody to spy on the communists and weaken the unions—and had gone so far as to get himself tattooed to show his allegiance to the clan. He had almost panicked the first time the cobra and centipede had come to life and slithered along his arms toward the woman he was fucking, but he had—after much effort—managed to control them by slowing his heartbeat. The other irezumi had been added later; the chain mail had proved useful on a number of occasions.

Tamenaga opened his eyes and slowly spun the chair around. After the focus, the most valuable item in the office was a picture of Hotei watching two birds fighting, painted by Miyamoto Musashi. It was one of the few artworks in the house that Tamenaga had actually bought. He was equally proud of the Murasama *dai-sho* that stood in the sword rack behind his desk; they had belonged to one of his superiors in the Fuki Bank, a man who was also a compulsive gambler. Tamenaga had slowly bankrupted him by manipulating the dice against him, all the while being careful not to win the game himself, until the banker had been forced to borrow from a *sarakin,* a yakuza loan shark. Eventually he had given the sarakin the treasured swords as security for a last loan—and committed suicide within a month, when the bank had decided against promoting him.

Tamenaga stared at the dai-sho and smiled. They were of no practical value to him, but they were a tangible symbol of his first victory, and not merely a victory over an unimaginative *sarariman*—a far more dignified term than the apt American expression of "wage slave." At the time, it had felt like a victory over the entire hierarchy of Japanese society. And Murasama blades were notoriously lethal. Legend had it that if one were dipped into a river, leaves floating in the water would be diverted toward the blade and their own destruction. The swords were also said to lure their wearer away from moderation and into conflict—and ultimately, to his death.

Tamenaga's fascination with the dai-sho had quickly faded; they soon made him feel less like Musashi and more like Kikuchiyo, the peasant masquerading as a warrior in *The Seven Samurai*. He had never learned to use them well. Knives and *mankiri-gusari* were easier to conceal and just as effective against unarmed opponents. But now he stared at the *katana* and *wakizashi* and brooded.

Which was the leader? Magistrale or Takumo? Or someone else? Perhaps there *was* no leader. Perhaps the drifters were more like the dai-sho: Magistrale the long katana, Takumo the small wakizashi. A partnership. . . .

Tamenaga reached for the katana and unsheathed it, admiring the keenness of the blade. How did you destroy a partnership? By dividing it. He returned the blade to its sheath and placed the sword back on the rack. Then he spun his chair around and reached for the dossiers on his desk.

18

Nothing Like the Sun

To Mage's profound irritation, the forensics team had not released his possessions by Saturday morning. He had little money left—he had refused to accept any more of Takumo's winnings or to borrow from Mandaglione—and after buying a new pair of Reeboks and a roll of Fuji film, he had barely enough for bus fares. He spent the morning sight-seeing and finally stopped, slightly footsore, at Echo Park, concluding that there was nothing to see except the occasional pretty girl—at least, nothing free.

Kelly spent the morning in court; the jury had acquitted her client of rape and she was now wondering whether justice had actually been served. She was in an even worse mood than Mage when they met, and five minutes into the conference she stood and snapped, "I can't win this without a little help! Maybe— *maybe!*—you could charm your way into an acquittal in Calgary: sex appeal and the presumption of innocence aren't going to help you here at *all*. All you have is the one alibi, and you won't even take a polygraph on *that!*" She sighed. "You know the cops expect you to jump bail, don't you?"

Mage shrugged. "Has forensics come up with any explanation for Amanda's not having leukemia?"

"What?"

"Have they even *tried?*"

"No."

"Has anyone?"

"I don't think so. The press hasn't got hold of it—"

"Because if they did, forensics'd have to explain it. Right?" He watched her face carefully.

"It doesn't really help your case—"

"Get off my case for a minute."

"Even if the body wasn't Amanda Sharmon's, it still matches your photo, and it was still found outside the youth hostel. Or are you trying to dispute the cause of death?"

Mage sighed. "I can just see the headlines if I did: 'Strangling Cures Cancer.' No, I was just curious." And wishful thinking had raised its artificially pretty head too—he was still hoping that Amanda might somehow be alive. Maybe if they let him see the body, he could believe, one way or the other. . . .

But the exchange had confirmed his suspicions about Kelly. She was still hell-bent on the cancer cure, and he might be able to turn that to his advantage. But best save it for emergencies or he might end up in a hospital, or worse, as someone's guinea pig.

He had no idea how soon an emergency would arise.

Takumo turned the table over, revealing the weapons gaffer-taped to its underside: a *ninjato* in a black scabbard, three star-shaped shuriken, and a black butterfly knife. He had just fitted the large square *tsuba* onto the ninjato when he heard a knock on the door. He sat there silently until the knock was repeated, then took the unsheathed sword and crept to the door. It hadn't been Mage's knock—too quiet for a New Yorker, and too quick. That, he suspected, also ruled out the cops and Mandaglione. It sounded like a child's knock, or a very small woman's. Of course, this could be a deception. He glanced at the window and was mildly astonished to realize that it was already dusk. Mage was late returning home; in the time it took to cross the living room, Takumo had thought of three fates that could have befallen the photographer and was imagining a fourth as he peered through the peephole.

Mika!

Hastily he slid the chain across, opened the door and welcomed the girl with open arms. She shrank back, and he suddenly remembered that he was still brandishing the ninjato. "Oh, shit, sorry. Forgot it was there. Come in! What's happening?"

She continued to stare at the sword. He backed off slightly and placed it on the kitchen counter. "Mike?"

"Hi, Charlie."

"Come in!"

"Thank you." She smiled prettily and closed the door behind her. They stood facing each other, and she stared at both of his hands, then down at his belt.

"Look, it's okay," he said. "I'm unarmed." He took a cautious step forward and slowly brought his hands up to caress her face. She flinched away.

"Mike . . . ?"

"Sumimasen, Charlie," she replied softly.

Takumo, equally sorry, looked at her and nodded. He stepped into the sitting room just as she reached out to touch him. They stood there, frozen off balance, and then she bent down to remove her shoes. Takumo cursed himself: on a good day, he could somersault over a five-foot fence, parry shuriken or arrows, walk silently over ice, escape from a straitjacket, climb a bare brick wall and defend himself against three opponents twice his size . . . and yet, a nineteen-year-old girl, barely five feet tall in stiletto heels, could instantly render him as clumsy as a newborn kitten. He took a deep breath, retreated slowly into a corner and sat down. She tiptoed toward him and knelt, her hand gently moving towards his—

The phone rang, making them both jump. Takumo hesitated, then decided that it might be Mage. He muttered, "Sorry," and reached for the receiver.

"Hello? Who's calling, please?"

"Charlie?"

It took him several seconds to recognize the voice: Elena had never called *him* before. "Elena?"

"Are you okay?"

I was about to ask the same question, thought Takumo, bewildered. "Yeah. Great."

"You sound . . . I don't know, worried. Uptight."

"No, everything's cool," he replied. "Mike's here." He glanced at the girl and smiled, he hoped reassuringly. She sat back on her haunches and seemed to fume slightly.

"Everything's *not* cool," replied Elena. "I just did a hexagram and it told me you were in danger. Two hexagrams, really; one told me a close friend was in danger, one told me it was you—"

"Hey, hey . . . I'm not in any danger. Not now, anyway."

"You *are,*" she insisted, "or you *will* be soon."

Takumo hesitated. Elena had been right last time, twenty-two thousand dollars worth of right—but last time he'd been using the key.

"Charlie, I'm *sure.* I rolled the hexagrams *twice* and got the same answer each time! And it's *now*—"

There was a knock on the door. Takumo froze.

"Shall I get it?" his guest asked.

"No!" he hissed. "Elena, I have to go, there's someone at the door. I'll call you back. Promise."

"Charlie—"

Takumo eased the receiver down. "Mike . . ." For the second

time in a week he cursed the lack of a fire escape. Where could he hide her? The closet? She was certainly small enough, and if he was killed, there was no reason for the attackers to look for her. Pity the bathroom cabinet was full.

Another knock, louder.

"Quick!" he murmured in Japanese. "Into the bedroom. Hide behind the door."

"Who is it? New girlfriend?"

He grabbed her hand and kissed it; she flinched and her sharp nails scratched him. He hurried toward the door, grabbed the ninjato and stared through the peephole. At that instant the door opened, batting him in the face—and then stopped. Mage peered around the edge.

"Sorry, Charlie. No one answered, and you told me to let myself in."

Takumo looked up at the photographer and opened his mouth, but whatever he was about to say was cut off by a feminine giggle.

"Hi. I'm Mike."

Mage smiled and bowed. "What a coincidence, so'm I. Short for Michelangelo. Call me Mage."

He shot Takumo a "hope-I'm-not-interrupting-anything" look; Takumo shook his head slightly—which Mage correctly interpreted as "Not yet"—and stepped back. Mage walked in, shut the door behind him and stopped at the edge of the tatami. The tension in the room wasn't quite thick enough to drive a nail into, but it was obvious that something was very wrong. He looked over at the girl. She was as pretty as her picture, but her body language didn't match her expression.

"I'd better be going," she said suddenly.

Takumo spun around to face her. "Mike . . ." he pleaded.

"Maybe *I'd* better be going," suggested Mage quietly.

Takumo hesitated, then bit his lip savagely. If Elena had been right—*if*—then it would be better, safer, to let them both go. He dropped the sword, said, "I'll be right back," and turned to

Mage, tossing his head at the door. They both backed out of the apartment, shutting the door behind them.

"Do you have anywhere else you can go?" Takumo asked after a long and uncomfortable silence.

"I'll find somewhere. Can I get the rest of my stuff?"

"Oh, for sure. Mage . . ." Oh, shit, he thought. If I tell him about Elena's message, he'll insist on staying. And why not? If the roles were reversed, I'd do the same. "Look, it'll just be for tonight. I'll give you the money for a hotel. Okay?"

"Okay. I mean, forget the money."

Takumo nodded, then turned, opened the door, and they both squeezed in. "Sorry, Mike." Mage was about to answer and then realized that Takumo was talking to the girl—who was studiously looking down at the tatami, meeting no one's eye.

Mage gathered his few belongings, said his good-byes, and furtively adjusted the shutter speed on his camera down to one-fifteenth of a second, the f-stop to 2.8. "I'll call you tomorrow," he said.

"I really should go too . . . It was nice meeting you."

"Hey, I'm just leaving," said Mage, smiling. He pointed the lens at her, held the camera as still as possible and continued to talk loudly to cover the click of the shutter, then picked up his carry-bags.

"Fifty?" asked Takumo.

"I said . . ." Mage began, then shrugged. "Make it twenty; I'll stay at a hostel or somewhere like that. Pity Dante's already gone." Takumo reached into his wallet, removed three tens and handed them over.

Mage nodded and called "Good night, sweet lady," as he walked away. As soon as the door was closed, he ran down the stairs to the street.

Kelly was rummaging through the back of the pantry for a can of cat food when the phone rang. She swore mildly and turned to face the Abyssinian standing beside her. "Could you get that for me?"

"Mrrow?"

"Didn't think so." She sighed and walked into the hallway. "Barbet."

"Kelly? It's Mage—Magistrale. Look, I can't stay at Takumo's tonight, I'll explain later, and I don't have enough for a hotel *and* a taxi."

There was a long pause.

"Hello?"

Kelly sighed softly. Logic said no; her instincts said why the hell not? She trusted him, didn't she?

"Where are you?"

"Somewhere in Santa Monica, I think," said Mage, twining the thong of hair around his fingers like a rosary. "A liquor store on Ocean Avenue."

"Okay. I have a couch, you know my address."

"Great. See you in half an hour."

Charlie, I'd better go . . ."

"You just *got* here! You come all the way from China and you're here for five *minutes* and—"

"I *knew* this was a bad idea!" she snapped, then stood. "You're just so *possessive* . . ."

Takumo drew a deep breath and held up his hands, palms forward, fingers spread. "Okay, okay. Look, at least let me give you a lift."

"I've got a car outside."

"When did you learn to drive?"

She stopped for a moment, her expression frozen, and Takumo wondered if he'd hit a sore point. "Over there," she said finally. "Sue—one of the other teachers—taught me. Goodbye, Charlie."

"I'll call you—"

She shook her head. "No. I really don't think that's a good idea. Look after yourself, Charlie."

For sure, he thought. No one else is going to do it for me. He accompanied her to her rental car and watched her drive away. He waved, then noticed the scratch on his wrist. Mike always was good at drawing blood, he thought sourly, and sucked at the wound before trudging back upstairs. So much for the invincible ninja, huh?

He shut the door behind him and padded toward the bedroom. The futon was still rolled up at one end, the compartment open. He sat down on the tatami, curled his legs into a lotus and sucked at his wrist again. The faint taste of blood reminded him that he hadn't visited the blood bank since before he'd left for Canada and that the night after tomorrow was Halloween: lots of parties, lots of road accidents. Have to make time for that, he thought, and then: time? Hell, what about now?

Elena had predicted that he was in danger. Hey, he'd known that before she'd rung. Why else had he been taking stock of his weaponry? So, he could sit here and wait for it—or he could go out and avoid it. Or maybe confront it. "'If it be now, 'tis not to come; if it be not to come, it will be now; if it be not now, yet it will come: the readiness is all.'" It was a very Japanese thing for an Englishman to have written.

Takumo inhaled deeply, slowly, and then stood—a little unsteadily. A moment later, clad in black, he jogged down the stairs to his bike and tore off into the night.

Thanks. I don't suppose you're into photography?" Mage asked as soon as the door closed behind him.

"*What?*"

"I didn't think so. Is there a twenty-four-hour developer near here, a quick one?" Everything else he'd seen in L.A. seemed to be open until very late—probably a reaction to the time it took to get anywhere.

Kelly merely stared at him, incredulous. Even her cat, a sphynxlike Abyssinian named Oedipus, stopped twining himself around Mage's legs to look at him strangely.

"Look, I *need* this roll of film developed. Tonight, if possible."

"You're insane."

"Well, I won't rule that out; it may be a good defense. Is there?"

She sighed and nodded.

"Walking distance?"

"Six, seven blocks, but—"

"All safe?"

"Fairly safe, as long as you cross with the lights."

"Great. I'll be back soon." He dropped his bags beside the door, narrowly missing Oedipus, and rewound his film.

It was more than seven blocks, it was ten and a half, and across two roads that pedestrians were obviously never intended to cross. The clerk balked at warming up the printer for one reel of film. It required all of Mage's charm and his last ten-dollar bill to persuade her.

"What's on here that's so important?" she asked as she shrugged her way to the developer.

"I don't know. That's why it's important."

"Why don't you buy a Polaroid?"

"I don't take that sort of picture," replied Mage dryly, then smiled. "Well, not often anyway. Besides, if you take a shot with a Polaroid, you're stuck with reality. Use a real camera and you've got the negative—you can do *anything* with that."

"What's wrong with reality?"

Mage paused. "You're not from around here, are you?"

"No," she replied with a slight sniff. "What's that got to do with it?"

"Never mind," he replied hastily. "I'm from out of town myself."

He realized that she'd taken the comment personally, and he

wondered at it. He'd always prided himself on his tact, never arguing with women, rarely even bantering, keeping his opinions to himself . . . no, that wasn't quite true. Suddenly he wasn't sure he'd ever *had* any strong opinions. Something very strange was happening to him. For one thing, he hadn't made a serious pass at anyone since his hasty departure from Totem Rock, and that was as difficult to believe as anything else that had happened to him, maybe more so. Granted that he'd been preoccupied, maybe even a little panicky, but even so, his recent lack of interest was almost unprecedented. Maybe, he thought, it was reluctance to get any woman involved in the mess he was in. He would have dismissed that as macho bullshit a month ago, but the mess was out of all proportion to anything that had ever happened to him before, and he couldn't think of any woman whom he could have asked to help . . . not including Kelly, of course, and that was her job, and he probably wasn't putting her in any danger.

With a slight toss of her head that showed her profile to best advantage, the clerk turned her attention back to the developer. Mage noticed that she was pretty enough—prettier than Carol or Jenny—but her hair was an unconvincing shade of blond, her suntan also came from bottle, and her makeup, though competently done, looked more like a disguise. She might have walked out of a commercial. Nothing wrong with reality, huh?

He reached into his shirt for the key. It felt more real (whatever *that* meant) than all of Los Angeles, and suddenly he was very glad of it.

Another customer entered and the clerk flitted off. Mage spared the man a glance, guessed what he had come for—condoms—and waited. The clerk returned a moment later, her expression slightly sour.

"You must get a lot of that, working alone here late at night."

"Oh, Christ, don't *you* start."

He shrugged. "Sorry."

The developer switched from shuddering to a faint whispering grind, or a grinding whisper, and Mage, no great reader, began to wish that he'd brought a book.

"I think you're out of luck," said the clerk.

"What?"

"Most of this roll is blank. What were you trying to photograph?"

"I know it's blank," he said a little testily. "It's the last shot I'm interested in."

The clerk glanced at the negatives and shrugged. "That doesn't look too hot, either. Just be a few more minutes."

He nodded, glancing at his watch. Half past eight. For once, he wished he'd *had* a Polaroid.

"*These* are the ones you were waiting for?"

"Yes. Why?"

"She doesn't have a face!"

He snatched the still-wet print from the clerk and stared. The shot was slightly underexposed, with appalling depth of field, but he could clearly distinguish small details: the buttons on the girl's blouse, her crimson nails, individual locks of hair. But her face was a void, utterly featureless, and somehow utterly terrifying. He tried to remember the list of monsters Takumo had told him about in Calgary, way back when he'd thought Amanda was still alive.

"Can I use your phone?"

"What?"

"Can I—" Mage realized that he was whispering. "Can I use your phone?"

The clerk stared at him, then nodded. She edged toward the cash register and—Mage suspected—the alarm button. Slowly, deliberately, he punched in Takumo's number.

"Hi! This is Charlie Takumo, and I'm far out! I mean, I am really out of sight! But if you leave a message after you hear the tone—"

Mage grit his teeth; it was that or scream. He disliked phones, and hated message recorders. "Charlie, this is Mage. I'm at

Kelly's. Ring me on—oh, hell—nine three six double two three
oh. Please. It's important. Ciao."

Packer sat back on the bed, watching *The Terminator* for the
twenty-sixth time. Schwarzenegger was aiming his laser-sighted
Longslide at Linda Hamilton, the red dot of light fixed on her
forehead like a third eye, and suddenly the phone rang. Packer
swore, reached for the remote control, switched it to "Pause"
and waited.

"Hi! This is Charlie Takumo, and I'm far out! I mean . . ."

Packer yawned. He wished that Inagaki, or Hegarty, or whoever was boss around here, would give him his guns back *and*
the order to go and blow both of those irritants away. Or *any*
guns. There was a pawnshop next to the video library, with a
collection nearly as large as his own—less powerful, of course,
unless there was some good stuff under the counter—but he
owed the Sunrise twenty or thirty thousand and didn't have any
cash. That still pissed him off; he'd been to Vegas before, for *Soldier of Fortune* conventions, and had never lost more than a
hundred . . . but then, there'd been other stuff to keep him interested. Now he was stuck with this chickenshit outfit until he'd
paid back his debts, and they wouldn't even trust him with beer
money; Hubbard, who had the shift from ten to eight, did all
the shopping. He wondered how long—

"Charlie, this is Mage. I'm at Kelly's. Ring me on—oh, hell—
nine three six double two three oh. Please. It's important. Ciao."

Packer sat up and grinned. *That* was what they'd been waiting for, the reason he'd been sitting in this dump. He picked up
the other phone and called Hegarty.

19

Bakemono

It was a wet and extremely irritated Kelly Barbet who opened the door after half a minute of heavy pounding. "What the hell—"

Mage took a deep breath and staggered inside before she could withdraw her invitation. "Charlie's in trouble . . . no, in *danger*. He—"

"Charlie? Your alibi?"

Mage collapsed onto the sofa, and Kelly, with a slight sigh, shut the door. "Huh? Oh. Yeah. I tried . . . ringing him, but he's . . . he's not answering. We have to go and . . . ."

"What sort of danger?"

"I . . . no time to explain," he panted. "The woman he's with isn't wh-who he thinks she is. Her face . . . ."

Kelly moved cautiously to a chair opposite him, carefully keeping out of his reach. Fresh out of the shower, she felt unpleasantly cool and extremely vulnerable; she was wearing nothing but a short bathrobe, which clung damply to her left breast and lay flat over her right.

"What about her face?"

"It's a disguise," he said, still reluctant to tell her about the bakemono, still afraid she wouldn't believe him.

Kelly nodded. "What do you suggest we do?" she asked, her voice and expression neutral.

Mage shook his head. "Can you drive me there?"

"Back to Charlie's?"

"It's just down the freeway. Please?"

That "please" rocked her with its concentrated sincerity—more sincerity than she'd heard in her six years of practising law and three of practicing marriage. Reluctantly she changed her opinion of her client. He was obviously insane.

"Okay," she said after a moment's hesitation. "Just let me get dressed first?"

He looked at her, noticing her bathrobe for the first time. "Yeah. Sorry."

She smiled, stood and walked to her bedroom, not taking her eyes off him until she closed the door between them. She decided against using the phone—he might pick up the extension in the hall—but there was the alarm, and her shotgun under the bed. She dressed quickly, not wanting to give Magistrale time to recover his breath from his run.

Mage, slumped on the sofa, looked blearily around the room and noticed the trophies on the ledge above the kitchen door: basketball (inevitably, he supposed), fencing, archery, target shooting. Oedipus suddenly looked up and launched himself from Mage's lap by planting his back feet firmly in the photographer's crotch and using it as a springboard.

A moment later Mage heard the hiss and yowl of an angry cat, and a slow flapping sound that he couldn't quite identify. He grabbed the camera, prepared to use the flash to startle the invader, and walked quickly toward the back of the house. The laundry was dark and he reached for the light switch. Silhouetted in the doorway, he made an almost perfect target for the rukoro-kubi, who hovered in wait near the ceiling.

The rukoro-kubi's right hand, brandishing a large switchblade, swooped toward Mage's chest. An instant later it was enveloped by a spitting, sharp-toothed, claw-raking cat. The knife twisted in the hand; the tip pierced Mage's T-shirt but missed scratching his flesh. The rukoro-kubi dropped the switchblade, and Mage knocked it aside before the other hand could catch it; then he grabbed Oedipus and the right hand, pulled them through the doorway and shut the door behind him.

"Kelly!"

The doorknob turned, but Mage managed to hold it firm, thanking the gods that he was stronger than the disembodied hand and that there wasn't a cat-door flap in *that* door as well. He dropped Oedipus—noticing that the cat had managed to rip the rukoro-kubi's leather glove—and looked around the kitchen for something that would wedge the door. Where the hell did Kelly keep her big knives?

A quick glance told him that Kelly wasn't an enthusiastic cook. The most frequently used items in the almost spotless room were the microwave, the percolator, and an enormous coffee mug with the inscription "Legal Grounds." Still grasping the doorknob tightly, he stretched as far as possible, opening all the drawers and cupboards within reach. The only knife with a point had a blade barely three inches long. The hand flung itself from floor to ceiling, wall to door, trying to dislodge the cat. Once, by blind luck, it hit Mage full in the stomach. Mage felt his hand grow sweaty, his grip begin to loosen; there was no weapon to hand, and still no sign of Kelly.

He tried to imagine some way that he could use the key; failing that, he forced himself to think logically. The rukoro-kubi had only one hand on that side of the door, and it couldn't be holding the knife. This would give him a momentary advantage—*if* he could arm himself.

He glanced around the kitchen again and noticed a pair of

salt and pepper shakers. A handful of pepper in the eyes would blind the rukoro-kubi for long enough to . . . well, he'd think of something later. He reached for the shakers. They were, as he'd expected, just beyond his grasp. He fumbled inside his T-shirt for the key, gripped it and stared at the shakers, imagining, *seeing* them glide across the counter like miniature Daleks.

When he stretched out his hand again, he was able to snag both shakers with his fingertips. He slid them a few cautious inches toward himself, grabbed the pepper and extracted the cork with his teeth as though pulling the pin on a grenade.

Kelly had nearly finished dressing when she heard the yell, and she hesitated for a few seconds, wondering which was the more necessary—her shotgun or her jeans. Mage had sounded genuinely panicky, but *that* was easy to fake. Finally she dropped to her knees and reached under the bed. If it were merely a ruse, the photographer's idea of a joke, then she could cheerfully blow him away.

Yukitaka Hideo felt the doorknob twist just a little farther and then finally yield. He raised his head to the ceiling, pulled hard at the door and waited.

To his relief, no shots rang out; Yukitaka hated guns almost as much as he hated cats, even though he doubted that a gunshot would kill him before sunrise. He released his grip on the doorknob and brought his left hand up to retrieve the switchblade from behind his ear. His right hand was still being mauled by that confounded cat, and he had only a vague idea of its location in the room. He counted to three and then dropped.

They saw each other at the same moment and acted in unison—Mage throwing the pepper into the rukoro-kubi's eyes, Yukitaka feinting with the switchblade and spitting a small envenomed dart at his enemy's face.

Mage, startled, blocked the dart with his left forearm and stepped backward, tripping over Oedipus and falling. The point of the switchblade scraped on his belt buckle, leaving a fine scratch and a faint brown smear. The Abyssinian leaped across the floor, releasing the flailing hand.

"Holy shit . . ."

Mage tipped his head back and saw Kelly standing over him, shotgun in her hands. The rukoro-kubi blinked and stared her in the face. She brought the shotgun to bear . . . and hesitated.

"Mage . . . what the hell *is* that?"

Yukitaka grinned as his right hand slid up the door frame and switched off the kitchen light. He was half-blinded by the pepper and saw no reason to play fair. Kelly certainly wouldn't risk shooting him in the dark. . . .

A moment later he felt the stock of the shotgun hit him in the side of the head. He barely noticed the lights going on again, but like a drowning man, he pushed his head as high as it would go. Kelly dropped the gun, leaped up and grabbed his head as though it were a hideous basketball.

Yukitaka blinked and dimly realized that Kelly's hand was covering his eyes. His knife hand feinted at her face and Kelly twisted, keeping the head between herself and the point. "What do I do with it?"

Yukitaka didn't hear Mage's reply. He circled with the knife, slashing toward the woman's fingers. Then he was shoved violently into a small white box. He twisted around as best he could—there seemed to be some sort of turntable beneath him—until he was staring out at Mage and Kelly through thick glass and a wire mesh.

A second later he realized where he was and hastily brought his right hand up toward the microwave controls. Mage grabbed it firmly.

"Either we kill him or we let him go now," he said. "If we hold him until morning, he'll die anyway. I say we kill him now."

"We could try to talk to him."

"I don't think he *can* talk. No larynx. No throat, even. Charlie stuck a knife through his hand last time and he didn't make a peep—"

"Last time?"

Mage kicked at the knife hand as it made another sweep toward his abdomen. "Yeah, I think this is the same one as before. Watch out for the knife—poison."

"What about your arm?"

Mage looked down at the dart, noticing it for the first time, and swore. Still grasping the rukoro-kubi's right hand, he reached into his shirt for the key.

"What're you doing?"

"Tourniquet. Oh, Jesus, this is ridiculous. I'm going to turn it on."

"No!"

"If you want to stop me, shoot me."

Kelly stared at him and then at the rukoro-kubi's hands—one struggling against Mage's grip, the other hovering between them. Slowly she dropped to a crouch, out of Yukitaka's sight. Mage followed suit.

"It's that or stay here all night—or capture both hands. Do you think you can do that?" Mage asked.

"What did you do last time?"

"Nailed one of his hands to a chunk of wood. We let it go before sunrise—but he wasn't trying to *kill* us then."

"What *was* he trying to do?"

"Frame me for Amanda's murder."

The microwave started to rock.

"Do you have any better ideas?" he asked. The knife jabbed at Kelly's chest, cutting into her prosthesis. She snarled, swatted the hand aside and stood, staring into the rukoro-kubi's face.

"You don't want to kill me," she said clearly. *"I'm* keeping you alive."

Yukitaka's expression didn't change. Kelly saw a large element of smugness in that stare. It was much the same smugness that she'd seen in the face of the rapist she'd successfully defended that day. They stared at each other for several seconds, and she smiled sweetly as she pressed the buttons. Yukitaka began throwing his head around violently, trying to push the microwave off the shelf, to tug the plug out of the socket—but Kelly reached out and held it still. She was still staring, and smiling, as his skull exploded like an eggshell.

Oedipus stuck his head around the door cautiously, saw that the hands weren't moving and crept up to lick the blood flowing freely from the left wrist. Mage grabbed the Abyssinian, stroked it, and carried it out of the kitchen. "You don't really want it," he crooned. "You don't know *what* it's been." He slid the door shut behind him, dropped the cat onto the sofa, ran into the bathroom and threw up in the sink.

When he returned, Kelly was scrubbing the floor where the hands had been. "Where's the rest of him?"

She jerked her head at the sink. "What should we do with them?"

"Dump them somewhere. If Charlie was right, there's going to be a dead body nearby for his boss to explain."

"His boss?"

"Yeah. Speaking of Charlie . . ."

She nodded. "Did you try calling him again?"

"No, but I will." He glanced at the digital clock on the microwave: nine fifteen. It felt more like three A.M., the hour when nightmares began.

"What's that on your arm?"

"What?" He looked down at the talisman, twisted tight around his biceps like a tourniquet. "Well, that's sort of what this is all about. Amanda's cure for cancer. It's a long story. . . ."

20

When Shall We Three . . .

"His bike isn't here."

Mage, who was already halfway up the stairs, turned on his heel and stared. "What?"

"His bike. If he were inside, the bike would be here."

Mage considered, and nodded. They stared uncomfortably at each other and Kelly asked, "Do you have a key?"

Mage grinned and reached for his tourniquet.

"It opens that door?"

"It opens *any* door. At least that's what Charlie said."

Kelly nodded, her expression doubtful. "How's your arm?"

"It's okay. I think I sucked most of the poison out. It hurts from the elbow down, but that could be from the tourniquet—or my imagination."

"Hurts how? Sting? Ache? Burn?"

"No—twinges. Like a pulled muscle."

"Badly?"

"No."

"I still think you should get to a doctor. It could be a digestive poison as well—"

Mage swore, then shrugged. "Later." He ran upstairs to Takumo's apartment and unlocked the door. It opened, confirming that Takumo was out—had he been home, it would have been chained and bolted. Nervously, Mage removed the key from the lock and held it tightly, then switched the light on. The apartment was almost exactly as he had last seen it less than three hours before.

Kelly appeared behind him and looked over his shoulder. The first thing she noticed was the unsheathed ninjato on the kitchen counter.

"His?"

"Yeah." He knelt, removed his sneakers and then stepped into the kitchen. He reached gingerly for the ninjato's hilt—

"Fingerprints?" suggested Kelly.

He stopped, glanced at the blade and shook his head. "It's okay. Hasn't been used."

"Is it real?"

"You mean sharp? I'd bet on it." He reached into his pocket, found a bus ticket and ran it along the blade; it was cut in two neatly and effortlessly.

"Can he use it?"

"I'd bet on that, too—but if you mean *has* he used it, I don't know. Have you ever used that gun?"

"Not against a living target. My husband used to like hunting, but there isn't anything left in America that needs shooting."

"Maybe that's why they shoot each other."

"What do you mean *they*, Paleface?"

Mage grinned, taking the ninjato and advancing into the apartment. "I don't know. People who like guns, I guess."

"I don't *like* guns, I—"

"Just know how to use one? How long did it take you to learn?"

Kelly was silent.

"Better come in, shut the door." He glanced around the sitting room and then cautiously opened the bathroom door. "Nothing in here. Me, I like cameras."

"My gun just saved your life."

"Yeah? If the safety catch hadn't worked, I could've been up for another murder; no one would've believed *my* story. What happened to your husband?"

"I dismembered him; he's in the deep-freeze. What the fuck do you *think* happened to him?"

Mage shut the bathroom door and walked into the bedroom without answering. "We're divorced," said Kelly flatly. "What exactly are you looking for?"

"I don't know. Something to say where he's gone."

Kelly relaxed slightly. "Write him a note. I'm taking you to a hospital."

"Just a second." He reached for the phone, pressed the redial and waited.

"Hello," came a cheerful voice. "Park Plaza Hotel."

"Sorry, wrong number," he said and hung up. Kelly looked at him blankly. "I just wanted to see if he'd called anyone." Dante had been staying at the Park Plaza—apparently Takumo hadn't used the phone since Mage had called his uncle the day before. "And if anyone had called him." He stared at the message recorder and switched it to "Playback." There was a faint churning sound.

"Try 'Rewind,' " suggested Kelly.

"I never *did* like these things. Where the hell could he have gone?"

"If he thought that creature was his girlfriend . . ." Kelly shrugged. "What made you think she wasn't?"

"Her body language was all wrong. *Seriously* wrong."

"Why didn't *he* notice it?"

"I don't know. I guess he saw what he wanted to see."

The recorder clunked and he switched it to "Playback."

"Charlie, this is Mage. I'm at Kelly's. Ring me on—oh, hell— nine three six double two three oh. Please. It's important. Ciao."

A blip, then a tired female voice: "This is the Emergency Ward at Good Samaritan. We have a Mr. Charles Takumo here, suffering from cryptogenic paralysis. If you can help us with any information, please call Dr. Barre on—"

Mage realized that he was brandishing the ninjato as though the recorder were about to attack him; he forced himself to relax.

"Where's Good Samaritan?"

"Off Wilshire. Do you want to call first?"

There were no more messages on the tape; Mage rewound it and shrugged. "I guess it'd save time . . ."

"I'll do it, if you like."

He nodded dumbly and she squeezed past him to grab the phone. He stepped back, looked at the ninjato and dropped it on the floor. *That* was trust, he dimly realized—letting a murder suspect stand behind you clutching a sharp twenty-inch sword. He had been outrageously lucky: first Charlie, then Kelly. . . .

"No, just a friend. Just a second, please. Mage?"

He looked up, startled. Kelly was watching him, her hand over the mouthpiece. "Takumo's next of kin?"

"His mother's dead, his father's . . . uh, unknown. No other family."

"He doesn't *have* a next of kin. Okay. We'll be there as soon as we can."

"He's alive?"

"Yes. Come *on* . . . and Mage?"

"Yeah?"

"Leave the sword here, okay?"

G oldin looked up from the computer when he heard the door open, then quickly looked away. "I'm a busy man. One coma case, looks like neurotoxic poisoning, and seven of the usual. What do *you* want?"

Kelly sighed. David Goldin was a sour, frustrated man who looked much older than his thirty-eight years. He was short, balding, diabetic, and terribly prone to ulcers and migraine. Kelly knew him as well as anyone did, and knew that "the usual" for him was an IV drug user whose heroin or crack had been laced with something even nastier. She also knew him to be a firm believer in the death penalty for offenses ranging from murder to tobacco growing, who suspected that most juries consisted exclusively of creationists, economists, flat-earthers, and other scientific illiterates. But he was an expert at his job in toxicology and, in his own quiet way, an enthusiast as well. She placed the switchblade and the dart on the bench beside him and waited.

"Well?"

"I think they're poisoned."

"You mean envenomed," said Goldin with a faint sniff. He lifted the knife gingerly and stared at the edge. "Could be poison, could just be oil or something. Is it urgent?"

"Yes."

"Let me guess. If I identify it in time, someone doesn't die and your client gets off with assault instead of murder and he's out doing this again in six months."

"It's not for a client."

"Uh-huh. What're the symptoms?"

"He's your coma patient. They were found outside his apartment. In his parking spot, in fact."

"Oh?" Goldin raised his skinny eyebrows. "Do the cops know about these?"

"Not yet . . . but if you don't want them, I'll give them to—"

"No, I'll look at them," replied Goldin blandly. "I was wondering about poison; the blood tests were negative for obvious gram-negative and gram-positive shit and all the usual drugs, and the stomach pump came up with nothing except his dinner. I thought it might be fugu, but it's not . . ."

"Fugu?"

"Blowfish poison; you get it from blowfish sushi. Idiots eat it to show they're macho, we had a case of it last month. I'd even thought of curare, but curare's *fast;* he would've died two or three times while they were doing the paperwork."

"What could it be?"

"Almost anything. Ask me again at the autopsy." Kelly waited, knowing that Goldin couldn't resist an opportunity to show off. "I don't have enough of the history. I haven't even seen him—"

"He drove from his apartment to the blood bank, apparently okay and feeling no pain. He passed out quietly on the table. At first they thought he'd fainted and didn't realize anything was wrong until they looked at his eyes."

"Uh-huh. What sort of time frame are we talking about here?"

"He blacked out at seven thirty-nine. He'd been at the blood bank for less than twenty minutes."

"And it's now . . . twelve past ten, so he's been paralyzed for nearly two and a half hours, unless he's died since you came down here." Goldin shook his head. "There weren't any needle tracks on him except from the blood bank, much less stab wounds, just a small scratch on the back of his hand . . . seems more like a snake bite or a spider, something like that."

"Aren't there—"

"Antivenins? Yeah, sure, but they're all specific and the wrong one can kill him. You better hope he's tough—and *lucky.*"

No, I'm *not* a relative. His relatives are *dead.*" Mage decided not to mention Manson. "His ex-girlfriend's teaching English in Beijing. I'm a friend of his—I was staying in his apartment."

The desk nurse looked uncertainly at the monitor. "He's still in a coma. We can ask him when he regains consciousness . . ."

"What if he *doesn't* regain consciousness?"

"I . . ."

"Oh, Jesus." The nurse flushed. Wrong approach, he realized suddenly; try charm, it's what I'm . . . what I *used* to be good at before this started. Kelly can intimidate her, if necessary; she's had practice. Softly, "Sorry. I didn't mean to snap. I'm under a lot of pressure. Look, can I talk to his doctor? Please?" He gave her his best little-boy-lost smile.

Most nurses, in his experience, saw themselves as ministering angels—why else would they work hours like this for such lousy pay?—and the hospital was, after all, called the Good Samaritan. He watched her face carefully and noticed a slight uncertainty there. He would have been crestfallen to realize that the nurse, thoroughly tired of deflecting passes from patients and visitors alike, was wondering how best to get rid of him.

"I don't know where he is."

"Can't you page him?" Mage asked instantly. "I can wait." They tried to outstare each other; he won. The nurse reached for the intercom and paged Dr. Barre.

"Thank you," whispered Mage as he backed away from the desk. The nurse smiled tightly and hung up. Mage took a seat, closed his eyes and waited.

"Any luck?"

He opened an eye and noticed Kelly sitting beside him. "Are you kidding? A *ninja* couldn't get into his room."

"Well, that's a relief."

Mage did a double take and then laughed. "They've paged his doctor. Maybe *you* should try persuading *him*. Ah . . . are you okay?"

"Yes," she replied automatically. "Why?"

"You look . . . I don't know. Shaky."

Kelly shivered slightly. "Hospitals scare me. I can cope with monsters if I have to—I *will* have to now, won't I?"

Mage shrugged.

"Can guns hurt them?"

"It worked on the rukoro-kubi."

"I meant bullets."

"I don't know. You'll have to ask Charlie. What did the toxicologist say?"

"Nothing very useful. How's your arm?"

"It feels—" He noticed a tall, silver-haired man in a white coat walking toward them and shut up.

"Mr. Magistrale?"

Mage decided against correcting his pronunciation. "Yes. Dr. Barre?"

"That's right. I understand you're Mr. Takumo's roommate?"

"Not really. I'm just passing through town. I'm his friend."

"How long have you known him?"

"About a week. We met in Canada."

"Know anything about his medical history?"

"Not really. He said he was taking codeine until a few months ago for a back injury . . . and that he didn't take any other drugs." Barre grunted. "What's wrong with him?"

"It's what we call a cryptogenic coma."

Kelly smiled thinly. "If I remember my Latin, 'cryptogenic' just means that you don't know what causes it. Am I right?"

"Actually, I believe the root words are Greek," replied Barre urbanely. "And the term also means that we've been able to eliminate the most common causes of coma. Apart from that, you're essentially correct. Are you a lawyer?"

"I'm with the P.D.'s office, yes, but that's not why I'm here."

Barre's toothy smile suggested that he was glad to hear it. He turned to Mage. "The nurse says you want to see Mr. Takumo?"

"Yes."

"Why?"

Mage looked to Kelly for help, but none was forthcoming. "You know he hasn't any next of kin?" Barre nodded. "If he were my brother—hell, my *cousin*—you'd let me see him, right?"

"Yes."

"I have cousins I've never met," said Mage, "and you'd let me see them? Charlie's my friend, and it's not as though there's a queue waiting to get in."

Barre raised an eyebrow at that and considered. Then he nodded slowly and glanced at his digital watch. "I really should check up on Mr. Takumo. You can come in with me. Two minutes, and don't touch anything—and the camera stays outside. All right?"

Charlie looked very small, bound in a web of tapes and tubes and wires. Mage stared at the EEG and EKG readouts, not understanding them, knowing only that a flat line would mean that his friend was dead. He unwrapped the talisman from around his arm and gripped it tightly. If you can cure leukemia, he thought grimly, you can help him.

Nothing happened.

"His heart—should it be that slow?"

Barre glanced at him, then shook his head slightly.

Mage grit his teeth. The tubes and wires made it impossible to hang the key around Charlie's neck, and his hands draped limply on the sheets, like dead flowers. Mage concentrated on the key. Charlie said that a god made you, he thought. Okay. *Make him well* . . . and he can have you back.

Nothing happened.

Mage stepped away from the bed. I didn't ask for this, but okay. You want something from me? *Cure him,* and I'll do it.

Charlie didn't stir. Mage glanced at the chart hanging beside the bed, did a double take, and stared. The red line on the graph had broken up into a series of Japanese-looking ideograms.

"Mr. Magistrale?"

Mage stared at the ideograms, concentrating, trying to remember. They didn't translate well into letters or shapes, and he had to absorb them as a pattern, a gestalt. Barre glanced at him, then at the chart, apparently seeing nothing unusual.

"I think you'd better leave," he said gently.

Mage nodded. He backed out of the room, still staring at the ideograms that only he could see, and immediately turned to Kelly. "Quick! Pen?"

"What?"

"I need a pen and paper, before I forget."

"Forget what?" she asked, already rummaging savagely through her handbag. A moment later she handed him a small notebook and a gold Parker pen. He transcribed the ideograms hastily.

"Do you know Japanese?"

She shook her head.

"Me neither. I just hope these are right. I'll have to ask Charlie when he wakes up."

If he wakes up, Kelly thought, and decided to change the subject. "Do you realize that the doctor thinks you're gay?"

Mage, leaning against the wall, shrugged lethargically. So much for levity, she thought. She was trying to think of something reassuring to say, when there was a sudden, urgent yell from inside Charlie's room.

21

Departures

"Boss?"

Tamenaga woke instantly but opened his eyes slowly, feigning torpor. The voice was one of Sakura's, but he had never entirely trusted the bakemono, much as he relied on them. He waited for a moment, concentrating, until he was ready to transform his tattoos into chain mail and mankiri-gusari, then murmured, "Yes?"

"Yukitaka hasn't come back."

That opened Tamenaga's eyes. "What's the time?"

"Seven. The sun's been up for a few minutes."

"You've tried his car phone?"

"Of course. No answer." Sakura's voice was harsh and slightly brittle, and so was the face she was wearing: a stylized, symmetrical, porcelain mask of the classical Japanese ideal of beauty, very different from the tanned features of Kayama Mika.

Tamenaga sat up and rubbed his chin. "Get Hegarty; tell him I'll see him in my office in five minutes. He's to have all the tapes and transcripts from last night ready for me."

Yukitaka, he thought as Sakura hurried out. Not Yukitaka-san, not Hideo. She's angry with him. Now isn't *that* interesting?

Man, of *course* I yelled," said Charlie, a shade petulantly, "waking up like this. Like I thought an octopus had fallen in love with me. Last thing I remember was lying down on the table to give blood, and *wham!* here I am. What the freakin' hell *happened?*"

Mage pulled the photograph out of his pocket and handed it to him. Charlie looked at it dubiously.

"She was a bakemono," said Mage. "I bet the real Mika is still in China."

"A mujina." Charlie shook his head. "First a rukoro-kubi, then—"

"The rukoro-kubi's dead."

"*What?*"

"Kelly killed it."

"*We* killed it," Kelly countered.

"Congratulations, *both* of you," said Charlie dryly. "How?"

They told him the story as quickly as they could; he, in turn, told them how "Mike" had left so soon. "Like she probably expected me to sit there and mope for a few hours—or maybe exercise, get the poison through my system a little faster—and didn't think you'd be here to help me. Man, we must've used up a lifetime's supply of luck in the past few days—What's that?"

"Can you read it?"

"I presume it's supposed to be *katakana*. 'Three focus—focuses?'"

"Foci."

"Foci. Thanks. 'Three foci exist. Tamenaga has two.' What's this from, a fortune cookie?"

"It was written on your chart after I used the key—"

"The—" Charlie shot a glance at Kelly.

"Would you rather I left?" she asked.

"Hell, no," Mage replied mildly. "I think we'd better stick together. I've told Kelly everything. False modesty aside, she saved my life—and without her, I could never have saved yours."

Kelly studiously looked away from them, apparently becoming fascinated by the ceiling—though she listened carefully as Mage explained his silent plea to the maker of the key.

"Okay. When can I get out of here?"

"They want you to stay another twenty-four hours, for observation."

Charlie shook his head. "I can check myself out, can't I?" he called to Kelly.

"Yes, but—"

"Neat. I'm out of here."

"What if you have a relapse?" asked Kelly softly.

"What if the mujina sneaks in here dressed as a nurse and puts a little drop of botulin or something on my thermometer? She could, and no sweat; she had me believing she was *Mike.*" He shook his head. "I should have noticed her nails."

"Nails?"

"Mike plays the guitar, so she always keeps her nails shorter than mine; a lot of people assume she's a lesbian. The mujina had nails like daggers—probably venomed. Old *kunoichi* trick."

"Kunoichi?" asked Kelly.

"Female ninja. Can you get me my pants?"

"I still believe you're safer here."

"Yeah? I don't think we're safe *anywhere.* Dig?" He turned to Mage for support, and the photographer nodded slowly.

"So where are you going to go?" Kelly asked.

"We're going to split. Hide."

"Until this all blows over?"

"It's *never* going to blow over. We're going to go somewhere

where *he* can learn to use that key"—Takumo smiled—"and *then* we're coming back."

Kelly stared and shook her head. "I hope you're not going to ride your bike in your condition. At least let me give you a lift."

As though in contrast to the huge and hideous sumo wrestler stationed at the door, the girl who ushered Hegarty into Tamenaga's office was the most beautiful the ex-soldier had ever seen. If she were six inches taller, he thought, with a less severe haircut, she would have been perfect. She slid the door shut behind them and sat on his right, at the very edge of his peripheral vision, so distracting that it was almost torture.

Tamenaga, clad only in a white silk robe, seemed to be meditating. The girl reached for a remote control on the desk, and Hegarty caught himself watching her hand—it was delicate and pale, the nails impractically long and painted an innocent-looking shade of pink.

He heard a very poor-quality recording playing on Tamenaga's expensive sound system: a female voice, with a lot of background noise. "This is the Emergency Ward at Good Samaritan. We have a Mr. Charles Takumo here, suffering from cryptogenic paralysis. If you can help—"

The hand stroked the remote and the voice stopped. Tamenaga opened his eyes and regarded the ex-soldier coolly. Hegarty met his gaze for a few seconds and asked, "Yes?"

"You've heard it before?"

"Yes, of course. Packer played it to me last night."

"And you didn't report it to me?"

Hegarty blinked. "You knew all that . . ."

Tamenaga nodded. The tape warbled briefly, then another voice said, "Good Samaritan."

A third voice—another woman, younger, and black if Hegarty was any judge. "Do you have a patient there named Charles Takumo, please?"

"One moment, please. Are you a relative?"

"No, just a friend. Just a second, please . . ."

Tamenaga nodded again and the tape stopped.

"He was still in a coma," said Hegarty, slightly puzzled. "Lamm's broken into the hospital computer—"

"Did it occur to you to wonder who was calling the hospital from *Takumo's* phone?"

"I didn't know; Packer didn't even report it. He must have stopped listening—"

"You sent my yojimbo, Yukitaka-san, to the attorney's house, neh?"

"Yes."

The kuromaku nodded again. "And well done, too. Have you heard from him since?"

Hegarty blinked. ". . . No," he said, his voice barely more than a whisper.

The sleeves of Tamenaga's robe had fallen below his wrists, showing the chains tattooed on his forearms. Hegarty had long known that his employer had links with the yakuza, but had never believed that he *was* yakuza. For one thing, all of his fingers were intact: yakuza *kobun* who erred would ceremonially cut off a finger joint to atone in a ritual known as yubitsume, so if Tamenaga had ever been yakuza, he'd never made a mistake. . . .

Hegarty tried not to stare at Tamenaga's hands, or at the girl's, or his own. He suspected that he'd screwed up royally . . . or more probably that Packer had, but Packer had been under his command and therefore his responsibility. He glanced at the kuromaku, but Tamenaga's face was, as always, unreadable.

"Neither have we," replied Tamenaga smoothly. "Nor does he answer his telephone. Did you send him on any other mission?"

Hegarty shook his head, glancing at the girl to see if *her* face gave any hints . . . but the girl's face had disappeared. In its place was a void, a dull dark gray, as deep and empty as the muzzle of a gun. Hegarty stared, fascinated, terrified, lost in déjà vu.

Hegarty had spent four years in Vietnam as a Green Beret, discharged via Section Eight after shooting two of his own men in self-defense. He had survived wars, invasions, coups d'etat, "police actions," the aftereffects of Agent Orange, three plane crashes, and innumerable bar brawls. He regarded death as a business partner, and they had been close enough to shake hands on several occasions. He gazed at the mujina, and then, without blinking, smashed the side of his hand into her throat.

He sensed movement behind him, but before he could react, the chain tattooed around Tamenaga's right wrist had become a mankiri-gusari whistling through the air. It hit Hegarty at the top of his spine, stunning him. His chair rocked, toppled, and he fell at Sakura's feet.

A moment later a gigantic right hand clamped onto his shoulders and lifted him from the floor, and the left hand slammed into his solar plexus. Hegarty sucked in enough air to last him the rest of his life and blacked out with the pain. The sumotori turned to Tamenaga and waited for his orders. Sakura created a face for herself—flat, nebulous, asymmetrical, and even uglier than the wrestler's—and looked up expectantly. Tamenaga nodded, and the sumotori broke Hegarty's neck.

"Thank you, Yamada-san." Yamada Kazafumi bowed, his forehead almost touching Tamenaga's desk, then backed out of the room with the corpse over his shoulder, as silently as he'd entered. Sakura, sensing Tamenaga's temper, concentrated on shaping her face into something more appealing.

"You left Takumo before he died."

"The venom can take an hour or more, but there's no cure. And it's hard to detect. I thought that if it looked like natural causes—"

"You left before he died!"

"Magistrale had been there, seen me, and he had the focus. He *suspected*. And Takumo had weapons ready. The risks . . ."

Tamenaga listened, his face as impassive as Sakura's Noh

mask. He had long known that the mujina was a coward, but it had rarely mattered. Worse still, Sakura knew that she was invaluable—that was why she had refused to become pregnant, lest her child become her replacement. The only other mujina that the Sumiyoshi-rengo had been able to find him had been Sakura's own mother, Oshima Zuiko: infertile (Tamenaga had offered the avaricious monster millions of yen for another child), nearly blind, cunning but slow-witted, and unwilling or unable to learn English. Sakura's father, and his short-lived successors, had been human, ensnared by the mujina and all but mindless. Zuiko was known to her enemies as "Kamakiri"—the praying mantis.

Zuiko/Kamakiri claimed not to have seen another mujina since Sakura's birth in 1944. Mujina children required years of practice to properly form human faces—Sakura had survived for years with a near-rigid mask of keloid skin, purportedly the result of radiation burns from the bombing of Nagasaki, before she learned to move her illusory lips—and hiding children was no longer easy.

By the turn of the century, Tamenaga estimated, bakemono might well be extinct. Those that could not pass for human had retreated to the remote mountains of mainland Asia, in groups too small to be viable. The shuten-doji, congenital idiot savants to whom every intersection was a fascinating maze, had also retreated to the dwindling countryside. Only Sakura seemed able to save her species (genus? order?), and she had shown no inclination to do so.

"Ah, yes, risks," said Tamenaga as though that were adequate explanation, ostentatiously concentrating on winding the mankiri-gusari around his right wrist. "That reminds me. With Higuchi dead, the Sunrise will need a new manager, and Nakatani-san would be utterly unqualified even if he were not so busy elsewhere. My daughter is willing to try, but she lacks . . . experience in dealing with . . . certain types of people. You would certainly be able to assist her."

Sakura's face remained immobile; pretty and false.

"Of course, if Yukitaka does not return, I will still need you here—perhaps more so than previously. Magistrale and his friends are becoming thorns." Tamenaga noticed her tense slightly, and he smiled inwardly. "Until they are dealt with, I doubt that I can . . . spare you. You're not pregnant, I suppose?"

If Sakura's eyes had been real, she would have blinked. "No."

"Good. If you were, I would have to temporarily relieve you of such hazardous duty—at your full salary, of course. Your child would be far too precious to . . . risk." He stared at his wrist as the chain became a tattoo again. Then, dismissively, "See that Hegarty's body is disposed of—an 'unexplained disappearance,' I think. I want to see Yukitaka as soon as he returns, or to be informed if his body is found. Send someone out to look for his car. And have Lamm watch Takumo's file; tell me the instant he dies. If he doesn't, if he is discharged . . ."

He stared unflinchingly into Sakura's phantasmal face. The mujina stood, backed away from the desk and bowed.

22

The Hard School

"So," said Takumo, pulling a pair of boots out from the closet. "You're going to need a hat, some long-sleeved shirts, and—believe it or not—something warm for the nights. I'll buy the munchies, and I've got nearly everything else." He unzipped one of the boots and removed a dark gray object that resembled a sandal with claws.

"So I see," said Mage. "What the hell is that?"

"*Neko-de*," replied Takumo, removing another from the other boot. "You put your hand through here, the spikes go over the palm, and you strap these to your wrists. You use them for climbing walls, or parrying swords, or minor damage—bleeding forehead wounds, stuff like that. Or you can envenom them, but I'd rather not at the moment, if that's okay by you." Mage nodded. "The thing on the bed's a *kyotetsu-shoge*. You can use it like a grappling hook, but the usual trick is to throw the ring end and tangle someone up with the rope, then pull him in close and stab him with the sharp end. The ninjato and *sawa*—the scabbard—have more uses than I've got time to explain."

"No shuriken?"

Takumo grinned. "There're a few hidden in the sitting room. See how many you can find."

Ten minutes later Mage returned to the bedroom gingerly holding three cross-shaped shuriken. "Where were they?" Takumo asked.

"Taped behind the *Ronin* poster, the block-mounted one." Takumo nodded. "Where're the rest?"

Takumo sighed, walked over to the library and passed his hand quickly under several shelves. Six shuriken—trefoils, stars, and a swastika—flashed through the air in quick succession, embedding themselves in a large chopping block that stood in the kitchen. He returned to the bedroom and produced another six from behind the framed Olivia print.

"You're taking those as well?"

"Yeah, why not? I could use the practice."

Mage glanced over his shoulder at the chopping block and shook his head. "Who made all of this?"

"My grandfather did most of the shuriken when I was a kid. I killed a pigeon with one once, and he damn near split a *shinai*—a bamboo sword—on my ass for it." He shuddered. "The neko-de and the iron sleeves were props from *Red Ninja*—stolen, I admit, but the bastards owe me residuals. And the armorer was a real buff, an old navy guy who really got off on doing good reproduction stuff; he did the ninjato and the kyotetsu-shoge for me, at cost and for fun. I made both the *shinobi shozuko* myself. Movie ninja suits are a joke, but I guess you can't have your hero and villain looking exactly the same. Besides, it makes it easier to switch between the actor and the stuntman."

There were two complete ninja costumes on the bed: multi-pocketed jackets, baggy pants, hoods, broad sashes, and split-toed moccasins. One of the sashes had been folded over, showing a gray side and a black. Mage picked up a black hood and realized that it was gray inside, and apparently reversible. The other suit could be either white or dusty brown.

"No jungle camo?"

"No need for it; not where we're going."

"Where *are* we going?"

"Death Valley."

"What?"

"I know this abandoned ranch where we can hide out for a while, out in the general vicinity of China Lake. It's where we did the locations, second-unit stuff, for *Age of the Sword.*"

"Why was it abandoned?"

"The wells ran dry a few years back. And it's kind of inaccessible: rough terrain, no real roads, no electricity, nothing. There is a house, but I don't know what sort of condition it's in. Even the *horses* thought it was the end of the world. Don't worry, the Family never squatted there—at least not as far as I ever heard. We won't dig up any bodies."

"What about our own?"

Takumo smiled thinly. "You want a safe place? Go back to jail; maybe they'll let you stay there, maybe not. Lots of people die in jail. Or you want to run? They found you in Calgary, they found you at Kelly's—"

"They didn't find me at Jenny's, and I wasn't *trying* to hide in Calgary. *Or* at Kelly's. I wanted you to reach me, I left a message on your machine. If they broke in, I was stuck—and maybe they did. If I *try* to hide, change my name—"

"They found Amanda, man."

Mage's face fell. He shrugged, turned and flopped onto the bed, carefully landing between the weapons.

"I *know* how to hide," said Takumo, "and they could catch me without any sweat. They got through my guard on the first attempt, sending around someone who looked like Mika. Old ninja tactic, *gojo-gyoku*—the five feelings and the five desires. *Aisha, dosha, kisha, kyosha* and *rakusha:* kindness, bad temper, lechery, cowardice, and boredom. Know your enemy's weaknesses and use them. You got any weaknesses that you can think of?" Mage glared. "Yeah, I thought so. Okay, so maybe you can protect yourself; make yourself a hard-hearted bastard, help no one, say no to all the pretty girls . . . because believe me, man, if you *do* try to run, you're going to end up scared of shadows. Like every girl you see could be another mujina, or just a kunoichi, female ninja—Tamenaga can probably afford dozens of them. You want to live like that?"

"Do you believe it's Tamenaga?"

"'Believe' isn't a word I use lightly; there's not a lot I actually believe. Let's say I suspect it. You?"

Mage shrugged slightly. Surrounded by blades, he reminded Takumo of a knife-thrower's assistant. "I don't know . . . but I get the feeling that if I *dis*believe it, you're going to keel over and die." He lifted his head, his expression sour, then struggled carefully to his feet. "No, I don't want to live like that, but that's not why I'm not going to run. If I'd known *yesterday* that the focus belonged to Tamenaga, I might have tried giving it back to him." He shook his head. "Or maybe not. He had Amanda killed. Maybe she stole from him, maybe not, but Jesus . . ."

"She had leukemia and the focus cured it."

"Maybe. Maybe Tamenaga cured her and she stole it later. Maybe I wouldn't die for Amanda, but that's not the issue anymore. He's tried to kill me, you, Kelly—"

"You killed the rukoro-kubi . . ."

"Self-defense," growled Mage.

"Hey, man, it's cool! I agree with you! I would've done the same! Like, that's why we're going! Dig?"

They stared at each other, and Mage relaxed slightly. "I guess I just had to talk myself into it."

Takumo smiled. "That's cool. If you hadn't, Kelly would've done it; that lady doesn't take shit from anyone. But you did such a good job that *you* get to talk her out of coming with us. Okay?"

In fact, it was Takumo who talked Kelly out of joining them. She had certainly dressed as though she intended to stand and fight, in hiking boots, dungarees, leather gauntlets, and a bulky down jacket. All she lacked, Takumo thought dryly, was a beret—and that would have looked silly on top of her afro. They had been driving for nearly three hours before she had carefully mentioned that she had her own camping gear in the back of the Range Rover. Mage spent twenty minutes trying persuasion, without any noticeable result; travel along the rough road was noisy and he had to raise his voice to be heard. Worse still, Kelly didn't seem to be listening.

Finally Takumo leaned over the front seat, poked his head between them and said wearily, "Miss Barbet—"

"Kelly."

"Kelly. For sure. When do you have to front up to your office? Monday morning?"

"I can phone in—"

"Yeah, you could. Buy another day that way, maybe two, before they come looking for you. They don't find you, they call the varks, they—"

"Varx?"

"Fuzz. Cops. So maybe they find us. What're you going to tell them? Like, *you're* going to be missed and we're not. Who's going to miss a couple of unemployed hyphenates with criminal records?"

"He's been charged and remanded. That doesn't constitute a criminal record. What about you?"

Takumo stared out the window and shrugged. "Assault. Three years ago. I broke up a domestic in the street, he filed charges; he had a better lawyer, the wife wouldn't testify, and none of the other witnesses bothered to show. Big guy against a little woman—I didn't know they were married; they didn't *look* married—and, like, I got carried away. Very uncool. They stuck me with carrying a concealed weapon too, though it never left my pocket."

"What'd you do to him?"

"Took a few teeth out of his smile. And, like, he kept punching this brick wall; broke a knuckle, they tell me. *She* needed an ambulance."

"Was she Japanese?"

"No. Filipina or Vietnamese, I think. Does it matter?"

The Range Rover lurched into the seventeenth pothole of the trip and Kelly carefully maneuvered it out again. "No. Did he hurt you?"

"Didn't touch me, which is not to say he didn't keep trying. Maybe I should've let him. There's the house."

The "house" had never been more than a shack, and now it was rather less. It looked decrepit enough in the headlights; close up, it was even worse, a peasant version of the House of Usher that no self-respecting ghost would deign to haunt. The visible windows were cracked, mostly held together by faded newspaper stuck to their insides; the roof sagged; the paint had vanished altogether. Kelly stopped the car and the three sat there, staring uncertainly at the ruin.

"Okay," Takumo murmured after nearly a minute of silence. "We get out simultaneously, so they hear only one door—"

"You said this place was empty," whispered Kelly.

"Yeah. You want to go first?" Before she could answer, he slipped his black hood over his head and reached for his flashlight: a heavy black club fifteen inches long. Mage nodded.

"Three . . . two . . . one . . ."

Three doors opened and slammed shut, and still there was no movement from the shack. Kelly flicked her shotgun light on, swept the beam across the wall and then stepped cautiously toward the porch. Takumo hurried ahead of her and crept silently sideways over the warped boards toward the door. He crouched and reached up for the handle with his left hand, brandishing the unlit flashlight in his right. The handle turned stiffly and he pushed at the door; it stuck, having warped in the weather. Takumo put his weight behind it and suddenly it swung open.

He let go the handle and somersaulted into the middle of the room. Kelly, behind him, stepped onto the porch; the board creaked loudly beneath her foot and Takumo whirled around, blasting her in the face with the beam of his flashlight. She started, thumbing the safety catch of her shotgun before both relaxed.

Takumo, barely visible in the beam of the shotgun light, waved her back, then looked around the room. Nothing. Slowly he walked through the shack, checking the other rooms—three empty bedrooms and a stone-floored kitchen/bathroom/laundry—glancing under the few remaining sticks of furniture, looking behind every door. Several minutes later he returned to the porch.

"It's safe."

Kelly nodded. "I can see why they didn't bother to lock it."

"So it's got character. Reminds me of Charlie Sheen's pad in *Wall Street.* I've stayed in camps and hostels that were just as bad . . . well, they would've been without the furniture. Besides, it's cover. We can rig up the tent in one of the rooms and no one'll ever see us."

"How long are you staying here?"

"We've got your basic life support for five days," replied Takumo. "Can you come back Wednesday? We'll need food and water, especially water. There's a shopping list in your glove compartment."

Kelly drew herself up to her full height and they exchanged glares in the near-darkness for half a minute. Finally she nodded. "Wednesday, then. Let's get the stuff out of the car."

Okay, that's everything. Don't forget your gun."

Kelly, at the door, looked over her shoulder and said blandly, "I wasn't forgetting it."

Mage grabbed the shotgun by the barrel and threw it to her. She caught it easily without even turning around.

"I can't use it," he said.

"It's like a camera. You point, and you pull the trigger . . ."

"You may need it yourself."

"I have a crossbow at home."

"Neat!" said Takumo brightly. "Bring it on Wednesday. *I* can use a crossbow."

Kelly looked down at the stuntman again. "What're you going to teach him? Karate?"

"No, just magic."

The lawyer shook her head and looked at her watch. "I hope you know what you're doing." Neither man commented. "Happy Halloween," she said and closed the door behind her. Takumo instantly wedged it shut.

"Okay," he said as soon as he heard the Range Rover's motor start. "First lesson. You don't plead with Amazons; it just doesn't work. . . ."

Mage? Wake up, man."

Mage opened one cloudy eye and stared crimsonly at the stuntman, who was clad in his dust-colored shinobi shozuko. "Wha' time is it?"

"Six thirty."

"Are they attacking?"

"No."

Mage began rolling over, but Takumo grabbed his shoulder and held it firmly. "It's cool out, and light; it'll be warm soon, and in a few hours it'll be as hot as Hiroshima. So. This is the only smart time to get outside."

"Why outside?"

"No room to throw a Frisbee in here. Come on, man, shake it while you got it."

Slowly Mage disentangled himself from his borrowed sleeping bag. "Do I at least get a coffee?"

"For sure. Make me a cup while you're there; the tea bags are on top of the stack."

A few minutes later the photographer stepped out onto the porch, a mug in each hand. Takumo was standing with his back to the sun, throwing a Frisbee so it boomeranged back in his general direction, then leaping and rolling to catch it.

"I thought you were kidding," muttered Mage.

"No."

"It's razor-edged?"

"No." Takumo moved back into the shade of the porch, accepted the mug of tea and leaned against the corner post. It creaked alarmingly, and he shifted his weight away from it and folded himself into a lotus position. "Have you used the focus—the key—since I gave it back?"

"Yeah, to get into your place. Oh, and when the rukoro-kubi attacked," and Mage quickly told him the story of the pepper shaker.

"Neat. So now you're a mover and a shaker. Finish your coffee and we'll get to work."

"Work?" repeated Mage dubiously, staring at the Frisbee.

"Work." repeated Takumo firmly. "I don't like the word either, but sometimes it's necessary."

They spent the next few minutes throwing the Frisbee to each other, until Mage had learned to grab rather than duck. "Yadomejutsu," explained Takumo. "The art of arrow cutting."

"What that's got to do—"

"Watch this." Takumo threw the Frisbee in an arc so that it passed just out of Mage's reach and returned to himself. "Okay?"

"I—"

"You saw it?"

"Yeah, I saw it."

"Great. You saw the shakers move, right? You moved them,

controlled them, dig? Okay, it was slow, for sure. You're going to have to speed it up. Like *this.*" And he threw the Frisbee directly at Mage's groin. Unable to dodge, the photographer knocked it aside.

"Okay. Send it back here and watch it fly. Experience it."

Mage threw the Frisbee back and Takumo caught it deftly, swinging on his heel and hurling it back on the same movement. Mage closed his eyes, stretched out, caught it, fumbled, and dropped it.

"That's cool. Confidence, man. Try it again."

A few minutes later Takumo tied Mage's hands behind his back, walked away, and sent the Frisbee spinning toward his navel. Mage grit his teeth and imagined it arcing off at the last moment.

It did.

Within an hour Mage was sending the Frisbee into boomerang curves, zigzags, even spirals. Seeing it rise from the ground and fly proved difficult, until Takumo advised him to watch the Frisbee hit the sand at the end of its flight and imagine it running through a projector in reverse.

A few minutes before nine o'clock, Takumo untied Mage's hands and instructed him not to use them. Breaking old habits took nearly an hour. When Takumo was convinced that Mage had mastered the trick, he walked inside and returned with another Frisbee, a Moonlighter.

By eleven, the Frisbee was orbiting the shack while the friends threw the Moonlighter to each other, catching it left-handedly. Takumo plucked the Frisbee from midair and returned it sharply; then, with his right hand, he threw a shuriken at the photographer's chest. Mage blinked, then stopped the Moonlighter short, dropping it onto the shuriken. The Frisbee also fell to the ground.

"Not bad."

"You—"

"I *told* you I'd teach you arrow cutting. Don't worry, it's a prop, a fake. It couldn't hurt you unless you tried to swallow it. Plastic, and *very* blunt. Getting warm, isn't it?"

Mage's shoulders fell. "You bastard."

Takumo nodded. "I guess that's enough for today. We'd better get inside. I, for one, could use some sleep."

23

Hide and Seek

Tamenaga, in his bath, received the news of Yukitaka's death with his usual monolithic calm; he had, after all, been expecting it. When Sakura added that the police had collected car and body, she noticed the cobra tattoo on his right arm swell slightly, but nothing more.

"Where are Magistrale and Takumo?"

Sakura blinked mentally. "I don't know. Packer hasn't reported any phone calls, there've been no sightings at the airports or the Greyhound depots, and your orders were not to have them followed or watched."

Tamenaga stared at her balefully and then nodded. Magistrale was learning to see even more clearly, and to use the focus. Tamenaga had not expected him to advance so rapidly, even with the threat of prison to goad him. And Takumo astonished him; his out-of-date affectations concealed sharpness, determination, and intelligence. And he was fond of playing ninja; his apartment would certainly be tricked out to show him if anyone had broken in, however carefully. Unfortunately, none of the nearby apartments were empty; there had been no chance of peering through the walls or ceiling, or even of recording their comings and goings along the balcony.

Of course, if Magistrale had killed Yukitaka and saved Takumo, then they *knew* they were being watched. . . . "Phone Takumo's apartment. If they answer, say . . . no, a wrong number's too obvious. Invent a charity or a survey. No, better still, offer him some life insurance." He smiled sourly. "If nobody's there, tell me immediately."

After an early lunch of tofu and fruit leather, Takumo scattered his shuriken in the front room and chalked a roughly sumo-shaped silhouette on the door. "Target practice," he said in answer to Mage's raised eyebrow. "Wake me up at six, okay?"

"But—"

Takumo yawned and stretched, and something whistled through the air barely a foot from Mage's ear. The photographer turned and saw a metal star embedded where the sumo-tori's right eye would have been. The stuntman smiled sleepily and walked toward the tent, shedding clothes and weapons as he went. He flopped down on the air mattress, closed his eyes and was instantly asleep.

The first thing that Anna Judd noticed was that Takumo's motorcycle was missing. It was three-thirty on a Monday morning, a time, she thought wryly, when even good little ninja should be home in bed. She sprinted silently up the stairs until she reached Takumo's apartment, listened carefully and then pulled a set of skeleton keys out of her pocket. The door opened easily and no alarms rang; she shut it behind her and waited before turning on the light.

Anna Judd was not quite a ninja—hardly even a *karima kunoichi*. She had become one of Higuchi's mistresses at the age of seventeen; Tsuchiya Shimako had recognized her intelligence and ambition and mentioned her to Tamenaga, who had recruited her to spy on Higuchi. When Higuchi began to tire of her, Anna had begun working at the Sunrise as a hostess, while being trained in ninjitsu by Shimako. In the four years since she had come to Vegas, she had helped to blackmail three businessmen, provided Shimako access to numerous wallets and briefcases, and given a double-dealing employee the kiss of death, luring him to his own murder. She had learned taijutsu, knife-fighting, and shurikenjutsu; she had learned how to kill a man with a hat pin and spit poisonous darts; she had learned stealth and disguise and burglary . . . and for four years, she had been kept in Vegas.

She examined the door and the floor around her feet, finding no gimmicks or traps that would let Takumo know anyone had broken in. The apartment was a mess; it looked almost as though another burglar had ransacked the room before her, yet there were still valuable items left—the sound and video systems, she estimated, must have been worth at least two thousand.

Within five minutes she had found Takumo's hiding places for some of his weapons and made an educated guess at what was missing. She also noted the chaos in the bottom of the closet, and the absence of Takumo's rucksack. She found nothing that obviously belonged to Magistrale anywhere in the apartment.

Anna continued to search, remembering her previous job for Tamenaga: sleeping with a middle-aged, hair-triggered Canuck farmboy, inept, inconsiderate, and probably virginal. Any other work had to be better than *that*. Besides, she had left a farm behind her five years before and had no wish to be reminded of it.

Nearly half an hour later she discovered Takumo's passport, and smiled.

* * *

He took weapons but no passport; he's not planning to leave the country," she reported confidently. "He seems to have taken very few clothes but a lot of underwear. He probably intends to buy more clothes in another city and set up a new identity."

Tamenaga, listening intently, immediately thought of several other possible explanations. A biker would not wish to burden himself with excess luggage. Takumo, with his erratic income and neo-hippy lifestyle, would have a different attitude to clothes than Anna Judd; he might have a spare passport, perhaps in another name, and he might not even *wear* underwear.

"You found nothing else to indicate where he might have gone?"

"No."

"What was missing from the bathroom?"

"Toothpaste, toothbrush . . . Band-Aids. There was a square in the dust, a large box: probably his makeup kit . . ." she handed the Polaroids to Sakura. ". . . but not the luxuries. As you can see, the shampoo and soap are still there."

"Luxuries . . ." mused Tamenaga. The girl had done her job well; still, it was a pity he hadn't been able to persuade Sakura to return there. He listened to the rest of her report in silence, allowing Sakura and Tsuchiya to ask the questions, and brooded.

Where would Magistrale go? He hadn't appeared in Boulder City or contacted his parents or sisters, and he certainly wouldn't have returned to Canada—but Magistrale, without intending to hide, had been drifting from bed to bed for years, accumulating friends, lovers, and acquaintances in many cities and towns. He used no credit cards or checking accounts, and rarely needed to register at a hotel. In Tamenaga's financial world, he was almost an invisible man; his dossier was very thin, and padded with guesswork, making him impossible to predict. He might return in time for his court case, but in that time he might have learned to use the focus.

Takumo, however, was a natural showman. He might be able to act inconspicuously and hide in a crowd, but only briefly. He was too easily recognizable; he would be far more likely to choose as secluded a refuge as possible. Perhaps a ghost town, or a bankrupt and semi-abandoned city, the sort they used for shooting post-Holocaust movies. Tamenaga reached for the photographs and stared at the film posters, smiling at the girls in skintight "ninja suits" and the incredibly clean-looking waste-land warriors.

Why would a man with shoulder-length hair leave home without soap or shampoo? Tamenaga shuddered slightly and glanced at the poster again, noticing the desert backdrop. May-be the stuntman was hiding somewhere where water was scarce. . . .

"I want everything you can get me on Takumo. I need to know everywhere he's lived—if possible, everywhere he's been. Information on his relatives, friends, lovers, enemies, employ-ers. Get copies of all his movies, and have somebody watch them."

He swiveled his chair around to stare at the Murasama dai-sho. It meant turning his back on Judd, but that didn't concern him; the chair was lined with kevlar plates, and as bullet-proof as the windows. "Magistrale had a visitor at the prison—his uncle, as I remember. Get me what you can on him, and put a tap on his phone."

"He wouldn't have gone *there*," Judd began before it oc-curred to her that she might be contradicting her boss.

"No, of course not," Tamenaga agreed. "But the uncle may know where they are, he may be supplying them . . . and if we need to lure Magistrale out of hiding, the man may be useful as bait."

Judd nodded. "What about his parents?"

"No," Tamenaga replied coldly. Involving a target's immediate family was always a last resort. "That won't be necessary. But his woman in Totem Rock, Mrs. Lancaster . . . have somebody watch her. Just in case."

I want to try something a little different."

"If it's bullets, I don't think I'm ready."

Takumo grinned. "No. Watch this." He walked back to the porch, donned his neko-de and grabbed his ninjato. He stood the ninjato against the wall and used the large square tsuba as a step, then climbed the wall and clambered onto the roof.

"Cute trick."

"That isn't the trick." He stood, turned around and jumped back to the ground.

"*That* was the trick?"

"Were you watching?"

"Sure."

"Okay. You ever watch any kung fu movies or Japanese TV shows? *The Samurai? Phantom Agents?*"

"Not since I was a kid."

"You ever see them jumping backwards, up cliffs or into trees?"

"Sure. They ran the film in reverse—every six-year-old knows *that* one."

"You think you can run it in reverse?"

"What?"

"Can you *see* in reverse? Put me back on the roof?"

Mage blinked very slowly. "Are you sure you want me to try? After what happened in Vegas?"

"That happened when *I* was using it. I don't have the talent, the knack. I think you do. Besides, what've I got to lose?"

"Your life, your mind, your soul—" replied Mage, counting on his fingers.

"Think of it as moving me to a higher plane of consciousness."

*M*anson?

Astonished, Tamenaga reached for the phone and called Lamm, asking for a printout of Manson's prison and police files. Then he returned his attention to the file on Takumo's mother. Compared to her, the young stuntman was a success story incarnate. It was as though every best-forgotten element of the sixties had chosen one girl to dump on: a loved and respected older brother disappearing in Vietnam, a gauntlet of sexual encounters as meaningless as a TV game show, bum trips and flashbacks, head injuries received in a riot, hitchhiking from San Francisco to Nirvana but getting no farther than Los Angeles . . . culminating in her joining the Manson Family in Death Valley. The seventies had been saner but even less kind, until finally she had broken and slowly died. . . . To Tamenaga, it endorsed what the focus had taught him: you had to know what you wanted, concentrate on it until you could see it. He had succeeded—become rich—because he understood large numbers, understood money, better than his competitors could. . . .

He shook his head; he was becoming sidetracked. He briefly wished he had Higuchi's knack for making lucky guesses, a knack the gambler claimed was enhanced by the focus—but the kuromaku rarely guessed, and never trusted his guesses without sound logic. He stared at the file, concentrating. Death Valley. . . .

Tamenaga drummed his fingers quietly on the desk, six slow beats and seven quick, as though stalking his intercom. He hesitated, then stabbed his index finger at the "Call" button and summoned Oshima Sakura.

"Yes, boss?" she rasped. The mujina's voice didn't come across well over the phone. She sounded desiccated and decayed, as though she'd died of old age thousands of years before.

"Who's watching those movies of Takumo's?"

"Hubbard and Packer."

Packer? "Are they enjoying them?" he asked dryly.

"Shall I ask?" Sakura had no sense of humor.

"No, but tell them that if they see anything filmed on location in Death Valley—no, make that in *any* desert—they're to call you immediately. Check the credits for a location service, or if that fails, have one of the girls call the production company, if it still exists."

"Anything else?"

Tamenaga glanced at his watch: nearly 1:00 P.M. They'd been working—he, Sakura, Tsuchiya, and Lamm—for twenty-six hours without a break; he hadn't even read the stock-market report to see how Pyramus was doing.

"Yes, have a rest," he said, choosing his words carefully. No one had ever seen the mujina sleep, except for her occasional mindless bedmates. Tamenaga wondered what happened to her face when she dreamed (if she dreamed). Maybe one day he'd have someone brave and dispensable watch her through a one-way mirror. Maybe Magistrale or Takumo. Maybe tomorrow.

Lamm, scarlet-eyed, wavered slightly on his feet as Tamenaga flipped through the printout. Eventually the kuromaku found the information he wanted and checked it against the other files on his desk; Manson's blood type proved that he could not possibly be Takumo's father. He wondered if the stuntman knew.

"Thank you, Mr. Lamm. What time is it?"

"Tuesday," replied Lamm fuzzily. "I mean . . ." He glanced at his watch. "Four fifty-one."

"Good. Call the kitchen, order yourself a meal and go to bed. Ask one of the girls for a massage if you like."

Lamm shook his head wearily. "Maybe after I wake up."

Tamenaga smiled. "As you wish. I'll call you if I need you again tonight. You do good work, Mr. Lamm."

"You pay good money," replied Lamm, returning the smile.

"Is there such a thing as bad money?"

Lamm looked at him cautiously. "I don't know."

"Personally, I've never met a dollar I didn't like."

The hacker shrugged. "They all look the same to me."

"Ah, but that's their beauty. Think about it. Pleasant—" The phone rang, cutting him off. "Excuse me." He reached for the button that opened the door and waited until Lamm had gone before picking up the receiver. "Yes?"

"Location shooting for *Age of the Sword* was done at Butler Ranch," rasped Sakura. "It's between China and Coyote Lakes, near the Naval Weapons Center."

"Good. Send"—Tamenaga thought quickly—"Tsuchiya, and let her pick whom she wants, but only kunoichi; I suspect that neither Mr. Magistrale or Takumo-san will willingly fight women."

"Tonight?"

"No, they'll be expecting us at night. Tomorrow afternoon." Tamenaga sat down and relaxed for the first time in two days. "And send Packer back to Canada—not to Totem Rock, he'll be recognized there. Let him go home. We don't need him anymore."

24

Again, Dangerous Visions

The shuriken veered away from Mage and embedded itself, two inches deep, in a splintered wooden corner post. Takumo stared at it, then blanched to a sickly yellow color.

"You said they were all fakes!" rasped Mage.

Takumo continued to stare, unmoving.

"You said they were all fakes!" repeated Mage stridently.

Takumo turned to him, his expression bleak. "They *were*," he whispered. He walked uncertainly to the porch and pried the shuriken loose. He nodded.

"Real?"

"*Now* it's real." He held it gingerly over the porch and dropped it. It thunked into a board, biting deep. "Let's not try that trick with the jumping again, okay?" the stuntman said, trying not to smile. "Not unless it's an emergency."

"Whatever you say."

* * *

Packer had never learned how to be demonstrative, and as much as he loved his guns, he would no more have kissed one than he would have kissed a man. He contented himself with staring fondly at his rack of rifles and shotguns while drinking a homecoming can of Coors. He then ritually crushed the empty can and threw it at the trash can with better-than-usual accuracy, sat on the bed and unlaced his boots, all without taking his eyes from the rack. A few minutes later he fell asleep, a smile on his face and the familiar smell of a recently fired gun in his nostrils.

It was three minutes to four and ninety-nine degrees inside the shack; Mage didn't even want to *wonder* about the temperature outside. He cast a glance at Takumo, wondering how he could sleep so peacefully in the stifling heat. Mage was lying on the stone floor of the kitchen/laundry, watching the key spin slowly on the loop of hair.

Bring Amanda back if you're so wonderful, he thought.

Nothing happened. Probably just as well, he decided. If Takumo was right, then the best he could do was to put flesh on his memory of Amanda, creating a good-looking puppet, a soft, warm ventriloquist's dummy obeying the commands of his imagination. Would it disappear when he stopped concentrating, he wondered, or become yet another corpse?

He blinked. What if Amanda *had* used the key to create a corpse-copy of herself and throw Tamenaga off the track? What if she were really alive? No, he thought, he knew her well enough to know she wouldn't have dumped him into this sort of shit . . . would she? *Did* he know her well enough? He'd always prided himself on being able to read women, but he certainly hadn't known Amanda for very long. . . .

Despite the heat, he shivered and wished there were something he could do to take his mind off— He stopped the thought half-formed and mentally trod on it. Unfortunately, he had already minutely studied every interesting crack and stain on the walls and ceiling. Their library consisted of a first-aid manual, a handbook on desert survival, and a few paperbacks of Japanese mythology and folklore that both he and Charlie had already read from cover to cover twice. Mage had never been an enthusiastic reader anyway. What was really bugging him was the lack of women. Not merely of sex, though that was a major part of it. A kiss—hell, a *smile*—would have tided him over for another few days.

I must be growing old, he thought. A year ago, if I'd spent more than a week celibate, I would've forgotten who I was. He stared at the key again. Okay, not Amanda. Just send me a woman.

The stone floor was hideously uncomfortable beneath his head. He turned sideways and heard, through the ground, the faint sound of hoofbeats.

He listened until he was sure that the sound wasn't merely an echo of his pulse, like the waves you hear when you cup a shell over your ear, and then he stood uncertainly, walked over to the nearest newspaper-covered window and peered through a crack, seeing nothing but desert. He'd always pictured deserts as being flat, but the broken land looked more like a moonscape. The horses could be on any side of the house, down any valley or behind any rise. He crept from window to window, looking, listening. Nothing. Finally he tiptoed into the room where Takumo was sleeping, peered into the tent grabbed the flashlight and waved the beam over the stuntman's face. Takumo blinked twice and reached for the ninjato beside his bed.

"Hey, relax. It's me."

"Is . . . what's happening?"

"Listen."

Slow, irregular hoofbeats could be heard echoing faintly from outside. Takumo's eyes opened wide and he jumped to his feet, scrabbling for his clothes.

"How close are they?"

"*Too* close. Get ready to—"

The hoofbeats suddenly became louder and faster. Mage slid over to the window nearest the front door and saw two women on horseback riding furiously up the road toward the house.

"Two of them—"

Takumo, pulling on his desert-brown *tabi,* shook his head. "I thought I heard *four* a second ago—unless it's an echo. Are they armed?"

"I can't see any . . . Jesus, they're only girls." Mage decided not to mention that he'd just wished for the focus to send him a woman.

The two young women seemed to be racing each other; the faster, olive-skinned and raven-haired, reined her bay stallion to a halt just short of the front porch. She was wearing khaki jeans, a loose brown jacket, fawn riding boots, and a soft brown Stetson. Her companion—a blonde, wearing white from her hat to her running shoes, her pretty face half hidden by mirror shades—stopped three lengths behind her.

"Anyone here?" she asked.

"Can't see anyone."

Mage looked toward Takumo and shrugged. Takumo quietly continued to don his weapons.

The woman in the Stetson turned her horse and rode slowly around the shack, counterclockwise. The blonde sat with her back to the sun and waited.

Suddenly there was a sound from the roof, and Takumo yelled, *"Out!"* Something landed in the fireplace and rolled onto the hearth. Mage yanked the door open and leaped out over the porch and into the Death Valley sunlight. A kunoichi, in a desert-brown shinobi shozuko, slashed at his legs with a knife, a fraction of a second too late.

Mustard-colored smoke billowed out of the cylinder on the hearth. Mage, sprawled in the dust, turned to face the kunoichi and yelled, *"Charlie! One at the door!"* The kunoichi started slightly and Takumo's hand, protected by a neko-de, smashed through the newspapered window and into the side of her head. The kunoichi staggered and dropped. Mage heard hoofbeats thunder-loud behind him and spun around.

The horse reared above him, its front hooves ready to smash into his skull and arm. He couldn't see the rider clearly; she was keeping the sun behind her, blinding him. One moment it was behind her head, then over her right shoulder, burning a round, blue-green hole into his vision. For an instant it seemed to Mage that he could see the sun through her chest.

The horse shied away from him, and Anna Judd fell from its back. There was a massive, cauterized wound above her right breast, as impossible to look into as the Death Valley sun. Mage stared at her in horror, until a flicker of movement attracted his attention; he turned, saw something flashing in the sunlight and reacted instinctively. Five venom-tipped shuriken reversed their flight in midair, hurtling toward the olive-skinned kunoichi on the roof. Two missed and she managed to deflect two more with her iron sleeves, but one hit her in the thigh, drawing blood. She cursed, then drew a large butterfly knife from inside her jacket and leaped from the roof. She landed lightly, catlike, but before she could run, a metal ring whistled through the air near her knife hand and jerked back as a tough, thin cord wrapped itself around her wrist. She looked along the cord and saw Takumo standing near her horse, the sharp end of a kyotetsu-shoge in his left hand. He jerked at the cord, pulling her off balance. Then, before she could recover, he hooked the sickle-shaped blade into the bay's stirrup.

The wounded kunoichi tossed the knife from her right hand to her left and slashed at the cord. Takumo swatted the stallion's rump as hard as he could and the bay reared and bolted, pulling the woman off her feet and dragging her behind him. Takumo turned toward Mage, and froze. A fourth kunoichi, almost invisible in her shinobi shozuko, had appeared from behind a rise and was running silently toward the photographer.

Mage, still staring at Anna's corpse, saw the new shadow and looked up just as Tsuchiya Shimako drew her ninjato and slashed. He raised his arm to block the blow and nearly lost the limb as the blade ripped through his biceps and grated on the bone.

Mage was conscious of more pain than he'd ever experienced, of the Death Valley heat and the retina-searing sun, of the smells of blood and flash-burnt flesh, but of nothing else. The world was a dusty red blur, too hellish to be real, a figment of some medieval priest's joyless imagination. I will open my eyes, he thought, and find myself safe in Carol's bed, shadows on the ceiling and this nightmare sweated out of me.

He opened his eyes and vanished, and the point of Shimako's ninjato slashed through the space where his kidneys had been a tenth of a second before.

Shimako's immediate response was to look down at Mage's footprints. Ninja are acknowledged masters of mysterious and sudden disappearances, and the kunoichi wondered briefly if her opponent had slipped into some concealed pit. But the ground appeared unbroken, even when she tested it gingerly with her toe. Only then did she notice the bloodless, fist-sized hole in Anna's body. No weapon, no force that Shimako had ever seen, could have made a wound like *that*.

An unusual sensation hit her: the knowledge of failure, of defeat. Mage had disappeared completely and—wherever he was now, dead or alive—had taken the focus with him.

She looked up suddenly and cut a star-shaped shuriken from the air with her ninjato. Takumo had recovered from his own astonishment enough to fight. More proficient at arrow cutting than the stuntman, she easily deflected two more shuriken while walking cautiously toward him. Takumo reached over his shoulder and drew his own ninjato. The edge of the unblooded blade reflected the sunlight into Shimako's eyes, but the kunoichi was prepared for the trick. She feinted, forcing Takumo back, and stepped sideways. Then they stared at each other for several agonizing seconds, their dusty hoods revealing little more than their eyes. She saw his reluctance to kill, he saw her indifference to dying, and neither moved.

For more than a minute they watched and waited—and suddenly Shimako crushed a packet of blinding powder in her left fist and threw it into Takumo's sun-seared face, simultaneously reaching under his guard and lunging at his chest. Takumo, startled, parried blindly and energetically, accidentally catching her ninjato's edge on his iron sleeve and deflecting it, and then crashed into her.

Shimako stumbled and they both fell, her sword arm pinned beneath his chest. She reached into her *obi* for a knife—her *fukiya* were in a pocket on her left wrist—but Takumo rolled away before she could stab him. She scrambled to her feet, and Takumo immediately scissored his legs around her ankles, throwing her onto the porch. Her head thumped against the boards, dazing her briefly, but Takumo made no move to attack; he merely waited, blinking in an effort to clear his eyes, ninjato ready to parry. Shimako sensed another body near hers and turned her head slightly. One of her karima kunoichi lay still beside her, eyes blank, blood on her lips. Shimako lay there motionless, feigning worse pain than she felt, allowing her head to clear, and then sprang to her feet. A half-rotten board cracked beneath her heel, and she staggered forward onto the point of Takumo's sword.

The knocking on the door was sharp and insistent but not loud; it filtered through Packer's sleep as slowly as a glacier. It was nearly a minute before the gunman, who prided himself on his combat reflexes, opened his eyes and glanced at his watch (he kept the windows shuttered and the blinds drawn to keep out prying eyes, and the darkness in his rooms was timeless).

The knocking continued, and he listened while he contemplated a course of action. Soft and staccato: not a cop, and probably female. He reached into the nightstand for his favorite pistol, a .357 Magnum Desert Eagle—Packer disliked Jews, but he had to admit that they made lovely guns—and hauled himself out of bed. He picked his bathrobe off the floor, wrapped it around himself and shoved the pistol into the large pocket, then strode over to the peephole in the door. A blonde, even prettier than the one he'd had in Vegas, was standing outside, looking at the peephole with large, slightly anxious blue eyes.

Packer was not accustomed to receiving visitors, and he noticed that the woman was carrying a shoulder bag large enough to hide a sawed-off shotgun or a mini Uzi. She was also wearing a bulky winter jacket, but that was hardly astonishing: it was November, and it was snowing nearly every night. Packer looked at her again, vaguely suspecting that something was wrong with the picture. The woman knocked again, her mitten-muffled knuckles making no more noise than a cat's footfall, and he wondered how long she'd been there before he woke up.

That she'd been sent by Hegarty, or Hegarty's boss, Packer didn't doubt; whether she was an assassin or a reward, he couldn't guess. He gripped his pistol in his right hand and opened the door with his left.

"Mr. Packer?"

"Yes?"

"May I come in?" She sounded puzzled, asking rather than demanding—it was cold out in the drafty hallway—and more than slightly amused.

Perhaps, Packer guessed, someone was supposed to have phoned him and warned him to expect her. He nodded and stepped back, then shut the door behind her, all without letting go of his pistol. She glanced around the room and nodded when she saw the locked rack of guns and the hand-loading equipment on the kitchen counter (Packer was no cook). She removed her mittens—her fingernails were painted pink, and too long to be practical—and then turned to face him. The dumb-blonde face—the Marilyn Monroe mouth and innocent blue eyes—collapsed into a gunmetal-gray void. Packer, who had just realized that her breath hadn't clouded in the cold outside, felt a sudden wet warmth in his groin as he pissed himself in mind-shattering terror.

Sakura grabbed Packer's right forearm gently and pulled his hand away from his pocket. If she'd had a mouth, it would have smiled as she steered her unresisting victim toward the bed and eased him into a sitting position. She left him there for a few minutes as she reached into her shoulder bag and removed three pairs of panties, holding them between the points of her sharp pink fingernails; she dropped one on the pillow, pushed one under the bed, and draped the third over Packer's empty left hand. Then she drew a Colt Python from inside her bag, placed the muzzle at the gunman's temple and blew his dead brain out of his skull.

25

To Leap in Ourselves

Mage opened his eyes and stared at the shadows on the ceiling. The leopard shattered into its component rosettes and became a map of the moon, and the Venus de Willendorf evolved into a four-armed Kali, complete with scimitar, skull-topped scepter, and severed head. He looked around the room and at the bed—Carol's bed, and unmistakably Carol's room.

He examined his arm and found it undamaged, but it still *hurt*. It was also entirely bare, and he realized that he was naked, except for the talisman wrapped around his wrist. He raised his eyes to the ceiling again and thought: when I look down at the floor, my clothes will be there.

He looked down and they weren't, and neither was the floor; there was *nothing*, no color, neither light nor darkness, not even an impression of distance. He grabbed the bed—it felt solid enough—and rolled over onto his back, closing his eyes hurriedly and trying to concentrate.

He couldn't remember having seen his clothes on Carol's

floor; he'd always reached over the edge of the bed and groped until he grabbed them, then dressed as well as possible without leaving the warmth of the blankets. He thought hard about Charlie's experience in Vegas, wondering what it was and wasn't safe to visualize. If he tried imagining his clothes, he was almost certain to get something wrong: the size, zippers that didn't work, buttons without buttonholes, sleeves sewn shut, whatever. It occurred to him that if he practiced, he might be able to imagine a pair of jeans that fit a normally shaped human comfortably. The thought cheered him slightly, even though he didn't feel up to trying at the moment. First things first: what had Carol's floor been like before he'd annihilated it?

A few seconds of memory-cudgeling told him that it had been carpeted—a slightly worn, gray shag carpet, reminiscent of an old and disreputable Persian cat. When he opened his eyes, it was there again, and in all the right places; when he touched it gingerly, it felt reassuringly furry, and when he rapped it, he heard the floorboards beneath it. Clothes, he decided, could wait.

The floor remained solid as he walked across it to the door and listened. No one else was home, and so he opened the door and looked into the living room. Everything in there seemed much as it had when he'd stayed there before. The Susan Seddon Boulet calendar on the kitchen door showed a new page: November. He glanced through the window and noticed snow on the rooftops. The clock told him that it was ten past four.

At least I didn't time-travel, he thought with mingled relief and disappointment. I didn't time-travel, and I haven't been dreaming—or if I have, I'm *still* dreaming, and dreaming that I haven't been dreaming. Or I . . . what would Dante call it? Teleported? Jaunted? Jumped?

He shivered, but more from the cold than from fear. Teleportation, he thought as he opened the closet door and looked for a robe. No more hitchhiking, no more airports or bus depots. A kitchen and a warm bed always in reach—*if* I can do it again.

He heard a key rattle in the lock, and froze.

The instructions Gacy received had been simple and the money was good; that took some of the pain out of sitting in a van day in, day out, but not all. Still, there was fuck-all else he could do; he'd had nobody else who could have gotten to Totem Rock in time. Packer had already been here, and though Gacy hadn't heard all the details, it was obvious that the farmboy had blown his cover.

Gacy had been more careful. He'd paid his secretary to play the role of his wife, then bought an old Citroën and carefully sabotaged the electrics so that it'd fail as soon as he arrived in town. He'd looked glum when the mechanic had told him how long it would take for the replacement part to arrive, checked into the only motel (conveniently close to the 7-Eleven, to his delight), and spread the story that he and his wife, accountants with a passion for bird-watching, were traveling to Winnipeg to see their first grandchild—a cover story carefully calculated to make them as invisible as possible and explain away a suit-case full of cameras and binoculars.

So far, the story had worked perfectly; not only had they been able to keep a near-constant watch on their target, but it had given him an excuse to buy some surveillance equipment from friends and present a heavily padded bill to Hegarty's anonymous and mysterious boss. After two days in town, they'd put a bug in the Lancaster woman's phone and a tracking device in her VW, and Gacy had decided that their worst problem would be fighting off boredom. Carol Lancaster's life seemed to consist of her job, sleep, and reading; she didn't even own a television.

"Why are we watching this poor woman, anyway?" Shirley, his secretary and sometime-mistress, had asked him.

"Because we're being paid to," Gacy had replied.

"Why? What has she done?"

"I don't know. I think she knows somebody . . . all I know is that this is where Packer was jumped."

"I guess there's a first time for everything," Shirley muttered.

Gacy grinned. "Not that sort of jumped, doll. I mean that somebody got the drop on him and knocked him out. He wouldn't tell me the details, which means he probably screwed up."

"And Hegarty thinks *she* did it?"

The grin broadened. "I don't think so. More likely it was the girl Pack was supposed to find—you remember, the blonde. The student."

"Amanda Sharmon?"

"Yeah, that's her. I guess this Lancaster woman's a friend of hers."

"But she's dead."

"What?"

"The Sharmon girl. Somebody strangled her. It's been in all the papers."

Gacy blinked. He'd heard about the murder but had never realized that it was the same girl; Hegarty certainly hadn't said anything about her having been killed. "You're sure it was her?"

"I think so. It looked like the same photo."

"Do the cops know who killed her?" he asked warily.

"The paper said they've arrested somebody in the States, but that's all I know."

"Uh-huh," he muttered and rolled over and tried to sleep. He'd always tried not to wonder too much about Hegarty's other business partners and contacts, and had stuck to smuggling and handling stolen property—usually car parts or electronics, some porn, some guns, even some marijuana, but no *hard* drugs—and if somebody hurt somebody else somewhere along the line, that wasn't *his* fault, was it? And Hegarty had told him he wanted the girl brought in alive and unharmed, said she'd stolen something valuable from *his* boss and they wanted to question her, so maybe it wasn't even Hegarty's fault that she'd been killed.

The worst thing about the job was the waiting; he had nothing else to do but *think*. At least one of them had to be awake at any given time, and he'd never been good at sleeping during the day.

"Jim?"

"Huh?"

"I can hear somebody in the house."

He sat up slowly and reached for his binoculars and his watch. The Lancaster woman wasn't due to finish work for another quarter-hour, and he couldn't see her car outside the house. He couldn't see inside the house at all, the shutters being closed against the cold. "Are you sure? It's not just the floorboards settling or something?"

"I don't think so." She handed the headphones to him. "I'm sure I heard a door open. *You* listen."

With a skill born of years of practice, Carol unlocked the door, pushed it open, pirouetted inside and kicked it shut behind her—all without removing her gloves, putting down her bag of shopping, or letting the warm air out. A moment later she saw Mage standing in the kitchen in her bathrobe, dropped the bag and screamed.

"Hi. Happy Halloween."

"Mage! Where did—how did you—Jesus, what the hell is *happening*? Last I heard, you were in jail for—"

He nodded. "Murder. I was framed; I'm out on bail. I'm sorry I didn't call you—"

"You—" She shook her head. "Why did you come *here*? What do you want *now*?"

Mage hesitated. "Mostly a place where no one's trying to kill me."

"I'm not promising anything," she replied sourly.

He tried to smile. "You remember the guy with the Ingram, at the laundromat?"

"I remember you telling me about him . . ."

"Okay. You'd better sit down; it's a long story."

Yოu're sure there's somebody in there?" growled Tamenaga.

"I'm sure," replied Gacy. "It's a man's voice, sounds like a New York accent. She called him 'Mage,' or something like that."

Tamenaga sat there, stunned into silence. Why on earth would the photographer have risked going back to Totem Rock? And *how?* He would have been arrested as soon as he'd shown up at the border. . . .

"He was there before she arrived," Gacy continued; then, more cautiously, "Or *somebody* was, anyway. And we didn't see him go in."

"You were watching the whole time?"

"Uh-huh."

"And there's only one entrance?"

"There's a fire escape at the back of the building, but we'd still see him on the street—unless he climbed over the back fence. But we didn't hear the window open . . ." Gacy sat there, trying to understand that. They hadn't heard him enter at all, either by the door or by the window, and the Lancaster woman hadn't let him in; she'd been startled as all hell to find him there.

"Don't let him leave. Don't let him past the front door. If he escapes"—Tamenaga took a deep breath, feeling the python tattooed around his waist beginning to writhe and squeeze—"I will make sure that you regret it."

"How do I stop him?"

"Wound him, kill him if you must, but *stop him*. Are you armed?"

"Yes, of course, but—"

"Good. Any more questions?"

Gacy nodded dumbly. There were dozens of questions he wanted answered, but none that he dared ask. "No."

He told her the story from the encounter with Packer in the laundromat to the fight with the kunoichi, leaving out nothing except Tamenaga's name. Carol listened without looking up, then sipped her coffee and said softly, "I've heard enough. Get out."

"What—"

"*Out!* Jesus, what do you expect me to say? Welcome back? First you find some younger girl and leave me; okay, so I was a fool to think you'd stay. Then someone kills her—don't worry, I told the cops I didn't think it was you, I still don't think you could've done *that*—and you get blamed. Who killed her, or why, I don't know. Her boyfriend maybe, or her husband. But you talk somebody into bailing you out, and you come *here* looking for somewhere to hide; give the old cow a good story, she likes murder mysteries, fuck her a few—"

"It's not—"

"*Shut up!* I've listened to you 'til I was ready to throw up; now you can listen to me! Okay. You're cute, you're sexy, you're great in bed, but there's a limit to the amount of shit I'm willing to put up with just to get laid. I don't *ever* want to see you again; now get the fuck *out!*"

Mage shook his head. "How do you think I got *in?* You think I caught a Greyhound dressed like *this?*"

She looked up uncertainly, then shrugged. "I don't know, and I stopped caring a long time ago. Get out or I'll call the cops— I bet they'd love to talk to you. And I'll have my robe back, too—and my key, please."

"It's still in my—" Mage began, then reached up and removed Amanda's key from around his neck. Maybe there was something he could do that would convince her—apart from teleporting out, which he didn't feel like trying again. He looked around the kitchen and noticed a large mug adorned with a computer-scanned photo, a souvenir of a visit to Fisherman's Wharf. He plucked it from the shelf, examined it—it was a pretty bad likeness—and asked, "Does this have any sentimental value?"

"Huh? That?" She grimaced. "Roy gave it to me."

"Okay." He looked long and hard at her, memorizing every detail, and then envisaged that image on the side of the mug. He glanced at the mug and nodded; the focus was pretty bad but it sharpened as he looked at it, like a print developing in a tray. "Here, look at this."

"What?" She glanced at the mug incuriously, without noticing it. Then she blinked and picked it up, examining the picture on its side. Suddenly there was a knock on the door; startled, she dropped the mug on the table. Mage reached out to grab it a fraction of a second too late; it fell to the floor and broke into three pieces. There was another knock on the door—louder, sharper, more insistent.

"Are you expecting someone?" Mage asked quietly.

"No . . . how . . ." She shook her head and stood.

Mage saw the doorknob turn and realized that the door wasn't locked. Before he could react, the door opened and Gacy stepped in, followed by a blast of cold air from outside. Carol wheeled around and yelled, "Shut the—" and then saw the small automatic in his hand and froze. Gacy kicked the door shut behind him, aimed the pistol at Mage and clicked the safety off.

For a long moment no one moved or spoke, and the loudest sound was the wind outside. Then Gacy said quietly, "I don't want to have to use this."

Mage looked at him and realized that that was true. "You Magistrale?" Gacy continued.

Mage stood and stretched. "You'd look pretty stupid if I wasn't, wouldn't you? Yeah, me Magistrale. Who the fuck you?"

Gacy flushed. "I'm the guy with the gun, remember?"

"Sorry."

"And you're coming with me."

"Dressed like this? It's cold outside." He considered teleporting out, but that would leave Carol alone with the gunman, whose reactions he couldn't predict. Better to get her out and— "My clothes are in the bedroom."

Carol blinked, but Gacy didn't notice. "You think I'm going to let you out of my sight?"

"She could get them," said Mage with a nod at Carol. Gacy seemed to consider this, then laughed. "And go out the window, call for help? Nice try."

Mage shrugged. "Yeah," he replied sadly. "I hope you've got a car outside?"

"You ask a lot of questions." Gacy edged around the table, reached for the phone and tried to pull it from its socket, without success. Mage and Carol watched, trying not to smile. "Okay," said Gacy finally. "*Both* of you, out."

"What?"

"*You heard me!*"

Carol took a half-step away from her chair and trod on a fragment of the photo mug; Mage heard the crack as it broke, and then stared at Gacy. Photograph. Still photograph. Freeze frame. . . .

The talisman was still wrapped around his fingers; he gripped it tightly, forming a fist, and focused on Gacy's gun hand, seeing it as an unmoving image, frozen in time like a three-dimensional photograph. He heard Carol take another step toward the door.

"Move!" Mage stood motionless, concentrating, *seeing*.

Gacy tried to gesture with the gun and grunted with surprise. He tried again, with no more success; his hand and the gun might as well have been encased in glass.

"Go!" hissed Mage, not looking away from Gacy's hand. "Get out of here, and don't come back!"

"But—"

"I can't hold him forever! Go!"

Carol stared and then nodded hurriedly, snatching her purse and her keys off the table and heading for the door.

Gacy yelled "Stop!" and put all his strength into trying to bring the gun to bear; there was an unpleasant muffled *click* and the gunman shrieked with fright and pain. His right hand still refused to move, and his frantic effort to free it had only succeeded in breaking his wrist. He looked around, sweating and whimpering, as Carol shut the door behind her and bolted down the stairs.

Slowly and cautiously, Mage edged closer to Gacy, never moving his eyes, watching the muzzle of the gun, seeing it become smaller . . . smaller . . . smaller. . . .

"I'm getting tired of this," he said softly.

"Huh?"

Mage took one last look at the pistol's tapering muzzle, now barely wide enough to admit a drinking straw, and sighed. "Drop the gun."

"I—I can't. I think you've broken my arm."

Mage shook his head sadly, then reached out for Gacy's right wrist and twisted it until the pistol was pointing at the floor. The gunman screamed and sank to his knees, the gun dangling uselessly from his trigger finger. Mage grabbed it with his left hand and took it away from him.

"Who sent you?" he asked, almost kindly.

"What?"

"Who's your boss?"

Gacy stared up at him, gibbering softly with pain. "He . . . He . . . Hegarty."

"Hecate?"

Gacy shook his head slightly. "Heg . . . Hegarty."

"Where can I find him?"

"Don't know."

"Who's *his* boss?"

"Don't . . . know his name. Only spoke with him once. Sounded like a Jap."

"Tamenaga?"

"I don't know. I always dealt with Hegarty, until yesterday."

Mage shrugged, slightly jerking Gacy's wrist. The gunman bit down to prevent crying out, drawing blood.

"What do you do for him when you're not pointing guns at people?"

Gacy was silent. Mage looked at him; then, giving his best impression of a Brooklyn tough, he said, "The only thing stopping me killing you is that I don't want to drag your body out of here. The only thing that's going to stop me *hurting* you is an answer. How do you contact this boss?"

"Phone."

"The number? I'll know if you're lying."

Gacy stared at him, tasting the blood in his mouth, and told him the number. Mage reached for the pen hanging from the corkboard next to the phone and wrote it down. "Okay, now call him."

"*What?*"

Mage began dialing the number. "Hand it over when you've got the boss," he said, listening to the ringing tone on the other end. He heard a woman's voice ask "Hello?" and passed the receiver to Gacy.

"It's Gacy. I—I need to speak to the boss," he muttered, trying not to whimper with the pain. "Magistrale—he's here. He's, uh . . ."

Mage listened intently as the secretary patched the call through to another extension. A deep voice replied, "Yes?" and Gacy handed the receiver back, almost dropping it in his eagerness to be rid of it.

"Gacy?" the voice asked.

"Tamenaga-san?"

There was a long silence at the other end, and then a sharp "Who is this?" Mage shrugged and hung up. Gacy stared at him anxiously.

"Tamenaga . . ." murmured Mage, sitting on a kitchen chair. "Do you know what he wanted?"

"What?"

"Your boss. Hegarty, Tamenaga, whoever. What were his instructions?"

"Stop you."

"Stop me what?"

"I don't know. Yeah. Going anywhere. Stop you getting away."

Mage stared at him and realized he was telling the truth. "So someone else is coming. Shit." He sighed. "Okay. One more thing." He stood wearily and suddenly reached for Gacy's damaged arm, pulling the gunman to his feet and turning him around to face the door. "Tell your boss, Tamenaga, this is between him and me now. If he hurts my family, my friends, any woman I've ever loved, any woman I've ever *known,* if he even *harasses* or *threatens* one, I will make him regret it. As for you—" He slammed Gacy into the door face-first, pulled him back, opened the door, and then pushed him through onto the landing. "Get out, and never come back to this town. Understand?"

"Yes."

"Good," said Mage, and threw him down the stairs into the snow.

26

The Burial of the Dead

Dear Carol, he wrote, then stared at the otherwise blank page for over a minute. *I'm sorry,* he began, and stopped again.

I'm sorry for everything that's happened. I mean, I was really glad we met and got together, but I'm sorry for all the other shit. Looks like I've become dangerous to know. I hope you realize now that everything I've told you is true.

I guess this isn't much of a love letter . . . and believe me, I do love you. I've never slept with any woman I didn't love. I'm sorry if I've hurt you. I didn't intend to, I really wanted to make you happy. Maybe I'm not as good at that as I thought.

Can't think of anything else to say. Look after yourself. Love,

Mage

He looked at the letter and shrugged, then picked up the shards from the floor, put them together and saw the mug whole, without cracks. Then he set the mug on the letter, walked back into the bedroom and draped the bathrobe over a chair. Exhausted, he collapsed onto the bed, eyes closed, trying to remember Takumo's apartment as he'd last seen it: the prints and posters on the walls, the books on the shelves. When he was sure that he could picture it accurately, he imagined himself into it, dressed as he had been before he'd disappeared from the desert.

In the same instant he fell flat on his ass as the bed disappeared from beneath him. The pain in his right arm was mindkilling; he had to force his eyes open and his mouth shut. He found himself lying on tatami and staring up at the library. He twisted his head around to look at his arm and saw that his wound had reappeared, reopened.

Going to have to be more careful of what I think, he decided, struggling to his feet. Don't think of the wound at all, even as an absence. He closed his eyes and concentrated on Kelly's living room, saw himself standing between the sofa and the coffee table, wearing what he'd been wearing three nights before, the night the rukoro-kubi attacked. . . .

An instant too late, he tried to amend that thought—then he heard Oedipus hiss and realized that he'd already jumped.

He opened his eyes to look around, and listened. It was day, not night, and the house was empty apart from the cat and himself. He drew a deep breath and reached out with his left hand to touch his right arm, feeling bare flesh, dry and unscarred. He muttered a Hail Mary in record time and collapsed onto the sofa. A moment later he felt hesitant paws walking across his chest, a sandpaper tongue licking tears from his face. He stroked the cat and rested.

I didn't time-travel, he thought, relieved. Maybe I can't . . . and then he shrugged. What if he could? Would he have changed the past? Refused to take the talisman? Would that have saved Amanda? No, probably not.

He stood, stretched, and walked around the room, glad to see that it was as he remembered it. Photographs, he thought.

I'll photograph all the places I'll want to come back to, photograph myself uninjured. . . . That's it, isn't it? he asked the universe in general. That's why you picked *me*, isn't it? Because I'm a photographer? You have one sick sense of humor, universe; did anyone ever tell you that?

He grabbed Oedipus gently and dropped him onto the carpet, then staggered into Kelly's room. The shotgun wasn't in the closet or under the bed, and he hoped she had it with her. He couldn't find the crossbow either, and the house was too large for him to search it; besides, he probably couldn't have cocked the damn thing, let alone fired it accurately.

There was a mirror above the dressing table and another inside the closet door, and he positioned them so they reflected each other. Then he stood between them and glanced at the images, focusing on the one in which his T-shirt was legible. Then he closed his eyes and *saw* himself on the porch of Butler Ranch.

He opened his eyes again . . . and wished he hadn't. Tear gas and smoke were still wafting from the doorway and the broken window. Apart from a few scattered shuriken, there was no sign of Takumo or the kunoichi.

He found them a few minutes later, at the bottom of a nearby ravine. The stuntman was doing his best to dig a pit in the loose, dead soil, and crying into the shallow hole. Mage, not wanting to sneak up on him, stood at the edge of the ravine and wondered what to say.

"Charlie?"

Takumo looked up, shading his eyes. "Mage?"

"Can I help you?"

"Can you help *them?*" He shot a bitter glance at the groundsheet behind him, and Mage realized that it covered the bodies of the four girls. He tried to think of them as kunoichi, as assassins, and failed; he tried not to think of his four sisters, and failed at that too.

"No."

Takumo nodded and returned to his task. "Can I help *you?*" Mage repeated.

"Not unless you brought another spade. Where the freakin' hell've you been, anyway?"

"Canada."

"Far out."

"And your place, and Kelly's. You don't seem surprised."

"'Frankly, mah dear, I don't give a damn,'" Takumo replied in the most unlikely Southern accent that Mage had ever heard. "What're you going to do with it?"

Mage shrugged. He'd had only one idea, and he didn't like it. "Is that grave for them, or for you?"

Takumo paused in his digging and then replied, "'For my part, I do not lie in't, and yet it is mine.'"

Mage, not recognizing the quote, pressed on regardless. "Isn't it too hot to be working like that? You could at least wear a hat."

Takumo hesitated. "The house is full of tear gas; it won't be bearable for a couple of hours at least, and it's cooler down here than it is up there . . . but yeah, you're right. Let's see if we can find some shade—or would you rather just beam back up to Canada? *Someone* has to bury these—" But his voice cracked suddenly and he dropped the spade into the pit.

"I'll go back to town and get another spade. Do you want me to bring you back a drink?"

Takumo tried to laugh but gave up in mid gasp. "Yeah. Grapefruit juice, okay?"

Kelly Barbet returned home that evening to find a hastily scrawled note in the microwave: *Kelly, please pick us up tonight. Mage. P.S. Don't believe the cat. I already fed him.*

* * *

I get the feeling we should say something," said Takumo. "Like if I knew the *segaki* rite, the Buddhist funeral ritual, I could recite that, but I don't. What do Catholics say?"

"'Man that is born of woman has but a brief time to live . . .' That's all I remember, and I think they've already guessed that." Mage shrugged, then recited:

"What are the roots that clutch, what branches grow
   Out of this stony rubbish? Son of man,
   You cannot say, or guess, for you know only
   A heap of broken images, where the sun beats
   And the dead tree gives no shelter, the cricket no relief,
   And the dry stone no sound of water. Only
   There is a shadow under this red rock,
   (Come in under the shadow of this red rock),
   And I will show you something different from either
   Your shadow at morning striding behind you
   Or your shadow at evening rising to meet you;
   I will show you fear in a handful of dust."

They stood there silently for a minute, and then Takumo asked, "What was that?"

"It's from *The Waste Land*, by T. S. Eliot. It's about the only thing I remember from college, that and a few lines of "Journey of the Magi." There was a girl doing Lit who was pretty obsessive about his stuff, and I was pretty obsessive about her for a while, so . . ." He picked up a handful of dust, stared at it for an instant, then threw it into the grave.

Takumo nodded. "I can relate to that." He looked down at the sand for a moment and shrugged. "If it's confession time, I've got a better one. Charlie Manson isn't really my father."

"Uh-huh."

"He probably *could* have been—I know he had at least one son—and my mother really thought he was, but she didn't know his blood type. I managed to find it out when I was seventeen; it couldn't have been him . . . but by then, it didn't really seem to matter. Mum was dead, and I'd been beaten up often enough for being the maniac's son, and had frightened a few bullies off by being the maniac's son . . . and frightened a few of the girls too, and fascinated a few others—I mean, like, crazy Charlie probably had more girls than you did and they wanted to see if whatever he had was hereditary . . . and it was a gimmick; agents and directors and casting consultants remembered me . . . but man, all I really wanted was to be someone, like in the Tracy Chapman song. I mean, that's what it's all about, neh? Not even someone *special*; I really, totally, didn't know who I was." He shook his head. "So, now I know something. I know I never want to kill anyone else."

"How did they die? I mean, apart from the one *I* killed."

Takumo held up a pair of fingers. "*Two* you killed. The one who went for a drag died of poisoning from that shuriken you threw back at her: I think it was curare. The one I hit with the neko-de swallowed her fukumi-bari, a poisoned dart, and it either tore her throat open from the inside or— And the one with the ninjato hit me with a blinding powder, and I was trying to parry, and I ran her through, don't ask me how. Karma, neh? But that's it. I quit. No more."

"I'm going to need your help."

Takumo stared at him wearily and then nodded.

They found the rest of the rukoro-kubi," said Kelly as soon as she was out of the car.

"Who?"

"The LAPD. They're treating it as a yakuza killing. He had the full-body tattoo, the—"

"Irezumi," volunteered Takumo.

"Thank you. Apart from that, they still haven't identified him, and it's driving forensics crazy. All the evidence suggests that he died in the car—there was even blood on the ceiling—but it looks as though the head and both hands were lopped off simultaneously. There's no trace of metal in the wounds and not even a scratch anywhere inside the car. It was a Japanese car, too—no room to swing a cat, let alone a katana."

"Stolen, of course," said Takumo dryly.

"Supposedly. It wasn't reported gone until after it was found, which means it must have been missing from the lot for more than twenty-four hours."

"Whose lot?"

"Taisho Tours; it's one of their rental cars. The company's owned by a Mr. Nakatani, who also owns the Sunrise Hotel in Vegas and is alleged to have yakuza contacts."

Mage glanced at Takumo, who rolled his eyes. "Can we skip the legalese for a moment? I used to work for Nakatani-san, and no one out here's going to sue you for libel."

"Sorry," Kelly replied, smiling slightly. "Mage, I remember you mentioning Tetsuo Tamenaga. According to the D.A., Tamenaga is involved in multimillion-dollar loan-sharking and money laundering, and Nakatani owes him a fortune. The LAPD's sure that the body they found was working for one or the other, and scared that there may be a war beginning between the two of them."

"Hey, *you* decapitated him," Mage reminded her. "Not the yakuza. Let's hope they never find his head."

"Who're they going to call in to identify the body?" asked Takumo.

"Probably the manager of Taisho if no one else comes forward. We don't know his next of kin. Why?"

"Not Tamenaga?"

Kelly shook her head. "He'd just send one of his secretaries. As far as we know, he rarely leaves his property—"

"As far as we know?" echoed Takumo. "Who's watching him?"

"I don't know."

"So make an educated guess."

"A guess? No one. The cops can't show probable cause; even if he's not paying them off, Tamenaga is much too clever to dirty his hands. Some reporters have tried to sneak in, or break in, or even fly low over the place, and have ended up with nothing to show for their pains except bruises."

"If he never leaves," said Mage, "I guess I'm going to have to go in and talk to him."

27

Face-off

They drove past the estate slowly, but not *too* slowly. There was no one visible at the gates; a single TV camera watched the road from behind a sheet of shatterproof glass. Beyond the barred gate, the driveway twisted around large trees that obscured any view of the house.

"I still say you're crazy to go in alone," murmured Takumo when they were well past the gates.

"*I* can always get out . . . and if I get a chance to take a photograph, I can always get back in again. I wish I *could* take you with me, but I can't." And if I die, Mage thought, I'm no great loss: Tamenaga gets his focus back, and hopefully he leaves you alone. "But I *will* need your help."

Kelly had obtained copies of the original plans of the house and estate, but neither she nor Dante had been able to find any recent photographs. Only one freelance journalist admitted to having been in and escaped alive; after a few bourbons, he'd described "gardeners" who resembled the Incredible Hulk, and mastiffs as large as racehorses.

"Yeah, I know," the stuntman replied sourly. "I get to kill the dogs."

"Don't think of them as dogs," suggested Kelly. "They're biologically engineered killing machines."

Takumo shook his head, his expression grim. "Like four-footed ninja, neh? It's not that I *like* dogs—I hate the freakin' things, I think they're evolution's greatest mistake since the dinosaurs died out—but I don't like *killing*."

"Can you think of a way around them?"

"Stop being logical. Logic has nothing to do with this." He grimaced. "I know, they'll have been trained not to accept baits, and we can't get a tranquilizer rifle without all sorts of paperwork, and they're too damn slow anyway, and a stun gun's next to useless—yes, I've *tried* thinking of ways around them—and that Tamenaga turned these animals into murderers—shit, he turned *me* into a murderer!" He closed his eyes and swallowed, trying to regain control of his breathing. Mage and Kelly watched and waited.

"If you get the chance," Takumo whispered, "tell him what he's done. And if you don't come back, I'm going in myself."

They returned at eleven, dressed all in black, and silent—except for Takumo, who chattered incessantly about land mines, envenomed *tetsubishi,* snag wires, pits, nightingale floors, oiled floors . . .

"Charlie?"

"Yeah?"

"No warnings. If I start looking for traps, they'll be there."

Charlie shut up, and no one spoke until they reached the edge of the property. Kelly parked the car fifty yards from the entrance, turned off the lights and handed the shotgun to Mage.

"I don't want it. What if I drop it and they trace it?"

Kelly shrugged. "It's my husband's."

Takumo smiled behind his mask. Mage opened his mouth to comment, thought better of it and grabbed the gun.

They crept toward the gate, and Mage lifted Takumo to the top of the thirteen-foot-high wall while Kelly crawled under the TV camera's field of vision and peered through the narrow gaps between the bars. Takumo, carefully avoiding both the cameras that he could see and the ones he knew *had* to exist, clambered over and hooked his kyotetsu-shoge onto the top of the gate before dropping to the ground.

Four heartbeats later three huge dogs raced out of the darkness toward the bars. Takumo grabbed the cord of the kyotetsu-shoge, back-flipped up and held himself out of reach. One of the mastiffs sprang at him and instantly received a crossbow bolt in the stomach. The second mastiff sniffed at the body and licked the blood while Kelly re-nocked hastily. Takumo descended like a spider lowering itself on its silk, and when one of the dogs snapped at his left arm, its teeth grating harmlessly on Takumo's iron sleeve, he drove the point of his knife into its eye. The third dog seemed torn between attack and flight, and fell victim to a second crossbow bolt before it could decide.

Takumo waited for a few seconds, then reached into his pack for a knotted rope, enabling Mage to climb over the wall. Kelly handed Mage the shotgun between the bars, then threw his camera, basketball style, for Takumo to catch—which, to Mage's obvious relief, he did without the slightest difficulty.

"Thank you—and now get the hell out of here," Mage said. Takumo nodded and swarmed up the rope. Mage didn't wait to see his friends leave; with the camera around his neck and the shotgun in his left hand, he set off in the direction of the house.

The door was opened a moment later by a sumo wrestler only slightly smaller than a football team. His face looked as though it had been drawn by a very young child. He didn't speak, and Mage wasn't sure that he could.

"I'm here to see Mr. Tamenaga."

Yamada Kazafumi's rubbery expression didn't change. He

looked Mage up and down, stared pointedly at the shotgun and shook his head.

Damn, thought Mage; I knew bringing the gun was a mistake. "Tamenaga will want to see me," he said, enunciating carefully and clearly, "and he will certainly want to see *this*." He opened his right hand, revealing the key and the braided hair. "So go tell him I'm here, before he gives you a job climbing the Empire State Building and swatting biplanes. *Capiche?*"

The wrestler stepped back slightly, but his massive arm blocked Mage's path. The plan, Mage guessed, was to delay him until reinforcements arrived to escort him to Tamenaga—or to wherever Tamenaga wanted him. He stared past Yamada to the end of the hall, noticing several doors and a staircase. Then he *thought* himself into the picture and teleported. He found himself at the foot of the stairs and heard the startled sumotori grunt behind him, but he wasted no time turning around until he was on the landing of the second floor.

Yamada was running upstairs with remarkable speed for such a massive man. Mage looked at the polished wood and remembered Takumo's warning about oiled floors—and the wrestler slipped, fell, and began to roll. He reached out and grabbed a banister, which slowed his descent briefly but cracked as soon as he tried to haul himself up. Mage allowed himself a slight smile, turned to look down the corridor . . .

. . . and saw Amanda Sharmon, wearing an expensive silk dress, emerge from a nearby door.

They stared at each other for nearly a minute, and she smiled slightly. "What kept you?" she asked softly.

Mage tried to swallow, and failed. "How long have *you* been here?"

"Ten days now."

It was an unusually pat answer, he reflected, but Amanda *was* a mathematician. "You were working for Tamenaga?"

"I wasn't when I met you," she assured him, "but he offered me a deal. If I'd refused, he would've killed me, and . . . I'm scared of dying. That's why I stole the focus," she said simply, softly. "All things considered, it was an amazingly good deal. Did you bring it?"

"It?"

"The focus."

"Focus?"

"The key."

"Oh, yeah." He threw it to her, whispering, "I guess it's yours." She was obviously too startled to catch it; it bounced off her breast and fell near her feet. "Can I go now?"

"I suppose so, if you want to, but Tamenaga-san would like to talk to you." She squatted slowly, not taking her eyes from Mage's pale face, and reached out for the loop of hair. "Would you like a job?"

It was Mage's turn to smile, and the smile became a chuckle, and the chuckle became a laugh.

"Mage?"

"He sent his thugs and his monsters to kill me, and now he wants me to work for him?"

She smiled again. "He pays well."

"I'm not interested in money."

"You'd be working with me, too."

Mage's smile twisted into something less pleasant. "Is that a proposition?"

She shrugged, and her breasts shifted enticingly underneath the tight silk. "He can get you anything you could possibly want."

"Oh, I doubt that," replied Mage heavily. "You know, the main reason I came here was because I thought he'd killed you. Okay, so he didn't kill you, maybe he just killed someone who *looked* like you, but I'm not going to forgive him that easily. Who was she?"

"Does it matter?"

"Yes!"

"It wasn't anyone you knew."

"That's not enough! Who was she?"

Silence. Mage pressed the button on the shotgun light and swept the beam unsteadily across her face. She stared into the muzzle of the gun without any hint of fear. Slowly, he lowered the gun, his hands shaking uncontrollably.

"If you don't want me," she said, "any woman in the world—"

He shut his eyes and squeezed the trigger, shooting her in the chest.

28

Kuromaku

He was still standing there, eyes closed, when one of the house guards hurtled around a corner barely ten feet behind him. The guard slowed, then noticed that Mage had dropped the shotgun and seemed to be crying. He hesitated, saying almost gently, "Okay, friend. Turn around."

Mage obeyed with agonizing slowness—and then pressed a button on his flashgun. The sudden burst of intense light startled the gunman, and Mage looked at the guard's black uniform, black-leather gloves and black-finished Uzi, and crossed his mind's eyes. The gun, now a toy of cloth and leather, drooped in the guard's hand and when he tried to pull the trigger, he found his hand encased in steel, his arms trapped in his metal jacket. He fell backward, and Mage knelt beside him.

"Where is Tamenaga?"

"Go to hell."

Mage shook his head. "I tried that, but he wasn't there. Those pants look very tight. If they cut off your circulation, you could get a very nasty localized case of gangrene. I hear that's what happened to King Herod. *Now, where the fuck is he?"*

"Let me up and I'll show you."

Mage sighed, plucked the limp Uzi from the iron glove and tied a reef knot in the barrel. The guard merely smiled.

"Where is he?" Mage repeated.

"Standing right behind you."

Mage glanced over his shoulder and saw a burly, middle-aged Japanese in a blood-red silk jacket and black pants less than ten feet away. Tamenaga Tetsuo was looking at the body at his feet and shaking his head sadly. The two magicians stared at each other, and then Tamenaga held his hands out, palms up and empty.

"It seems I misjudged you, Mr. Magistrale. You may be better suited to the job than I had dared to imagine. Why did you have to kill her?"

Mage stood, turning his back on the helpless guard, and didn't answer.

"Because she betrayed you?"

"She didn't betray me," Mage replied, careful to keep his voice steady despite his fear and anger. "That isn't Amanda Sharmon."

"What makes you—"

"It's your creature," snapped Mage. "The mujina. She actually had me fooled for a minute; I made the mistake of *thinking,* hoping you'd used the focus to create a phony corpse, instead of *looking.* Then I noticed that the body language was wrong, and the perfume, but I thought she might still be human—until she forgot to blink, or even to dilate her pupils when I shone a light in her eyes. And her nose didn't cast a shadow either."

Tamenaga knelt by the body and turned the head face-up, knocking the platinum wig askew. The mujina, dead, lacked any features, and her skin was the color of old ivory, with the faint sheen of a dull mirror. Tamenaga picked up the key and grimaced.

"A fake. Your own hair, I presume?"

Mage nodded. "But the key was Amanda's. I thought that was where the magic was stored, but I've been experimenting and I found that it was in the hair; the key didn't make a difference. Whose hair is it, anyway?"

Tamenaga stood. Higuchi had told him how Amanda had tied a key onto the focus, enabling him to open any lock—until she'd stolen both key and focus. Higuchi's stupidity and her brilliance had gotten them both killed.

"This is no place for a civilized discussion, Mr. Magistrale," he said rather sadly. "Would you care to follow me?"

Mage cast his eyes around the antiques and artwork in Tamenaga's office. "Very impressive."

"They have a certain sentimental value. I suspect you would consider my aesthetic sense rather limited; I find nothing else so beautiful as money." Tamenaga smiled. "But like you, Magistrale-san, I have taken care to surround myself with beauty."

"Money doesn't impress me."

"I know. You don't really understand it—so few people do. After all, you're not a mathematician. You think almost entirely in images: women, landscapes, telling a story in one frozen moment. Like your lady Amanda, I think in numbers, numbers that do not fit in ordinary minds. I can think of hundreds of billions of dollars and *know* every one of them.

"To you, this may be meaningless. But most of the world's money now exists only in the form of numbers, in the memories of computers, and I can influence it in subtle little ways: rounding down a decimal on an exchange rate, collecting real interest on imaginary investments, adding a few extra expenses onto a Department of Defense contract. And the stock exchange, of course—you'd be surprised at how a slightly inaccurate quote can cause a rise or fall. I made millions out of the eighty-seven crash."

"You caused it?"

"Yes and no. It was inevitable; I merely hastened it by a few days. I cannot buy this country—not yet—but I can buy anything in it. I could probably buy New York, if I wanted it. What would *you* like?"

"Some answers would be nice."

Tamenaga reclined in his leather-and-kevlar chair, smiling. "Ask."

"Who killed Amanda?"

"Yukitaka—the rukoro-kubi. The mujina lured her into the car by assuming the appearance of her friend, the Holdridge girl. Yukitaka was waiting in the back seat."

"Why?"

"Amanda Sharmon stole from my organization; she took the focus from Higuchi, who must have been fool enough to tell her about it, maybe even taught her how to use it. I regret her death—I was impressed by her mathematical work, and she could have been a valuable asset to us. She obviously had a great talent for magic, as well as intelligence and imagination, just as you do—but I *cannot* allow people to steal from me with impunity; I have a reputation to maintain. I'm sure you understand."

Mage didn't comment. "Why did the rukoro-kubi—Yukitaka?—attack me? To recover the focus?"

"He didn't mean to attack you. He was merely defending himself, he hadn't expected you to be so alert. Most people who see—*saw* him late at night refused to believe their own eyes and assumed they were dreaming. You knew better. And we didn't know then that you *had* the focus. When Yukitaka didn't find it on Amanda's body, we thought she had hidden it, but it had never occurred to any of us that she would give it away."

"You haven't answered my question."

Tamenaga sighed. "He wanted to take something of yours to plant on her body, or to photograph it with your camera."

"To frame me."

"Yes. She might have left evidence somewhere to implicate Higuchi, or even myself—we needed to give the police a more obvious suspect. We assumed that she'd hidden the focus somewhere; I never imagined that she might have given it to you, simply handed over an item of that power to a complete stranger, but perhaps she thought she had no further need for it." Tamenaga was silent for a moment. "Later it occurred to me that you might have it and that if you were arrested, the focus would probably end up in an envelope full of personal effects—very easy for us to recover. If not, it would give us a lever—your freedom, which was obviously invaluable to you, in return for the focus.

"But, quite frankly, you and your friend astounded us. When it became obvious that Mr. Takumo had also learned how to use the focus, however imperfectly, I decided to recruit you."

"By sending ninja and a rukoro-kubi to kill us?"

Tamenaga smiled toothily. "A simple test of your ability, no more. You passed. Where *are* my kunoichi, by the way?"

Mage tried to think of a flippant answer and failed. "We buried them," he replied bleakly.

Tamenaga bowed his head for a moment, his expression neutral. "Any more questions?"

"Who made the foci?"

"A good question; I only wish I knew. They were already old when I found them; the legend attached to them attributed them to the god Hotei, patron deity of the yakuza—but as I do not believe in gods, I find the legend unhelpful. May I ask *you* a question?" Mage shrugged. "Why did you come here?"

"I had nowhere else to go."

Tamenaga nodded, careful not to show his triumph. "And where will you go now?"

"I don't know."

"Come work for me. I'll need someone to replace Higuchi, and I don't see why Mr. Takumo couldn't learn the job. And you—well, work can always be found for a man of your talents. Removing flaws from diamonds should be easy for you, and good practice. Shall we say a hundred thousand a week, to begin?"

Mage was silent.

"Two hundred thousand, then. I know, you're not interested in money, but imagine all the women you could buy—oh, don't look so shocked. All women can be bought, Magistrale-san. Your precious Amanda sold herself to Higuchi for a cure for cancer—cheap at twice the price. Others will do it for diamonds, for furs, for Maseratis, for drugs, for a shot at stardom —or for a large donation to Greenpeace or Amnesty, if that's the sort you prefer. Or for a few effortless miracles."

"What about the trial?"

The kuromaku smiled. "There won't be a trial. The police in Edmonton have already found some of the girl's belongings in a man's room—the man who held you up in Totem Rock, incidentally. He won't be able to testify, of course—he blew his brains out last night with a fragmenting bullet."

"How did you arrange that?"

Tamenaga ignored the question. "Do we have a deal?"

"What about Kelly?"

Tamenaga raised an eyebrow and shrugged. "I can find her a job somewhere and triple her salary, if that's what you want."

"What if she says no?"

Another shrug. "She needn't know we had anything to do with it."

"What if *I* say no? Hand over the focus and never come back to L.A.?"

Tamenaga studied him and nodded. "If you wish, you may."

Mage smiled sourly. "And what's to stop you from having me killed as soon as I walk outside this room?"

"Only the fact that I do not need to, or wish to. Mr. Magistrale . . ." Tamenaga pulled his jacket open at the collar, revealing the braided black hair looped around his neck. "You're not a stupid man, and you show considerable potential as a magician, but you are hardly my equal—and I have worn this for nearly half a century. You cannot *hope* to defy me."

Mage pulled up his right sleeve, showing the focus tied around his wrist. "Maybe not, but I can't trust you, either. Maybe I'm no threat to you without this—"

"You're no threat *with* it," scoffed Tamenaga. "Don't you understand? I can turn any magic of yours around and against you in an instant. I may not have your vision, but I *do* have a memory. Anything you do, I can undo."

The photographer shrugged. "Maybe you can." He closed his eyes and concentrated on Takumo's apartment, *saw* himself sitting on the futon bed and staring at the Olivia prints.

He opened his eyes and the vision flickered; an instant later he was staring at Tamenaga, seeing the dai-sho behind him. The old magician smiled broadly. "Have a nice trip, Mr. Magistrale?" Seeing the horrified expression on Mage's face, he burst out laughing.

Fighting off panic, Mage croaked, "One more question."

Tamenaga yawned and raised a hand to cover his mouth. His sleeve slipped down, showing the chain tattooed around his wrist. "Yes?"

"Where's the *third* focus?"

The inscrutable Tamenaga started, very slightly—a man less observant than Mage would not have noticed it at all—and for a fraction of a second, the answer showed in his eyes as he glanced toward the hallway outside. The mujina had been wearing the third focus—and it hadn't saved her. Tamenaga recovered his composure instantly and yawned again, without closing his eyes.

Mage stared past Tamenaga's shoulder at the dai-sho, and remembered glancing through the first few pages of *Ronin,* remembered the young samurai throwing his katana. If he couldn't teleport, maybe he could perform some lesser magic, something the older man wasn't expecting. He concentrated, and the two Murasama swords flew from their scabbards, turned about and headed for Tamenaga. The old magician didn't even deign to look at them; the chains tattooed around his wrists became mankiri-gusari instantly, and he lashed out, entangling both blades. His tight jacket all but exploded as his irezumi transformed into chain mail and monsters. With a flick of his wrists, he snatched both swords out of the air.

Three pairs of eyes stared into Mage's and someone hissed, "That was *stupid!*" Tamenaga touched the tip of the katana to Mage's throat and smiled.

"Maybe I won't kill you," he said. "Yakuza who make mistakes can cut off a finger joint to atone. Which would you rather keep—your cock or your eyes?"

Mage resisted the temptation to shrug; even the slightest movement might cost him his life. The swivel chair, he decided, was too well balanced to be toppled. "I don't care," he muttered.

"You don't?"

"I'd grow them back."

The sword point retreated by a millimeter or two, allowing Mage to breathe. Tamenaga seemed to be hesitating. "Amanda cured her leukemia, didn't she?"

No answer. Tamenaga's face remained inscrutable, but his eyes seemed distant, as though he were meditating. Even the snakes seemed to be fascinated. Moving very slowly, Mage grabbed the blade of the katana and pushed it away. The edge cut deeply into his fingers but he ignored the pain; if he escaped alive with the focus, then he could cure the wound. If not, it hardly mattered. Tamenaga snapped out of his reverie, and the cobra widened its hood and arched its head back, ready to strike. Mage slid out of the chair and ducked beneath the level of the desk. If he were able to teleport away *now*—

No, he thought. If he escaped now, he would never again

summon the courage to face Tamenaga. The rest of his life would be spent running—not merely traveling or wandering, but *running*. His freedom, which he had given almost everything to keep, would be gone. Tamenaga stood, slashed downward with the katana and chopped the desk in half. Mage stared into the six eyes above him and waited to die as Tamenaga, his face contorted with fury, raised the sword to strike again.

Mage *saw* the corridor outside and teleported out, knowing that he had less than a second before Tamenaga brought him back. He grabbed the shotgun he'd dropped near the mujina's feet and was pumping another round into the chamber when he reappeared in Tamenaga's office. He saw the old magician's eyes widen momentarily before he swung the gun around to point it at his chest and squeeze the trigger. The blast sent Tamenaga flying back into his chair, and Mage pumped the shotgun again, leveled it at his enemy's head and fired. Tamenaga blinked, and the shot parted like the Red Sea, scattering around his face and leaving a halo of holes in the leather headrest. Mage lowered the empty gun and stared at Tamenaga's chest. The python and the chain mail had absorbed or deflected most of the pellets, though bright red blood was bubbling rapidly out of a few small wounds in the kuromaku's lungs, and Mage suspected that the blast had broken a few ribs. The python was writhing furiously, obviously in pain, as Tamenaga struggled to control his own heartbeat.

Mage jabbed at Tamenaga's face with the butt of the empty shotgun; Tamenaga parried expertly with the katana, removing much of the stock, and then kicked the gun out of the younger magician's hands. The cobra hissed, and Mage realized that Tamenaga—furious and in great pain—had lost control of his monsters. Mage stared at the python, concentrating on it, charming it, directing it—and the great snake twisted its head and bit into Tamenaga's right arm just as the blade was descending toward Mage's shoulders.

Tamenaga, startled, dropped the katana. The python twisted its tail around the kuromaku's left leg, anchoring itself, and began to tighten its coils, squeezing Tamenaga's broken ribs into his already damaged lungs.

Tamenaga tried concentrating on the python, willing it back into a tattoo, and Mage turned his attention to the cobra. The serpent struck at Tamenaga's right ear, drawing blood. The kuromaku flinched, and Mage saw the python swell and resume its attack. Tamenaga, his attention divided, began hacking at the huge snake with his wakizashi; the shortsword sliced cleanly into the python's scaly hide, but had little effect. Mage could not even be sure of whose blood it was spurting from the wounds— Tamenaga's or the monster's. Without taking his eyes from the snakes, Mage reached out for the fallen katana.

The cobra became a tattoo again. Tamenaga, his face twisted in agony, looked away from the snakes and at Mage. "A million," he whispered.

Mage, holding the katana before him, backed away toward the door and realized suddenly that the old magician, however brilliant he was, had never learned how to heal himself. Maybe he had never needed to, maybe he had never been injured since finding the foci, or maybe his money-cluttered imagination had simply never stretched that far. Mage doubted that Tamenaga would ever have thought of healing anyone else.

A slight movement caught Mage's eye as the mukade slithered out from under the bisected desk to become an ink drawing on the tatami. Mage looked away from Tamenaga for less than a second and felt him struggling vainly to regain control of his monstrous pets. He heard the old man's labored breathing, heard his heart beating far too fast—and then heard the popping of cracked ribs as the python tightened its coils about him.

But Tamenaga wasn't finished yet; he closed his eyes for a mere instant before driving the point of the wakizashi through the python's skull and into the wood of the desk, then teleported out of its writhing coils. Unable to concentrate long enough to envision anyplace outside the room, he appeared immediately behind Mage and wrapped the mankiri-gusari around his enemy's throat.

Mage dropped the katana and grabbed the chain, trying to loosen it, but Tamenaga was stronger and heavier. Mage let go of the garrote and jabbed back with his elbows, but he only succeeded in smashing his funny bone into the kuromaku's chain mail. He dropped to his knees, but Tamenaga held on fast.

"It was a good effort, Magistrale-san," croaked Tamenaga. "But it seems I'm going to have to kill you anyway. *Sumimasen.*"

Mage looked up at the Musashi painting of Hotei and the fighting birds and *saw* the birds fly out of the frame, over his head and toward Tamenaga's eyes. Tamenaga, startled, raised his left arm to cover his face, letting go of the chain an instant too late. Mage broke free, reached for the fallen katana and turned to face the kuromaku. Tamenaga had hurled the birds back into the painting, but blood was pouring from the remains of one of his eyes as well as his innumerable other wounds.

"You're going . . . to have to do . . . better . . . than that," Tamenaga panted as the shotgun wounds in his chest suddenly stopped bleeding. "Such a simple . . . trick. Thank you . . . for teaching it to me . . . Magistrale-san. If I'd known about this . . . I would never have let myself . . . become so old." His hair darkened suddenly from iron-gray to black, and his face became more youthful, until he appeared only slightly older than Mage. He laughed raspingly. "Wonderful! I might even . . . live forever."

"One-eyed and full of poison?"

Tamenaga smiled. "A temporary inconvenience." He was silent for a moment, concentrating, and Mage took a half-step into the kuromaku's blind side and slashed at his neck with the katana. The Murasama blade was sharp enough to decapitate, but Mage's skill wasn't equal to it; instead, he sliced through the loop of braided hair around Tamenaga's neck. The focus fell silently to the floor, and the old magician's mankiri-gusari became mere tattoos. Tamenaga stared at Mage and staggered backward, holding the wound in his neck closed with his fingers.

"Two million," he wheezed.

Mage shook his head, and Tamenaga wavered for a moment, then lunged for the fallen focus. Mage thrust the katana into the floor like a stake, blocking his path, then grabbed the focus and *saw* himself on the other side of the office, out of Tamenaga's reach. The kuromaku looked up at him, opened his mouth to speak, reached for the hilt of the katana and succeeded only in grabbing the blade, then died without another sound.

Mage, exhausted, leaned against the shelves and waited until he was sure the old man was dead, then stared at his hand and *saw* it whole. The pain remained, but he was almost glad of it. Ignoring the treasures in the room, he collected the pieces of Kelly's shotgun and *saw* himself into the corridor, standing near the mujina's body.

The house guard had passed out. Mage considered helping him but decided against it; he knew there were other guards nearby, who would almost certainly find their way up here before long, and he didn't have the strength or the will left to fight them.

He knelt by the mujina's body and tore her silk dress open. The monster had dark, eye-like spots where her nipples should have been and a large navel that he suspected was actually a mouth. There was no sign of the focus. He glanced at the featureless yellow-gray of her face, noticed the blood-spattered platinum wig and reached down to pick it up. The focus was sewn into the hairnet. "Shades of 'The Purloined Letter,' " he muttered, then shoved the wig into his pocket and *saw* himself in Takumo's apartment.

He opened his eyes an instant later and stared into the smiling face of a bald, fat Japanese. Mage dropped the pieces of Kelly's shotgun, knowing that he had no energy left for fighting, and collapsed on the tatami.

Mr. Magistrale?"

"Yes?"

"Congratulations, sir. But there's no need to kneel. I don't insist on ceremony."

Mage opened his eyes warily. The intruder wore a thin orange robe and did not appear to be armed. "Who are you?"

"A good question. People—and gods—call me Hotei, and I don't remember ever being anyone else, so I suppose that Hotei is who I am."

Mage blinked and tried to remember the Japanese mythology Takumo had taught him. "The God of Gamblers?"

Hotei shrugged, and his massive belly shuddered. "I suppose so."

"You made the foci?"

"Did I? I'm afraid I don't remember that, either."

Mage shook his head, as though trying to dislodge a particularly stubborn idea. "Do you want them back?"

"No, they're of no use to me. Keep them, or give them to someone deserving, or whatever you will. You've earned them."

"Have I?" Mage sat up painfully and stared at the god, his expression sour. "You know, I get the horrible feeling I've been set up. You arranged things so that Amanda would meet Higuchi and I'd meet Amanda, and Charlie, and that maniac with the machine pistol . . ."

The god merely smiled broadly.

"Why did you do it?"

"There was no one else I could trust who could have learned how to use the focus in time. You had the vision and the courage—you're *much* braver than you believe—and you were the sort of man who would follow the ghost of a girl halfway around the country without wasting time wondering why. And I didn't think Tamenaga would be able to buy you; *that* was a gamble, I admit, but—"

"That wasn't what I meant."

"Tamenaga had had the foci for too long," said Hotei gravely. "He was hoarding too much luck, becoming an oppressive force. If you hadn't reclaimed them, he would have destroyed your country economically and left it with only one asset to hire out—its military capabilities. America would have become a geopolitical soldier of fortune, working for the highest bidder."

"You mean Japan."

Hotei shook his head. "The yen will collapse within a decade, and you heard that from the God of Gamblers. I mean *Tamenaga*. He owned politicians in both countries; Japanese politicians need a *lot* of campaign funds. Do not try to hate a whole nation, Mr. Magistrale—the Japanese people do not deserve it, and besides, you cannot possibly *imagine* so many people. Even *I* could not, and I have had centuries of practice."

"And you have the advantage of being Japanese."

"Maybe I have—I don't know," said the god, wrinkling his massive brow. "I can't remember anything earlier than, oh, two centuries ago, and I think I've been Hotei for much longer than that. I suspect I was mortal once . . . I've no way of being sure. But you see, the rich and the powerful don't need gods. The poor do."

"Is that why you created them?"

"It's more likely that *they* created *me*," said Hotei cheerfully. "Billions of poor have a *lot* of imagination—or faith, if you prefer. And they believe in luck." He stood and waddled toward the door, then turned around. "And don't judge gods too harshly, Magistrale-san. You may be one yourself one day. Good luck."

He bowed deeply, and Mage yelled, "Wait!"

Hotei paused and looked up from his bow. "Yes?"

"Did you create me?"

"Of course not," the god replied, a little huffily.

"Then how long have you been interfering with my life?"

"Only since the day Amanda Sharmon wished for someone like you to come along—slightly less than a month. I'm a busy god." He grinned. "It takes a lot of work to create someone like Charlie Takumo." And he vanished, leaving Mage with the three foci and a thousand questions.

Epilogue

"No," said Takumo firmly. "I don't want it, and I won't take it."

"Why the hell not?"

"Because it scares me. I'm allergic to power, even more than you are. Besides, I'm no magician; my mind doesn't move in those sort of circles. Look what happened last time. I might hurt someone, without meaning to."

Mage thought of the dead kunoichi and winced. He turned to Kelly, who was lounging on the sofa with Oedipus on her lap. "Don't look at *me*," she said.

"Don't tell me *you're* scared of power."

"No . . ." she replied carefully. "Only when it's abused."

Was I *really* expecting a straight answer from a lawyer? Mage wondered, and shrugged. Then he stared at her long and hard for nearly a minute. "Go look in a mirror," he said mildly.

"What? Why?"

"Go into the bedroom. Take a good long look at yourself and tell me what you see. Humor me, okay?"

She stared at him, puzzled, before stalking off into her room. Mage waited and then heard a shriek. Takumo leaped to his feet, but Mage shook his head.

"You *bastard!*" she screamed. Mage blanched, turning to stare at the closed door. Oedipus hid behind the sofa, and Takumo blinked. "I think you'd better split," he whispered, and Mage *saw* himself into the stuntman's apartment an instant before Kelly, naked to the waist and protecting her breasts with one arm, threw the door open and stormed into the room with murder in her face.

He sat in the darkness until he heard the unmistakable growl of Takumo's Ninja from the car park, and then he walked slowly over to the kitchen and filled the kettle.

"Where's Kelly?"

"Back home. Sorry I'm so late, but she was really freaking out badly and I didn't want to leave her alone; if my bike hadn't been there, I probably would've stayed the night."

"Yeah, I used to use that excuse too . . ." Takumo glared. "Sorry. You know, I used to think I understood women."

Takumo laughed and latched the door. "Yeah? I used to think there was a Santa Claus."

"Why did she—"

"How's she going to explain to her friends that her breast grew back? Tell'em she got a freakin' transplant? She'll be *weeks* just getting used to the *concept.*" He shook his head. "Most of us just aren't equipped to handle miracles, man. I'm not sure that *I* am, not without being seriously stoned. Okay, so we all managed when we didn't have a choice, but like, we have to live in the real world. Okay, so maybe we don't *have* to—personally, I'm just visiting—but it has its creature comforts, and Kelly *likes* living there. Come to that, so do I. You—"

"It's not my town."

"I wasn't just talking about L.A., man, and you don't *have* a town. You don't have a job, and you sure as hell don't have a home. If you want my advice, you'll split as soon as this murder rap has blown over, go back to being the wandering magician, and hide the other two foci in a safe place until you meet someone who can use them—and you will. It's a big world out there, and there's nowhere you can't go."

"Nowhere . . . ?"

The magician spent the afternoon at the Victoria and Albert Museum, looking at the netsuke and the Japanese porcelain. A few people noticed his camera: an old Hasselblad, equipped with oversized controls and designed to function perfectly in free fall. His tan marked him as a recent arrival, probably fresh off the plane and still jet-lagged. They had no way of knowing that he had spent the morning in a darkroom in Boulder City and would sleep the next day in a youth hostel in Inuyama, or that he had just cured himself of the worst case of sunburn in human history.

In the Littrow region, east of the Mare Serenitatis, rest the relics of the last men to walk on the moon: the lower stage of a LEM, a Lunar Rover, an array of scientific instruments, and assorted items not wanted on voyage. And the footprints, which give a human scale to the picture. A few of the footprints were made by size eleven Reeboks, and in the compartment under the Rover's seat, there lie two braided loops of black hair.

Glossary

aisha: manipulating an overly sympathetic or softhearted person

bakemono: Japanese goblins

bakuto: gambler; one of the traditional occupations of the yakuza

chambara: martial arts movies or TV shows emphasizing action over authenticity

chi: literally, "breath." Life force, inner energy.

chunin: ninja officer

dai-sho: pair of swords, the *katana* (dai-to, great sword) and *wakizashi* (sho-to)

dosha: taking advantage of a person's bad temper

fukiya: poisoned darts, usually fired from a blowgun

fukumi-bari: pin-sized darts, held in the mouth and spat out at point-blank range

fundoshi: loincloth

genin: lowest rank of ninja

giri: duty

gojo-gyoku: principle of five feelings and five desires: *aisha, dosha, kisha, kyosha,* and *rakusha*

irezumi: large and elaborate tattoos worn by the yakuza

jonin: ninja general

kabuto: samurai helmet

kamikari: praying mantis

karayuki: girls forced into prostitution (not to be confused with *karaoke,* which is legal)

karima kunoichi: a girl or woman recruited by a ninja clan as a spy or assassin

katana: samurai longsword

ki: see *chi*

kirisutegomen: "killing and going away": the samurai's traditional right to kill any commoner who offended him

kisha: taking advantage of an enemy's lechery

kitsune: fox

kobun: "child role," yakuza term for an underling

komuso: wandering priest

kuji-kuri: ninja method of focusing ki, using finger movements

kumo: spider

kunoichi: female ninja. See also *karima kunoichi* and *shima kunoichi*

kuromaku: literally "black curtain"; yakuza term for the power behind the throne

kyosha: taking advantage of an enemy's cowardice and phobias
kyotetsu-shoge: ninja weapon, consisting of a length of rope
  with a heavy ring at one end and a double-bladed knife at
  the other

mankiri-gusari: a heavy chain, weighted at both ends
mujina: a *bakemono* with the power to appear human. A *mujina*'s true face is a featureless, terrifying void.
mukade: centipede

neko: cat
neko-de: "cat's claws"; a band fitting around the ninja's hand,
  with claws protruding from the palm. Could be used for
  climbing or combat.
netsuke: small ivory carvings
ninja: "invisible person"
ninjato: ninja sword
ninjo: compassion
ninjutsu: "the art of invisibility." Often used to describe the
  training of the ninja, including stealth, climbing, unarmed
  combat (taijutsu), and weapons skills
Nisei: second generation
nunchaku: Japanese flail; two short clubs joined by length of
  chain or rope

obi: sash
oyabun: "parent role," yakuza equivalent of "godfather"

rakusha: taking advantage of an enemy's boredom
ronin: "wave man," a masterless samurai
rukoro-kubi: human-looking *bakemono*, with the ability to sep-
  arate its hands and head from its body

sarakin: yakuza loan shark

sarariman: "salary man," employee

sawa: scabbard

shima kunoichi: a girl born into, trained by, and loyal to a ninja clan

shinai: bamboo sword

shinobi shozuko: ninja costume

shoto: shortsword

shuriken: ninja throwing weapon, frequently star-shaped

shurikenjutsu: art of throwing shuriken, knives, and other small weapons

shuten-doji: a *bakemono,* similar to a European vampire

sumimasen: so sorry

Sumiyoshi-rengo: a Tokyo-based yakuza syndicate

sumo: Japanese wrestling style

sumotori: sumo wrestler

tabi: thick-soled split-toed "shoe-socks"

taijutsu: ninja unarmed combat style

tatami: woven straw mats

tenuki: badger

tessen: iron war fan, usable as a bludgeon or a parrying weapon

tetsubishi: caltrops

tsuba: sword guard. *Katana* and *wakizashi* traditionally have ornate tsuba; ninjato have plain square tsuba, large enough to use as a step.

wakizashi: shortsword

yadomejutsu: "the art of arrow cutting"; the technique of parrying arrows, shuriken, and other thrown weapons

yakuza: the Japanese criminal underworld

yama-no-kami: mountain deity

yojimbo: bodyguard

yubitsume: yakuza ritual of slicing off a finger joint to atone for
a mistake

About the Author

Stephen Dedman's award-nominated short fiction has appeared in most major genre magazines, including *The Magazine of Fantasy and Science Fiction, Asimov's,* and *SF Age,* and in such highly regarded anthologies as *Little Deaths* and *Dark Destiny III.* He lives in Perth, Australia.